The Tomb of
the Chatelaine

Karen Baugh
MENUHIN

Front cover: Shutterstock : Scotney Castle by Frank Parolek

First paperback and ebook edition March 2021

ISBN: 978-1-9162947-6-9

Aaron, Merle, Arthur, Vera,
Ava, Edgar and the bump.
With love...

CHAPTER 1

Autumn, season of mists and mellow fruitfulness.

October 1922.

'There's been a murder, sir! Really, it was a murder.' Tommy Jenkins called to me as I swung the axe down to split another log.

'What?' I tossed the wood onto a pile next to me, then straightened up to regard the lad. He'd come running up the hill from the house with one hand on his school cap and a slip of paper in the other.

'Miss Persi telephoned, and you wasn't there and neither was Mr Greggs, so I wrote it down!' He waved the paper again, an excited grin on his face. 'Some bloke died an' it was supposed to be an accident, but it wasn't because of the gun.'

I leaned the axe against the nearest tree trunk; it was late afternoon, we were up in the woods behind my old manor house. Now that autumn was upon us I'd thought to cut logs for winter and there were fallen trees ready for

1

splitting. I'd been enjoying the exercise under a clear blue sky with my little dog and the trill of birds for company.

'Persi rang?' That caught me by surprise.

'Yes, and she asked if you was home, but I said you was out with Mr Fogg. It was a terrible crackly line, I couldn't hardly hear what she was sayin'.' He passed me the ink-spotted paper.

I straightened it out. He watched with brown eyes, bright with enthusiasm. Tommy was the boot boy; a scruffy lad in grey school uniform, skewed tie and thick dark hair under a crumpled cap.

I read the message, written in his straggly handwriting.

Miss Persi said Lord Sinclair's chauffeur was killed at Lanscombe Park yesterday. It was supposed to be an accident, but she didn't think it was, on account of the parcel with the gun in it. It caused great ~~constirnashion~~ worry for Auntie and Uncle St George and everyone. I'd like you to come to Lanscombe and investigate.

'How can St George be Miss Persi's uncle?' Tommy pushed his cap back from his face. 'Wasn't he the knight who killed a dragon?'

'This is a different knight, one of the ordinary sorts.' I hadn't actually met Sir Bertram St George but was pretty sure he hadn't clashed with any mythical creatures.

'It's a good name though, ain't it.' Tommy fidgeted. 'I'd like to be a knight an' have armour an' a sword. I'd go fightin' monsters and…'

'Where was she calling from?' I interrupted his excited chatter. Persi lived at Hope House and I didn't understand why she would ask me to come to Lanscombe Park.

'Don't know, sir.' Tommy continued. 'It must be a long way off. It sounded like it on the telephone.'

'Sussex,' I muttered, staring at the message. 'She doesn't actually mention murder.'

'Aye, but then she said the gun was for Lord Sinclair. I asked her what she meant, but it was all garbled, on account of the cracklin'.' He was irrepressible. 'I think it's jolly suspicious an' it stands to reason that, if it wasn't an accident then it must be murder, mustn't it? That's why she wants you to go, so you and Inspector Swift can find the murderer, like you always do. An' it's better than choppin' wood, and fishing 'cause that's not really doin' anything and…'

'Swift's an ex-Inspector now and this hardly warrants a trip from the Highlands.'

'But he'll want to go, just like always.' Tommy was almost hopping, a flush to his freckled cheeks. 'Can I come too, sir, can I?'

'No, and I'm not going either.'

'But… but…' The grin fell from his face. 'You have to…'

'I can't go to Lanscombe Park without a proper invitation,' I tried to explain. 'And the local police will have already made investigations, there's no reason for me to be there.'

'But it's Miss Persi, sir. She wouldn't have telephoned if it wasn't important.'

'Look, I'll telephone her later, or write, or…' I ran

fingers through my hair. 'Tommy, will you find Greggs and remind him it's almost time for tea.'

'Oh, sir...' He was inclined to argue but noted my expression, so gave up and ran back to the house.

I contemplated returning to chopping wood, but the message was as perplexing as it was unexpected and I had no idea what to make of it. Mr Fogg, my little golden spaniel, had been digging in the blackberry bushes. He broke off when called and came bounding through the trees. My house lay in a shallow vale amid the gentle Cotswolds hills. I wound down through long meadow grass, swallows swooping low about me as the sun dropped in the sky. Foggy raced ahead with ears flapping, he galloped across the stable yard and through the overgrown walled gardens. He was sitting panting on the stone flags outside the front door when I caught up with him.

Greggs, my butler, wasn't about, so I had to let myself in. I headed for the quiet of my cluttered library and warm fireside to contemplate the message from Persi, or rather, Persephone Carruthers. We'd had an unconventional courtship, if you could even call it that, various adventures had thrown us together where murder had featured more heavily than romance. I'd fallen for her before really getting to know her and now... and now she wasn't even speaking to me. Or at least she hadn't been until the telephone call. I sat down in my favourite chair and pulled out the crumpled note to read again.

'Sir.' Greggs arrived with a tray of tea and hot buttered scones. 'There was a telephone message.'

'Yes, I know. Tommy gave it to me.'

He poured tea into a china cup before depositing it on a low table at my elbow, along with scones on a plate. I noticed he had a smudge of dust on the sleeve of his butlering togs.

'I have commenced packing, sir.'

That made me look up. 'What the devil for?'

'The investigation, sir.'

'Greggs, what are you talking about?'

'The suspicious incident at Lanscombe Park,' he intoned.

'But it's... we don't... Persi doesn't even live there,' I objected. 'I can't just barge into a place like Lanscombe Park on some flimsy pretext.'

'It was not Miss Persi, sir, it was ex-Chief Inspector Swift.' His eyes moved to a distant spot above my head, a sign he thought I was being obtuse, or merely idiotic.

'What? You mean Swift rang?'

'Yes, sir.' He sounded mildly exasperated. 'He left information that he would arrive this afternoon.'

'How could he possibly travel from Braeburn in an afternoon?'

'He wasn't in Braeburn, sir, he was in London. The message was quite clear, I left it by...' He suddenly stopped and felt in the top pocket of his tailcoat. 'I, ahem... I may have forgotten to...' He turned pink and handed me a carefully written note.

12.30 pm. Telephone Message received from ex-Chief Inspector Swift. "Persi sent a telegram to Braeburn about the death of the chauffeur and the gun in the parcel. Her Aunt and Uncle St George are distressed. She believes it is suspicious and wants us to investigate. I'm leaving London now, we must go to Lanscombe Park. Swift."

I read it twice, wondering what the devil was going on. 'Did he say anything else?'

'He did not, sir.' He cleared his throat. 'I understood Lanscombe Park to be the home of Lord Sinclair.'

'Yes, but it's the St Georges' old family seat, Persi's related to them.' Persi had a great many relatives, as I'd recently discovered.

'And they still reside there?' He sounded surprised. 'With Lord Sinclair?'

'Well, it may be a little eccentric, but I'm sure it's all perfectly amicable.'

He sniffed, Greggs could be a bit of a stickler for protocol. 'I believe Lord Sinclair made his fortune in the sale of weapons, sir.'

'He develops them, Greggs. But you're right, and the war was particularly profitable for him.' There was an edge of distaste to my voice.

'You encountered him when you were in Sussex, sir?' He tidied a few books and whatnots I'd left on my desk.

'No, it was his wife, Lady Penelope, who was there.' I took a sip of tea.

'You mean at the reception prepared for you and Miss Persi when you arrived back from Egypt, sir?'

'You know very well it was, Greggs,' I gave a sharp reply.

'Indeed, sir.' He straightened up, his chins wobbling above his stiff collar. 'If you will excuse me, I will complete the packing.'

'No, I'm not going.'

'But… but, sir,' he stuttered, consternation on his face. 'Inspector Swift is on his way and Miss Persi… she will expect…'

'Greggs, I have no idea what she expects…' I snapped, then felt ashamed of my bad temper. 'I mean, well, she hasn't replied to any messages I've left, or written, or, or…' I blustered. 'Look, we should wait until Swift arrives.'

'Very well, sir. If you insist.' He went off with an air of injured martyrdom. Greggs had been my batman during the war. Upon its end, we'd retreated to the quiet haven of Ashton Steeple where he'd developed a taste for amateur dramatics, operetta and good Irish whiskey. I'd taken to rural pursuits and more recently murder; uncovering it, I mean, not committing it.

I picked up a scone and shared it with Foggy while contemplating the news from Sussex. It wasn't that I didn't want to see Persi, and I knew it was my fault. I'd tried to apologise, but she was so damn stubborn… and hurt. Recently I'd begun to accept that it really was over… but now this. Quite frankly, it all sounded rather histrionic, and that would be very unlike her. She was forthright, quite blunt actually, and she certainly wouldn't have telephoned unless it were serious… so perhaps it really was murder?

A sharp rap on the front door, followed by a shout from Tommy, broke into my musings. Foggy ran off and the hall echoed with joyful woofs and the boy's eager greeting.

'He's in the library.' The lad's high voice rang out. 'I reckon it was murder, you'll make him go, won't you, Chief Inspector?'

Swift mumbled something indecipherable in return; various noises ensued, including the clunk of a suitcase being deposited on the tiles, then Tommy rushed in.

'He's here, sir!'

'Lennox.' Swift strode into the library, wearing a heavy wool coat over a natty city suit, his dark hair neatly combed above lean features. 'Are you ready?'

Typical of the man; always in a hurry.

'There's a storm coming,' I countered.

'Nonsense, it's miles away, the clouds were barely above the horizon.' Swift was dismissive.

'The swallows were swoopin' low, that means it's goin' to rain,' Tommy broke in. 'They hunt insects, but they can't go high when there's damp in the air. The gardener told me an' I've watched them, an' it's true!'

'There you are then, Swift,' I told him.

'It's hardly...' The sudden sound of rain pattering on the window panes undermined his objections. He frowned. 'Right, fine. But we leave at the crack of dawn.'

He tugged off his overcoat to toss over a chair.

'Tommy,' I told the lad. 'Go and tell Cook we'll have the trout for dinner.'

'Aye, sir,' he said, but didn't go. 'I've started on my Christmas list and I've asked for a magnifying glass and a fingerprint kit. Aunty said you can't have fingerprint kits 'cause it's special and only the police have them. Could you get me one, Inspector Swift? 'Cause I'm goin' to be a detective an' I'll need to have everythin' proper to find murderers…'

'Tommy,' I cut in. 'Go.' I pointed towards the door.

'Will do, sir.' He jumped off his chair. 'But Inspector Swift – will you get it, will you sir?'

'I'll see what I can do.' Swift smiled at the lad. 'But you'll have to wait for Christmas.'

'That's just smashing, that is!' Tommy skipped off, grinning with excitement.

'No trench coat?' I remarked.

'Florence said it was becoming worn.' Swift's face fell. 'And the buckle didn't work.'

That made me grin. 'Come on, Swift. Sit down. Why were you in London?'

'I had a meeting about the whisky.' He dug about in his inside pocket to pull out a small bottle and handed it over. 'The Braeburn Malt.'

'Excellent.' I unscrewed the cap and breathed in the fumes.

'Yes, and I must thank you again, Lennox. Your idea to sell our whisky to the London merchants has turned everything about.' He smiled and dropped into the wing chair opposite me. 'The distillery has never been so busy and we're employing more men. Florence is thrilled, even the Laird is impressed. It's… it's marvellous.'

Swift had married Lady Florence Braeburn and given up Scotland Yard to move to the Highlands. It hadn't been an easy transition for any number of reasons, but the new enterprise seemed to have helped.

I poured two fingers of malt into tumblers and handed one to him. 'Is this all you brought?'

'I hadn't intended coming here until Florence called and told me she'd received the telegram.' He sounded tetchy.

I sipped the whisky, it was superb. I leaned back in my chair, Tubbs, my little black cat, emerged from a cozy nook to jump onto my lap, demanding to have his ears rubbed.

'How's the baby?' I asked.

'Growing!' Swift chattered on with news of Braeburn and his and Florence's baby boy, Angus. I wasn't particularly listening, but talk of Scotland made him happy. He stopped abruptly, possibly having noticed that my eyes had glazed over.

'What happened in Egypt?'

'What?' That brought my gaze back into sharp focus.

He sipped his whisky and waited.

'I... um... we,' I spluttered, then pulled myself together. 'Well, we came back together. It was supposed to be a leisurely cruise across the Mediterranean, but the weather was appalling.'

He cut in, 'I meant, what happened between you and Persi.'

'I proposed to her, of course.' I finished my whisky and poured another. 'I had to travel the length of Egypt to find her. It was worse than Damascus – unbelievably hot, sand got into everything and nobody spoke a damn word of English until I tracked down the consulate...'

'Lennox,' he broke in again. 'Did she accept your proposal?'

'Yes, why wouldn't she?'

'So, you're actually engaged?' He sounded surprised.

'No.'

His dark brows furrowed further. 'Lennox...'

I hadn't wanted this conversation. I took another gulp of whisky. 'I proposed, she said yes, then she said I should meet her family, because I might want to change my mind. I thought it was nonsense...'

'And...?' he prompted.

'When we docked in Marseille, she sent a telegram to her parents, telling them the news. We caught the Train Bleu to Paris, which was...' I paused, recalling the pure joy of travelling in luxurious comfort after the camels and carts of the Middle East, not to mention the heaving ship.

'Was what?' Swift cut across my dreaming.

'Sublime. The food, the service, the champagne....' Memories of Persi and me dining together, as the world flew past the carriage, flooded my mind. I sighed again, because it had been rather magical. 'Anyway, we arrived at Hope House just after dark to find hordes of them waiting for us... it never occurred to me...' I stuttered to a halt at the memory.

'You'd just become engaged to Persi, her family were bound to want to meet you.' Swift remarked dryly. 'What did you expect?'

'Just her parents, of course, and I can't say I was even ready for them. As it was, half the damn county seemed to be there.'

He seemed more interested in the myriad relatives than my tirade. 'Persi is a Carruthers, where do the St Georges fit in?'

'Her father is a Carruthers, her mother is a St George.' I took another drink. 'Sir Bertram St George is the oldest of eight siblings, Persi's mother is the youngest. There are dozens of cousins, second cousins and the like and they all...'

'And what about Sinclair?' He interrupted.

I tried to recall what Persi had told me about her family while we were travelling through Europe. 'Sir Bertram's only son and heir, Randolph, was killed in an accident. His widow married Sinclair, she's called Penelope.'

'Hum.' He fixed his dark eyes on me. 'What happened at the reception party, Lennox?'

I took another sip and tried an evasive action. 'Has Persi talked to Florence?'

He nodded. 'Yes.'

'So you know what happened, Swift,' I accused him.

'We've heard Persi's side,' he admitted. 'What the hell were you thinking?'

'Nothing... I told you, we arrived at the party...' I stammered, then took a breath. 'I'm the solitary sort, Swift. You know that. I loathe all the niceties and point-less chatter.' I knocked back my drink. 'When the dinner gong rang, they all walked one way and I walked another.'

'So you left! Just like that? You left Persi in the middle

of the reception which had been organised to welcome you into her family?'

'It wasn't as bad as…' I reached for the bottle but he swiped it away.

'And now?' he demanded.

'I've telephoned, sent telegrams, written letters; it hasn't achieved a damn thing. She won't even speak to me.'

'Well, she's speaking to you now.'

'You mean she's snapped her fingers and expects me to come running.'

'That's unfair, she's asked for our help.'

He was right, but I was bemused by Persi's sudden volte face. I'd been desperate to talk to her for weeks and now, out of the blue, comes a demand to rush off to Sussex on nothing more than vague suspicion. She hadn't even said she'd be there.

'I just don't know what to make of it.' I slumped back in my chair.

'Lennox, are you coming or not?'

'No…' I let out a sigh of exasperation. 'Damn it, yes. Of course I'm coming.'

CHAPTER 2

It was after nine o'clock before we set off the next morning. I'd tossed and turned half the night, then overslept. I'd insisted on a proper breakfast, the Bentley wouldn't start, and, after much cursing and cajoling, she burst into life and we all climbed in. Swift was in the passenger seat, Greggs sat in the back with Foggy on his lap and next to him was Mr Tubbs in a wicker hamper. The Bentley lacked a roof, so we were bundled up in coats, mufflers and hats because the storm had lingered to whip dark clouds across a sullen sky.

They complained about my speed, the rain and the racket from the engine. I wore my flying helmet, scarf and goggles which rendered me practically deaf and mostly dry. We travelled winding roads peppered with fallen leaves, puddled potholes and mud-spattered verges. Swift was supposed to be navigating, although I didn't agree with most of his directions, which caused a few sharp words and any number of wrong turns.

We came upon Lanscombe Park in the late morning;

serene in a vale enclosed by rolling downs. The estate consisted of the entire valley and was the reason for its secluded setting. The clouds cleared and the sun came out as we approached; the scene spread out before us like a landscape painting. A tree lined road led to an impressive entrance with elegant stone pillars supporting wrought-iron gates. They were firmly closed.

I drew to a halt and sounded my horn.

'Somebody's watching, sir.' Greggs sounded anxious. I'd told him he didn't have to come, but he'd insisted, I've no idea why. I suppose he was curious to see Lanscombe Park in all its reputed glory.

'The gatekeeper's supposed to be watching, it's his job,' I replied, noting movement behind the gates.

'Stop!' The guard had slipped through a side gate. He marched in front of the car with a hand held high. 'Names?'

'Major Lennox, Chief Inspector Swift and...'

'We're the police,' Swift shouted from the passenger seat.

The guard regarded the car, my butler, dog, cat in a basket, and me, with a look of patent disbelief.

'On whose authority are you here?' he demanded.

'Miss Persephone Carruthers,' I told him.

'She's not a resident.'

'But she must be staying here,' Swift put up an argument.

'She isn't.'

That took the wind out of Swift's sails. I can't say I felt any more buoyant.

'Lord Sinclair, then,' I said.

'There's no-one listed for today.' The guard turned hostile. He looked to be the military sort, short hair, dark moustache, smart black and red uniform and a holster on his hip.

'Right, Sir Bertram St George,' I tried.

'He doesn't have visitors.'

'He does now,' I retorted.

'I repeat, he doesn't have visitors.'

I swore under my breath, I may have been wary of coming, but was damned if I was going to drive all this way for nothing. 'Call the house and check.'

He glowered at me, I glowered back, Foggy growled; none of it helped.

'Stay where you are,' he rapped out and marched back through the side gate and into a lodge house set behind the walls.

'Sir, he has a gun,' Greggs hissed loudly.

'I know, Greggs. I saw it.'

'It's private ground.' Swift was leaning forward in his seat. 'It's permitted under licence.'

We waited with the engine idling until the guard returned.

'You can enter. Drive to the rear of the house and wait in the car until someone arrives to meet you. I repeat, *do not* leave your car without an escort.' He instructed, then went to a discreet box set in the wall and pressed a red button. The gates started to open.

'Oh, sir, they're electric,' Greggs uttered in awe.

17

'They must have powerful generators to run the motors.' Swift observed the gate's mechanism.

They swung in a slow arc until wide enough to pass through. I'd heard of such things, but it was the first time I'd seen them.

'The guard could have opened them perfectly easily himself,' I muttered, and slipped the Bentley into gear.

I raced the car down the long drive, the roar of the engine reverberating across the perfect expanse of manicured lawns to bordering woodland and the hills beyond. The mansion was huge and white with a portico of towering columns in the Palladian style. We pulled up in a spray of gravel beneath the colonnade.

'Sir, the gatekeeper said we should go to the rear,' Greggs exclaimed.

'Nonsense, why should we.' I pulled off my cap and goggles.

'But…' he began, as Foggy escaped his grasp and jumped out to run about the lawn, barking with excitement.

I hopped out and walked up the sweeping steps with Swift beside me.

The door swung silently open to reveal a butler within a vast hallway. He did not look amused.

'The guard telephoned to advise of your presence. Sir Bertram and Lady Millicent St George can be found at the rear of the house,' he instructed, then the door began to close.

Undeterred, Swift put a hand to the door and strode in. I followed, so did Foggy. He ran twice about the snooty butler then straight up the elegant staircase, which dominated the grand hall.

'I'm Detective Chief Inspector Swift and this is Major Heathcliff Lennox. We're here to investigate a death,' Swift announced to an ensemble of footmen liveried in black and red, a pimply hall boy and the forbidding butler.

'I cannot allow...' the butler continued to protest.

'Yes, you can,' I told him firmly.

'You must have his Lordship's permission to enter here.' The butler was tall, square shouldered with cropped grey hair, steely eyes, a sharp nose and chin. His face was taut with an expression of open animosity.

Another standoff loomed, an ormolu clock on a marble-topped table chimed the hour, and I considered retreat.

'Oh, my goodness. It's you!' A voice suddenly called from an upper floor. 'Heathcliff Lennox.' A young lady came down the thickly carpeted stairs, carrying Fogg in her arms. 'What on earth possessed you to bolt like that? And in front of everyone, it caused such a fuss...' she chattered on, in blithe fashion, as she crossed the hall, then suddenly stopped. 'You don't remember me, do you?'

'I... um.' She was quite right, I hadn't the faintest idea who she was.

Swift broke into my feeble excuse. 'DCI Swift, delighted to meet you.' He made a neat bow.

'Oh, gosh, the detective. Persi told me you're a professional. I'm Lydia St George.' She smiled up at both of us, white teeth behind pretty pink lips. 'Is this your dog?'

'Yes,' I admitted.

'He's scrumptious.' She laughed and put him down. 'Did you bring him to help your investigation? I don't think he'll like it; the accident was simply horrible.'

'Persi mentioned it was suspicious…' I realised the butler, hall boy and footmen were listening intently, and decided to shut up.

'It is, I've said so all along. The local force are jolly keen, but I really don't think they know anything at all.' She regarded me with dark brown eyes. Her hair was the colour of roast chestnuts, cut fashionably short. She wore a pale peach frock of finespun wool, a matching scarf in silk and a gold necklace around her slender neck.

She turned to the butler. 'Trent, take them to the old wing, it's terribly important. Tell Grandpa that these are the detectives and they simply must stay and discover what happened.'

'Do you mean they should stay *here*? In the house?' He asked in an incredulous tone.

'Good heavens, no. They can stay in the old wing with my grandparents where they will be properly welcomed,' she replied, sarcasm in her voice.

'I was merely suggesting that a formal invitation hasn't been sanctioned, Miss Lydia.'

'Well, if they're staying with my grandparents, it hardly matters, does it,' she retorted.

'I must consult his Lordship…'

'Lydia, who are you talking to?' A woman's voice came from upstairs.

'Oh, Mama, it's Heathcliff. And the detective,' Lydia called back.

The lady walked calmly down the stairs; her chestnut hair curled in cultivated waves, she wore a simple twin set and tweed skirt in dark green.

'Oh, Heathcliff, I'm so pleased to see you again.' Lady Penelope Sinclair crossed the chequered tiles to greet us. I remembered her very clearly, she was a striking woman; pale skin, large brown eyes under slender brows, a straight nose and softly curving lips.

'Ah... pleased to see you again, Lady Penelope.' I bowed over her proffered hand. 'But not Heathcliff, if you, erm... it's Lennox.'

Swift cut into my babbling and introduced himself.

She offered him a pleasant smile. 'A genuine detective. I do hope you haven't had a wasted journey.' She laughed suddenly. 'Oh, heavens that was a terrible thing to say, I'm so sorry.'

'No... I...' Swift stuttered to a halt, no doubt as confused as I was by her words.

'Trent,' Lady Penelope turned to the butler. 'Take these gentlemen to the old wing, they will be staying as long as they require.'

Trent didn't attempt an objection, he simply bowed. 'Certainly, my lady.'

Lady Penelope turned her steady gaze back in our direction. 'You must join us for dinner tonight, it will be the immediate family only, I'm sure you'll wish to meet them.'

'No...' I began. 'I mean, yes, of course.'

She smiled again and walked back to climb the stairs.

'There you are then!' Lydia laughed with delight and turned to follow her mother.

'Wait… is Persi coming?' I called out.

'Possibly. Who knows?' 'Jerome,' a man's voice suddenly bellowed from above. 'Where the hell are you? Get that bloody lawyer on the phone, now.' We all looked up although we couldn't see anyone. The servants froze, the tension was almost palpable.

'Sinclair.' We could hear Lady Penelope's voice. 'We have guests, it's…'

'Shut up, woman,' the man yelled. 'I'm in the middle of a deal and Jerome has left the paperwork in his room, the bloody imbecile. If he doesn't shake himself, he'll be out on his ear.'

Lydia had turned pale.

'Mama,' she called, then ran upstairs.

'Sinclair, please…' Lady Penelope spoke.

'I've got a call to make.' The sound of a door being slammed reverberated down the hallway.

Lydia's voice could be heard, but not the words, her mother answered, then they drifted away.

A number of the footmen let out their breath.

'I assume that was Sinclair,' I remarked. No-one replied. The butler muttered something to one of the men, then stalked off, presumably expecting us to follow. We passed through a procession of stately rooms, vacant of humanity apart from an occasional bustling maid or liveried footman, who sprang to stiff attention when they spotted Trent. I noticed it was quite warm, despite none of the fireplaces being lit.

The interior was as prestigious as the exterior; lofty ceilings painted in renaissance style. Sofas and chairs perfectly contoured in rich satin and silk. Large paintings of war ships, battlefields and military might lent animated drama to the rooms. The whole show shrieked of new money, invested to impress.

'Is he always like that?' I asked Trent as he marched ahead of us.

'This is his Lordship's house.' His tone made it clear he wasn't going to elaborate.

We walked in silence for a while, then Swift launched into action. 'What was the name of the chauffeur killed in the accident?'

Trent maintained his silence.

'Did you hear me?' Swift tried to pull his notebook from the pocket of his damp overcoat.

'The local police have already been informed of the facts, sir,' Trent gave a short reply.

'And now you can inform me,' Swift retorted.

The butler didn't attempt to hide his irritation. 'His name was Monroe, he was Lord Sinclair's chauffeur. It was an accident.' He didn't sound concerned about the death of the man.

'Was he a skilled driver?' Swift began an interrogation.

'He wouldn't have been employed as a chauffeur if he weren't.'

'How long had he been in Lord Sinclair's employ?' Swift

handed me his notebook, I've no idea what he thought I was going to do with it. I shoved it in my pocket.

'Twelve years,' he replied.

'How old was he?' Swift continued.

'Nearing fifty.'

I guessed Trent to be the same age.

'Was he liked? Did he have a wife or girlfriend?' Swift rattled out questions.

'No and no.' Trent replied through gritted teeth.

He led the way through another magnificent sitting room, then opened a narrow door which I'd mistaken for part of the panelling.

'Come this way,' he ordered.

Swift and I stepped through into a wide hallway and halted in surprise. We were in a scruffy back corridor which stretched about ten yards. It was draughty and cold with a profusion of pictures hung haphazardly along the walls; cosy cottages, cows in meadows and a large painting of a castle on a lake. I paused for a moment to gaze and wonder. It was a pretty scene; a romantic ruin under a blue sky, trees and shrubs grown wild around tumbled walls, one high tower reflected in the still water. It held an aura of mystery and memories of days long ago.

Trent had continued along to the end of the corridor and we had to extend our stride to catch him. He'd stopped at the only door and rapped loudly on it.

'Go away,' a voice called from the interior.

'Sir Bertram, there are visitors here for you.' Trent raised his tone.

'Not today, thank you.'

'They have come about the accident,' the butler persisted.

'Busy. Off you go now,' came the reply.

Swift stepped forward and shouted. 'Persi Carruthers asked us to come.'

'Persi?' Surprise sounded in the voice. Shuffling footsteps grew nearer, muttered curses were heard amid much fumbling. The door was opened by an elderly man in a thick, red dressing gown, tartan slippers and a deerstalker hat. He peered up at us through wire-rimmed spectacles.

'Who are you?' He adjusted his glasses and stepped closer to bring me into focus.

'Lennox,' I informed him.

'Ha! You're Persi's beau. The bolter! Lydia told me all about you. Where d'you go?'

'I... um, I had to go home,' I gave a stumbling reply, then attempted to divert his attention. 'This is Fogg.' I pointed to the little dog at my feet. 'And Swift, he's a detective.'

'Good morning...' Swift tried a greeting.

'Ah, you don't squirm out of it that easily.' The old chap raised a finger at me. 'Not done, young man. Not done at all.'

'No, I have apologised...' I began.

He gave a chortle. 'I'd have done the same in the face of the massed ranks. Run like a jackrabbit! Haha. Come in, come in.' He suddenly glowered at the butler. 'Not you, Trent.'

'I had no intention of doing so,' Trent replied coldly and marched off.

Sir Bertram St George waved us through the open doorway.

Fogg ran through, tongue out and tail wagging.

'I believe you were concerned about the accident to the chauffeur,' Swift stated as we strolled into a room reminiscent of the Old Curiosity Shop.

'Was I?' St George's thick brows raised.

'Yes, Persi told us,' I mentioned. 'We're here to investigate.'

'Really? Well, you'd better get on with it, then.' He was a chap of comfortable proportions, a round, ruddy face below the deerstalker with proper tweeds under the dressing gown. I assumed it was worn for warmth as there was a chill about the place, despite a blazing fire in the generous hearth.

'I have a wife about somewhere.' He looked around, then yelled, 'Millie.'

We waited, nothing happened.

'Kitchen,' he said. 'Baking probably. Very good cook, my wife.' He stopped by a table heaped with books and picked three up, before shuffling off through an archway. Fogg followed him, quite aware that the word 'kitchen' meant food.

'He wasn't expecting us,' I remarked. 'Nobody was expecting us, Swift.'

'I thought this house had been renovated.' Swift tried switching the subject. 'Someone said Lanscombe Park was a marvel of modern technology.'

I wasn't interested in technology. 'Swift, this investigation isn't something concocted by Florence and Persi, is it? Because it's beginning to feel like we're here under false pretences.'

'Don't be ridiculous, Lennox.'

I stuffed my hands in my pockets, feeling out of sorts.

We were in a large room with a beamed ceiling; rugs scattered about, armchairs and sofas squashed together and heaped with colourful cushions. The walls were lined with bookcases stuffed with tomes of every size and where there weren't books, there were curios and relics of the past. A theodolite, a transit, numerous measuring devices in silver, ivory and brass and a human skull on a dusty shelf staring from the shadows.

We retreated to the log fire and stood with our backs to it, contemplating the clutter. Despite the disorder, it was a homely place with the sort of hushed atmosphere usually found in a cloistered library.

A tap on the door disturbed the peace and we both looked in that direction. Nobody came to answer it, so I volunteered.

'I'll go.'

It was Greggs with Mr Tubbs in his hamper.

'Sir, they drove your car around to the rear with me in it.' Greggs' colour was high with indignation. 'I protested, but they wouldn't listen.'

I took the hamper from him. 'Well, never mind, old chap. You can stay here, out of the way.'

'They have left the luggage in the outside porch, sir. They refused to bring it any further.' He was quite agitated.

I placed the hamper on a dusty table, unbuckled the straps and released Tubbs. My little cat jumped out and strolled to the hearth, sat down and began washing himself. He was a composed creature, perturbed by very little.

'Good heavens, such a crowd of you.' An elderly lady entered carrying a large tray laden with a porcelain teapot, cups, saucers, creamer, sugar bowl and a sponge cake. 'Are you a butler?' She peered at Greggs.

That put Greggs on his mettle. He straightened up and gave a stiff bow. 'Indeed, madam.'

'You're not from the other side, are you?' Her gaze slid in the direction of the door and the Palladian splendour beyond.

'Certainly not, madam.' He was quite adamant. 'May I be of service?' He didn't wait for an answer, merely stepped forward and took the tray from her trembling hands.

'Oh, how splendid,' she said with the glimmer of tears in her faded blue eyes. 'You've brought a butler.'

CHAPTER 3

'Yes, please. Milk, sugar and a small slice of cake.' Lady Millicent St George was seated by the fire with a look of pure joy on her face. Greggs hovered at her side, ready to serve from the tea tray placed on a nearby stack of books.

'Lost our butler years ago,' St George was seated opposite her. 'Died poor fellow. Only eighty-seven.' He shook his head in sorrow, or possibly disbelief.

'And we don't have any money, you see, so we can't afford another. But we make do and mend.' Lady Millicent was pushing a silver fork into her Victoria sponge, causing a billow of cream and jam to ooze from the centre. Foggy watched with round spaniel eyes; the little duo had already enjoyed a huge fuss and too many treats. Tubbs was now ensconced on his own footstool by the hearth while Swift and I were on a sagging sofa opposite St George and his wife.

'Doesn't Sinclair provide you with staff?' Swift asked, as Greggs handed him tea and cake.

'Good Lord, no.' St George nearly choked on a crumb.

'Can't have that. Not going to be indebted to Sinclair, the bounder.'

Having heard a sample of the man's temper back in the main house, I could sympathise with the sentiment.

'But Sinclair owns Lanscombe Park, doesn't he?' Swift was fishing for information.

'Humph! The St Georges have always been masters of Lanscombe, and always will be.' The old man bristled. He had removed the deerstalker and tied a napkin about his neck.

Lady Millicent intervened. 'We can stay as long as we want to, and we do want to, don't we Bertie. We're waiting for Randolph, he's our son...'

Her husband waved a hand to quiet her. 'Now then, hush, old girl. You know it does no good...'

Lady Millicent wasn't about to be hushed. She was an elderly lady with an air of fragility, her lace blouse too large on her slight frame. She wore a long dark skirt, her white hair caught in a bun. Her face maintained a faded prettiness, creased and etched by time.

She leaned forward conspiratorially. 'Randolph is in America, he's seeking his fortune.'

'Erm... is he?' I was pretty sure he was dead.

'Yes.' She smiled sweetly. 'He's prospecting for gold in the Klondike, in Alaska. He must have found a great deal, he's been there such a long time.'

Swift and I exchanged glances. The Alaskan gold fields had been abandoned over twenty years ago, and Randolph's widow, Lady Penelope, had since married Sinclair.

'Millie, there's no need to go into that,' St George tried again to quieten her. 'These chaps are here about that rascal who crashed his car.'

'Monroe, wasn't it?' Swift was quick to jump on the subject.

'Yes, an absolute menace. Always racing about. Killed our cat. Ran her over! Flattened. Didn't even come and tell us; just left her on the grass. Had to bury her myself.'

'How did the accident happen?' Swift's lean face sharpened.

'She must have run out and he hit her,' St George glowered. 'The blaggard.'

'I meant Monroe's accident,' Swift said.

'Oh, that. He came along the back way, through the Dell. Dark there, bad place, crossed the bridge and hit a tree. Bang. That was the end of him. Destroyed the car. Good thing it was his own or Sinclair would have docked his pay.' St George took a large bite of cake and chewed it.

'What do you mean by the Dell?' I asked, as Greggs finally handed me a slice of the goodies.

'It's the name for the old woods,' Lady Millicent answered. 'It's rather wild and overgrown. There's a ravine with a humpback bridge. I never liked it. We don't go there, do we Bertie.'

'No, no. We don't go anywhere, old girl,' St George mumbled between bites.

'Were there any witnesses?' Swift continued.

'Oh no,' Lady Millicent answered. 'It's the tradesman's

road, nobody is allowed there without permission and it was Sunday teatime.'

'The servants' tea or the family's?' I asked, thinking that she seemed perfectly sane when she wasn't talking about her dead son.

'The servants, they take their tea between five and six,' she explained. 'It is quite usual.'

'Did that include all the staff?' Swift continued questioning.

'No idea, hardly going to go and count 'em, are we.' St George seemed to have cheered up.

'Lennox, you could take notes,' Swift suggested.

'So could you,' I replied.

He frowned, then turned back to St George. 'Why was Monroe on that road if the staff were supposed to be having tea?'

'Coming back from the village. Had a fondness for the bottle and didn't dare take any from the cellars. Always went Sunday teatime when he was here. Trent turned a blind eye, wouldn't let anyone else get away with it.' He looked to his wife. 'We could hear Monroe's car from our kitchen window.'

'It was such a noise.' Lady Millicent nodded, her cup held in both hands.

'Had he been drinking on the day of the accident?' Swift persevered.

'Couldn't have been if he'd run out, could he?' St George chuckled.

'Did you mention this to the local police?' I finished

my cake. Swift's notebook was still in my pocket, so I gave it to him. He didn't seem grateful.

'No, the bobby's a local, he'll know what's what without us telling tales,' St George answered.

'What marque of car was it?' Swift had begun making rapid notes in his neat hand.

'Fiat, a sporting car,' St George answered. 'Horseless carriages we called 'em in my day. Never mastered the things, hopeless with mechanicals, aren't I, old girl?' He patted his wife's hand.

'Oh yes, but Randolph is terribly clever with them. He invents things; machines and experimentals, he's had his own workshop since he was a boy.' Lady Millicent's face lit up as she talked. I thought she seemed rather tragic.

Swift gazed at her for a moment, then returned to his questioning. 'Monroe was Sinclair's chauffeur?'

'He was, went everywhere with Sinclair,' St George replied, 'Ex-military, some of the other menservants are too. Carry guns! Notorious for it.'

'Why?' I asked, wondering who they expected to shoot.

'Blueprints. Sinclair keeps them in the house,' St George rumbled. 'Thinks it's safer than a bank with all those ex-soldiers about the place.'

'Blueprints for what?' Swift looked up from his note taking.

'Armaments, weapons. He buys inventions from boffins and the like, then has 'em built. That's the secret to his success. Knows artillery and rockets inside out; knows what they do, knows how they kill. Sinclair's a merchant of death.'

Everybody knew Sinclair's reputation. His name was synonymous with war and weaponry.

'You said your son was an inventor?' I risked mention of Randolph while Lady Millicent's attention was on Greggs; he was wielding a silver server over the sponge cake.

'That's it. Met Sinclair through inventing.' St George's face clouded.

'What happened?' I asked quietly.'No use turning over old stones, lad,' he mumbled. 'Let it be.'

Swift was still making notes. 'What can you tell us about the gun that Lord Sinclair received. It was in a package, wasn't it?'

'No, no,' St George became flustered. 'Not a word. Mustn't mention it, not in front of Millie.' He flapped a hand as though to ward off the topic.

I glanced at Lady Millicent; tears had welled in her eyes and were beginning to spill down her thin cheeks. Her husband tugged a handkerchief from his pocket and handed it to her.

'Ahem… More cake?' Greggs stepped forward, the perfect butler, defusing the discomfort. He was just showing off because he never did it at home.

'Ah, yes, excellent idea,' St George agreed. 'Lennox, I don't care what they say about you, any man prepared to share his butler is a good 'un in my book!' He slapped the arm of the chair, causing dust to rise.

Swift sneezed.

'Who was in the house when Monroe had the accident?' I turned the conversation.

'We were here.' Lady Millicent had dried her tears and held the handkerchief in her lap. 'Lydia and Max and Penelope were home.' She paused, her brow creased in a puzzled frown, then said. 'And Sinclair, of course.'

Swift's pen was moving rapidly across the page. 'Are these members of the family?'

'Not Sinclair. He's not,' St George instantly retorted.

'And there's Jerome, he is Sinclair's assistant.' Lady Millicent ignored her husband. She was watching Swift as he listed the names, then whispered. 'And there's that young man, Finn…'

'Finn?' Swift stopped writing to question her.

A loud rap at the door interrupted us. Greggs made a show of answering it. Tense murmuring was heard, along with some harrumphing from Greggs. After more exchanges, he closed the door firmly and returned to address me.

'Lord Sinclair has requested your presence, sir, with Inspector Swift.'

'Trent, was it?' St George asked loudly.

'It was, sir. He is waiting in the outer corridor,' Greggs replied.

'Good, because he's not allowed in here,' St George shouted towards the door.

'He failed to bring a written message,' Greggs informed us, 'or a silver tray. I did bring it to his attention.'

I laughed. 'Butlering one-up-manship, old chap?'

35

Lady Millicent turned to gaze at Greggs. 'Isn't he marvellous.'

He simpered and picked up the teapot. 'More tea, m'lady?'

We left them to it, at Swift's insistence. Trent was waiting in the corridor, he didn't say a word, merely turned sharply on his heel and marched off. We retraced our steps back through the procession of palatial rooms to the grand hall. There was no sign of Lydia, or Lady Penelope, nor anyone apart from various liveried footmen standing at strategic points.

The staircase was in sweeping style fashioned with a curving bannister rail in glowing Honduras mahogany. The carpet silenced our footsteps as we trod the stairs and reached a balustraded landing, which ran in a full square around the upper hallway. More artistry in military fashion hung on richly papered walls. A few side tables bearing porcelain vases of carefully arranged flowers took up any spare space. I looked about at the lavish magnificence and preferred the cosy clutter of the St Georges' old wing.

Trent knocked tentatively on the grandest portal, then waited with a white-gloved hand poised over the brass doorknob.

'Come,' a voice called.

Trent opened the door and stood aside. A paper aeroplane whizzed past our ears.

'Sir!' Trent exclaimed in anger.

A young man was sitting in a large leather chair, looking relaxed, his feet up on a gleaming black modernist desk.

'Jerome called Sinclair away, something about his stocks on the ticker, it was all terribly urgent.'

'Mister Max, this is his Lordship's office. You must leave immediately.'

'He told me to wait, so that's what I'm doing. You can go and ask him if you like.' The young man, Max, was folding another sheet of thick creamy paper between long fingers. He wore casual slacks and a linen shirt without a tie under a beige sleeveless jersey. He had dark brown eyes and hair, and bore a close resemblance to Lydia.

'These are the gentlemen his Lordship asked to be brought to him.' The butler barely contained his ire. 'They can't stay here unsupervised.'

'Don't worry, I'll keep an eye on them. Off you go.' Max glanced up from under dark brows, his face devoid of expression.

Trent hesitated, then went with obvious reluctance, the paper plane following closely behind him. He'd deliberately left the door wide open and a footman sidled into view a moment later, no doubt with instructions to watch us carefully.

Perhaps he thought we might steal something, there were plenty of pricey pieces in the room. A silver ink pot and stand, gilded desk calendar and leather-bound blotter. A gleaming glass and walnut drinks cabinet against one wall, opposite a large portrait of a battle-hardened warrior scowling beneath an iron helmet.

'You're Lennox, Persi's bolter, aren't you,' Max announced in my direction. 'Lydia told me you were here with a detective.'

'I'm not a damn bolter, I just needed some time,' I objected.

He laughed. 'Can't blame you.' He swivelled in the chair to drop his feet to the carpet. 'But you do realise this whole incident has been exaggerated. It's just a ploy to reel you in.'

I frowned, because that had been my fear all along.

'Inspector Swift,' Swift told him in a cool tone.

The young man didn't get up or offer a handshake. 'I'm Max St George. Scion of the house, son of Lady Penelope, brother of Lydia. Twin brother to be precise.'

'Grandson of Sir Bertram and Lady Millicent St George,' I added.

He gave a wry grin. 'Quite the sleuth, aren't you.'

'You're Randolph's son,' I stated.

'Got it in one, yes. Grandma been talking, has she?'

'She said Randolph was in the Klondike, searching for gold,' Swift took up. 'But we understood he was dead.'

'Poor old Grandma.' Max stopped folding the sheet of paper in his hands. 'Likes to keep the memory alive, so she pretends he's still out there somewhere. She's not gaga, it's just her way.'

'What do you know of the accident?' Swift asked.

Max looked askance. 'Are you really going to keep this pretence up?'

Swift sat mute, his arms crossed, waiting for an answer.

'Oh, for heaven's sake,' Max swore in irritation. 'Monroe hit a tree. It was five thirty in the evening. He died, there were no witnesses. I was nowhere near it at the time.'

I had something else on my mind. 'There was talk of a parcel with a gun in it, it was given to Sinclair. Was it something to do with your late father?' That was a guess on my part after observing the reaction of Lady Millicent.

'You're grasping at straws.' Max screwed up the paper and tossed it into a waste bin. 'Look, you weren't asked to poke your noses around, you don't even have permission to be here.'

'Lady Penelope said we could stay as long as required,' I replied, trying to contain my irritation.

'Mama's just humouring Lydia while she plays cupid, you sap.' He laughed without humour.

'Answer the question about the gun,' Swift demanded.

Max turned sullen. 'It was a stupid prank to annoy Sinclair.'

'By you?' I asked.

'No, I've no idea who did it.'

'Why would receiving a gun annoy him?' Swift continued. 'He's an arms dealer.'

'Because the parcel came from Alaska, that's why. And I've already told you, it was just a stupid prank,' he fumed, then stalked out.

We watched him leave before Swift spoke.

'Alaska?'

'Where Randolph is supposed to be,' I replied.

'Where Randolph is supposed to have died,' he corrected.

Well, that merely answered one mystery with another.

'Come on Swift.' I'd had enough and was riled by Max's insinuations. 'I'm not kicking my heels here, let's go.'

'Wait.' A voice hailed us.

We left the office as a chap came bounding along the landing. 'Just a moment, I've come to apologise, Lord Sinclair has been delayed.' He was a trim fellow, almost as tall as me. Black hair, good features and dressed in a tailored city suit. He was smiling in a friendly manner.

'We're leaving,' I told him.

'You're Persi's bolter and the detective, I presume? I'm James Jerome, Lord Sinclair's assistant.' He gave a disarming grin and held his hand out.

'I'm not a bolter,' I retorted sharply.

'No, of course… sorry, I'm being crass. Would you like to wait, gentlemen?' He dropped his extended hand.

'How long will Sinclair be?' Swift asked.

'I really don't know. I can have a bite of lunch brought up if you wish.' Jerome was the epitome of the good lieutenant; well spoken, pleasant in manner and form, probably capable of charming the birds from the trees. I didn't trust him an inch.

'We have an investigation to carry out,' I told him curtly and walked off towards the stairs.

Swift caught me up in a few strides. 'Lennox, that wasn't helpful.'

'I know, but I don't give a damn, Swift. We're being played for fools. If we can't find any evidence, I'm leaving and that's the end of it.'

CHAPTER 4

The pimply hall boy was lurking near the front door, I called him over. 'Do you know where the Dell is?'

He glanced at the other footmen, then nodded mutely.

'How do we find it?' Swift pressured him.

The lad's cheeks flushed as red as his jacket. 'I'm not supposed to talk' he whispered. 'I just take hats and coats and put them in the cloak room.'

He was a placid looking lad, pale blue eyes with sandy hair and downy growth on his chin.

'We're investigating a suspicious death,' Swift told him. 'You're obliged to answer our questions.'

'But… but,' the lad stuttered. 'You can't go wandering about without permission.' His eyes flicked again to the footmen watching every move.

'Just tell us,' I said.

He leaned forward to whisper. 'Cut southwest across the lawns to the big bushes, follow the deer path through the woods 'til you reach the tradesman's road on the other side, then follow the track downhill.'

'Right, come on, Swift.' I strode to the front door, yanked it open and led the way out into the fresh air.

A few calls of 'wait!' followed us as we exited between the white pillars of the portico and made an escape.

'Slow down, will you, Lennox.' Swift was breathless as we strode across the lawn.

'Fine.' I moderated my pace. The grass was wet, my leather boots showed dark splashes above thick soles, the sun shone between gathering clouds. The storm was still circling.

Swift muttered something, then said. 'Look, Max was goading you. We can't let him drive us away.'

'Swift, you heard him. He said Lydia's playing cupid and I'm being reeled in.' I was angry and raised my voice. 'Lydia probably exaggerated the accident to provoke Persi into calling us.'

'Persi isn't gullible, Lennox, as you very well know.' He was walking with his hands stuffed into his coat pockets.

He was right about that, but I wasn't ready to back down. 'Someone's playing games.'

'Yes, to cover up a murder.' Swift was very single minded.

'We don't know if it was murder,' I snapped.

'Then we'll find out, won't we,' he retorted. 'And there's more than just the accident, there's that parcel from Alaska.'

'Hum,' I muttered and made an effort to calm down. 'Lady Millicent spoke about Randolph without any distress until the gun was mentioned.'

'Yes, and Persi said they were upset in her telegram,' he replied.

'They were upset by the gun, but not anything else,' I remarked.

'No...' He replied meditatively. 'They weren't, were they.'

We found a gap in the row of thickly grown bushes to enter a belt of woodland. The trees were mostly ash, beech and oak, with silver birch on the fringes. We followed a track with small hoof prints amid a layer of yellow and orange leaves; it was a pretty place, where squirrels gathered acorns and birds hunted beetles and bugs among the leaf litter.

'Max was evasive,' Swift continued. 'No-one has explained how the gun and parcel relates to the death of Sinclair's chauffeur.'

'Perhaps it's aimed at Sinclair,' I remarked, which gave him something to think about.

We emerged from the trees to find ourselves in a landscape given over to simple agriculture. Fields and meadows predominated, with clumps of gorse and brambles forming islands of spiny thickets. Bleating sheep scattered as we walked across close-cropped grass to a narrow tarmac road.

'The Tradesman's route,' Swift remarked as we stopped to look about.

'Swift.' I pointed down into the valley. 'There's a lake.'

It lay in a dip in the distance, a silver expanse partially obscured by specimen trees, their foliage turned bright with autumnal colour. There was a ruined castle on a promontory with a tower jutting into the water; it looked like the painting I'd seen in the hallway of the old wing.

'It's beautiful,' Swift muttered.

'And not far from the house,' I remarked. We'd walked in a wide loop and now stood above the mansion, looking down.

We gazed for moments more, before a shout returned us to reality.

'Stop right there.' A man limped up behind us. 'The house telephoned, Mr Trent has made checks on you. He said you're retired from Scotland Yard.' He was short and wiry, with sparse hair under an ill fitting cap, he wore the house livery of black and red and had one leg shorter than the other.

'Ha, they found you out, Swift,' I said with a grin.

'Who are you?' Swift demanded.

'I'm the gatekeeper for the tradesmen's entrance, I am.' The chap was out of breath. 'I saw you from the lodge.' He flicked a hand to indicate a small house away in the distance. I could see the outer wall and a modest wooden gate set between plain columns.

'We're investigating with Lady Penelope's approval,' Swift replied coolly.

'Aye, but you should be authorised by Lord Sinclair…' The guard squinted up at us in the sunshine. 'Mr Trent has rules you know…'

'Trent isn't the law and I suggest you cooperate.' Swift was in no mood for an argument. 'Did you know Monroe?'

'Ay,' he replied with a nod.

'And you're um…?' I encouraged him.

'Hodges,' he saluted, then grinned. 'From Hereford, I am. Gone and got me leg twisted round in the war, Hop along Hodges they call me.'

There wasn't much I could say, but I returned the smile.

'Did you witness the accident, Hodges?' Swift continued in a more friendly tone.

'Nope, I heard it though. Nasty bang, followed by a wallop. I came down here an' found 'im, or what was left of him.'

'Was it instant?' I asked.

'Oh aye, I'd think he was gone in a flash.' His eyes darkened. 'A right mess he was. I went straight back to me lodge and called the house, then the police.'

'Did you see anyone else in the vicinity?' Swift questioned.

'Not a soul,' Hodges replied. 'You goin' to catch the blighter then?'

'You don't think it was an accident?' I asked.

Hodges shook his head. 'Monroe were too good a driver to die like that.' He leaned forward. 'But don't you tell no-one I said so, or I'll get me marchin' orders.' He stepped back. 'Now, I'll be off, before I say anythin' else out of turn.'

He limped back up the road at a reasonable rate given the handicap.

'He's fearful.' Swift remarked.

'Not of us,' I replied.

'No, of Trent,' Swift was thoughtful. 'He didn't believe the official version of events, either.'

I returned to the task. 'The hall boy said to follow the road downhill,' I indicated where the track ran towards sprawling woods.

'The Dell,' Swift said. We strode towards it as the sun slipped behind massing clouds.

Shadows engulfed us as we entered the wood. It would have been a shaded place at any time, but it felt dark and sinister in the gathering storm. Toadstools sprouted from decaying stumps; lichen, bracken, brambles and ferns grew wherever a patch of light filtered through the high canopy. Dead leaves littered the road and ancient tree trunks crowded the tarmac's edge as it twisted and turned downhill.

'Humpback and narrow,' Swift said, as we approached the bridge spanning the deep ravine.

'Designed for horses and carts,' I replied, glancing about in the gloomy light. I'd driven over any number of humpback bridges, or rather flown over them at speed. They were common in the countryside and usually rather fun, but there was nothing fun about this rank spot. I buttoned up my collar against the creeping cold.

We paused at the highest point of the bridge. Swift pulled a torch from his inside pocket and lit it.

'He must have hit here first.' He shone the beam at the left side of the parapet.

'Strange, why here?' I bent over to run my hand along where the car had gouged red paint into the dank green stonework.

Swift walked slowly forward, keeping the torchlight steady.

'The car veered along the wall and smashed through it near the end.' He stopped to gaze at the pile of rubble.

I moved to join him and looked over the broken parapet; chunks of shattered stone, white against black earth, had been thrown down the steep bank. 'He must have been driving at speed.'

Swift stooped to peer at the road surface covered in a fresh fall of yellow and brown leaves. He swept them aside with his hand, then pointed. 'He braked here, you can see tyre marks.'

'If he flew over the hump, he'd have left the ground and skidded on landing.' I stared at the traces of burnt rubber. 'Perhaps he lost control.'

'No, if he'd lost control, he'd have bounced off both walls,' Swift disagreed. 'He only hit the left side.'

'Wet leaves can be as lethal as black ice,' I reminded him.

'How many motor accidents have you attended, Lennox?'

'None, obviously.' I'd seen a number of aeroplane crashes, I'd even been in one, but that probably didn't count.

'I was a bobby in London and I've examined enough of them,' Swift remarked and paced along the bridge, directing the beam. 'He broke through the wall then hit this log.' He aimed the torch at a fallen tree by the roadside, the mass of splinters telling its own story. 'That caused the car to catapult into the air and smash against here.' He pointed at an ancient beech, its dark trunk riven by deep gashes, the exposed sapwood showing bright against the black bark.

'Poor soul,' I muttered under my breath.

We paused for a moment, trying not to imagine the hurtling vehicle crashing into the massive solidity of the tree. I sighed and sent a silent prayer to the man above, before turning back towards the bridge.

'The police must have collected the debris when they removed the car,' Swift continued, sweeping his torch in an arc across the ground. Scattered slivers of glass, metal and red paint chips shone in the light. Other, darker remains, lay mixed with the detritus and mud. 'They'd have gathered evidence if there were any.'

'Which means there wasn't,' I concluded.

'There's nothing here.' He sounded dispirited.

I dug into my jacket pocket to find my own torch and aimed it at the intact wall opposite. 'He swerved to avoid something. A deer, perhaps?'

We crossed to the other side, which was entirely unaffected by the catastrophic events.

'He was a professional driver, he'd have run into an animal rather than risk hitting the wall,' Swift countered.

'So, someone stepped out in front of him.'

'Impossible, he wouldn't have been able to avoid hitting them. It would be suicidal.'

I had to agree; the road was too narrow for a car and a person.

'What if they stood just behind the end of the parapet?' I suggested.

'If they had, Monroe wouldn't have had to swerve.'

He was right, but we both leaned over the wall anyway.

'Footprints!' I exclaimed.

Swift shone his torch onto the mud. 'They're full of water, you can't be certain.'

'Somebody stood here, Swift,' I exclaimed

'It could have been the police,' he tried to sound sceptical, but I heard an undertone of excitement in his voice.

'No, look. There's only one set. Someone stepped off the tarmac there,' I aimed my beam at the sequence of hollows. 'And they took two steps, turned to stand behind the wall, then walked back to the road again.'

'We can't prove anything. It's impossible to take an impression; the storm has washed away any details.'

'But it's evidence, Swift.' I was certain.

'It's muddy puddles, Lennox.'

'Let's search by the bridge.' I stepped into the morass, my boot slipped and sank. I swore.

We slid and slithered down the bank among the bracken and moss until we reached the bottom. I was relieved I hadn't brought Foggy, and not just because of the mud. He wouldn't have liked it any more than I did.

'No-one's been down here,' Swift said as we peered below the arch of the bridge.

'We'll try along the bank.' I turned and clambered along the edge of the ravine.

'Swift...' I stopped. 'Look.' I shone my torch onto a freshly broken branch.

'It's a stick, Lennox.' He was unimpressed.

I picked it up. It was almost as thick as my wrist, about a yard in length and forked at the end to form a 'y'. Bright splinters showed it had been snapped off a tree not long ago.

'It's sweet chestnut. It wouldn't grow here, it's too dark.'

'Are you sure?' He frowned.

'Yes, of course I'm sure. We gather chestnuts for Christmas every year.'

He took a closer look, then shone his torch onto the surrounding trunks. I've no idea why, I doubt he'd recognise a sweet chestnut if it fell on him.

'We should find out where it came from,' he announced.

'Well, it's not from these woods, it's too densely grown.' We climbed back up to the road, drops of rain began to spatter through the trees.

'Wait, I want to try something.' I stepped into the muddy footprints behind the parapet wall. I'd been thinking about how I'd cause a car accident in this confined spot without risking my life. 'What if someone held a coat or jacket?'

'So that it looked like a figure?' He regarded me, his brow furrowed. 'It's possible, I suppose.' He shrugged off his overcoat and hung it on the end of the branched 'y', then handed it to me.

I leaned over the wall and waved it into the road. 'I think that would work. Monroe could have mistaken it for a person, he'd only have caught a glimpse in his headlights. His reaction would be instant.'

'You're right.' Swift's smile suddenly flashed in the grim

light. 'He'd swerve, but there would be nowhere to go. He'd crash into the wall as soon as he turned the wheel.'

'Someone caused the accident! It's murder Swift.'

'It's not proof.' Swift preferred his evidence cut and dried.

The rain had turned into a downpour and was drowning out my words. 'Come on. We're in for a soaking, we'll have to run.'

CHAPTER 5

'Sir,' Greggs swung the back door open. 'It is raining, you are wet.' He was a master of understatement.

I was too breathless to reply; we'd raced through the storm but were still drenched and dripping. My old butler ushered us into the rear hallway, a place as homely as the rest of the St Georges' quarters; faded wallpaper, umbrella stand and a bunch of wild roses in a vase on a window sill.

We began shrugging off our wet gear.

'And the stick, sir?'

'It's evidence,' I told him.

'Really, sir,' he sounded unimpressed. He went off with our sodden coats, presumably to a boot room or some such.

'We'll examine it upstairs.' Swift was keen. 'Did you bring a magnifying glass?'

'No. Didn't you?'

Swift usually carried a complete detecting kit with him, despite being retired.

'I was in London for meetings about the whisky,' he replied.

'Your rooms are prepared, sir,' Greggs announced on his return. 'If you would like to come this way.'

A bare pine staircase ran up from the hallway, typical of servants' stairs. The treads creaked as we traipsed up behind my old retainer.

'What's for lunch, Greggs?' I was feeling distinctly peckish after the day's excursions.

'I'm afraid lunch was taken some time ago. It is almost three o'clock.'

'What?'

'Inspector Swift, your room, sir.' He opened the door.

It led to a comfortable chamber as cluttered as the drawing-room below. The fire was lit, the windows had misted and the smell of wood smoke and damp hung in the air, but Swift seemed happy with it.

'Won't be a moment, Lennox,' he said and went in.

'Fine.' I followed Greggs to the next room. It was similar to Swift's, an oak-framed bed, a desk under the window, various small tables, a dresser and a merry fire with chairs set before it. 'Where's Fogg?'

'With Mr Tubbs, in the kitchen, sir. Lady Millicent has cooked steak and they are waiting for it to cool down.'

I sat on the bed. It creaked. 'I hope they've saved some for me.'

'Should I prepare a repast, sir?'

'Yes please, Greggs.' I don't even know why he asked, he knew I was starving.

'It will be ready on the hour.' He went off.

Swift entered without knocking. 'Did you find it?'

'Find what?'

'The magnifying glass, of course.'

'No, give me a minute, will you.' I opened the bedside cabinet to discover my gun. I took the little pistol and slipped it into my inside pocket, not with anything particular in mind, but if everyone else in the place was armed…

'Lennox.' Swift had gone to the window and now held up the magnifying glass. 'It was on your dresser.'

'Why did you ask me to look then?' Really, he was always so damn precipitous.

He found the stick where I'd left it and laid it on the low table in front of the fire. 'We should have worn gloves.'

'Well, we didn't.' I sat down to watch as he played the glass along its length. 'Would we be able to see fingerprints on a stick?'

He considered it. 'Probably not, but we should try. We'll need to make some powder, unless you've brought any.' He sounded hopeful.

'Of course I haven't brought any.'

He moved the lens closer to the forked ends of the stick. 'There are fibres.' He broke into a grin and indicated the fine filaments caught in the splintered ends.

'You hung your coat on it,' I reminded him.

'Ah, um, yes.' He looked a bit crestfallen.

'Ha,' I laughed. I was the one who usually spoiled the evidence.

He went to the desk-top and picked up an envelope. 'Do you have tweezers?'

'Probably.' I dug around in drawers, trying to discover

where Greggs might have squirrelled things away, and found the tweezers on the washstand.

'I'll send them to London for analysis. There's a laboratory specialising in forensic testing.' He teased tiny fibres from the broken splinters and carefully placed them in the envelope, which he tucked into his jacket pocket. 'If I add some fabric from my coat lining, they can exclude them.'

'Are you sure it's worth checking for prints?' I looked again at the stick on the table. It was wet, grimy and distinctly lacking in promise.

'Yes, we must be thorough, Lennox. We can make powder with soot and talc, I've got some talc in my room.' His enthusiasm had returned.

'Fine, I'll scrape some soot from the chimney.'

We gathered our ingredients and he mixed them in a bowl in front of the fire.

'I'll brush it on.' Swift offered and carefully stroked the grey powder with a shaving brush over the stick.

I followed his movements with the magnifying glass. It took ages. He was finicky and pedantic, as usual. We sat back in our chairs once he'd finished.

'Nothing.' His face fell.

'Last night's storm could have washed it away,' I reminded him. 'We need to find the sweet chestnut tree it came from.'

'It could have been carried by anyone.' He was becoming despondent.

'Nonsense. Why on earth would anyone carry a stick into a forest?'

'I don't know, to walk with probably.'

'With a stick shaped like that?'

He ran fingers through his dark hair. 'What if there isn't anything, Lennox? Even if it was murder, we may not be able to prove it.'

My heart sank. The contretemps with Max had unsettled me, and all we'd really found were puddled footprints and a stick in a wood. Perhaps we were seeking things that weren't there? I knew I'd come in the hope of seeing Persi and I was certain Swift had been cajoled into coming by his kind-hearted wife. Perhaps we really were deluding ourselves.

I gave a sigh of exasperation. 'You're the professional, Swift. What does your training tell you?'

A clock on the mantelpiece ticked while he said nothing, but then he raised his dark eyes. 'That it's only circumstantial evidence and supposition... And yet, I believe it was an act of premeditated murder.'

'Ha!' That cheered me up. 'So, we're not on a fool's errand.'

'Well, I wouldn't go that far.' He grinned.

The little clock suddenly chimed the hour.

'Food, Swift,' I remarked and headed for the door.

He muttered something about the investigation having priority, but followed me downstairs anyway.

Fogg greeted me with excitement when we reached the kitchen. I made a fuss of him, as Gregg placed two plates of delicious cold cuts, slices of pork pie, apples, nuts and freshly baked bread with pats of butter, on the table. There was a glass of claret each too.

'Marvellous, old chap,' I congratulated him.

'Aren't the St Georges here?' Swift asked as he sat down, his eyes on the meal.

'They are taking an afternoon nap, sir. Would you like tea?'

'No, thank you. Claret is exactly what we need,' I told him as I tucked in.

Greggs pootled around the place while we ate. He wore an apron made for a girth of lesser proportions. Swift droned on about procedures and the like, I nodded in the right places. The claret was rich and warming and I looked about for more.

'Ah, sir, I forgot to inform you that Mr Trent returned.' Greggs paused while drying dishes at the sink. 'Lord Sinclair has been asking for you again.'

'Well, he can wait until I've had another glass of claret,' I replied, placing my knife and fork on my cleared plate.

'No, Lennox, we need to go.' Swift was already on his feet.

'Wait…' I called, but it was too late, he was heading for the corridor. I strode to catch up. 'Swift, we don't need to jump at the snap of Sinclair's fingers.'

He wouldn't listen, despite my objections. We lost our bearings at one point, which didn't help. Swift found a footman to point the way and we reached the grand hall with tempers frayed. Well, mine was anyway.

'Lennox, Swift, I've been waiting for you.' It was Jerome, the perfectly polished professional. He led us upstairs and back to the office where we'd met Max earlier in the afternoon. He knocked at the door.

'Come,' a voice called.

I'd half expected another paper plane, but there was no such light-hearted nonsense. Sinclair didn't look up as we entered, he was reading a document, it looked like a legal contract.

'Please sit down,' Jerome whispered, indicating the same chairs we'd occupied earlier. There was a silver sixpence on the floor. Someone must have dropped it, so I picked it up and placed it on the shiny black surface of Sinclair's desk.

Jerome left, closing the door quietly behind him. We watched Sinclair, or rather his hair; it was silver grey, plenty of it, lightly oiled to keep it in place. I didn't find it particularly interesting and was about to say so.

'Ah, gentlemen, apologies.' Sinclair stopped reading and straightened up. 'My lawyers had spotted some tricky wording in the small print and wanted my opinion.' He picked up the contract and crumpled it with large, workman-like hands, then tossed it into a waste bin. 'That's what I think of it.'

We watched him without a word.

'So, you're Lennox, and you're the other one.'

I almost laughed. Swift wasn't amused. The flush to his lean cheeks gave him away.

'I'm...' Swift began, but was cut off.

'You're *previously* of Scotland Yard, a fact you omitted

when you barged into my house.' Sinclair reached for the silver sixpence and pocketed it. 'Drink?'

'No, thank you,' I answered, because I didn't want to accept anything from the man. Swift didn't reply, he was frowning with his lips closed in a thin line.

Sinclair poured himself a glass of whisky from a decanter on the desk, then sat back to regard us. Well built, fleshy about the jowls, pale blue eyes, light tan and a look of steel about him. His jacket fitted him loosely, made for a man on the move, not a stuffed shirt putting on the style.

'Now, you're here on some pretext about Monroe,' Sinclair said, as though it were somehow amusing.

I shifted in my seat.

'Not just Monroe, there's the gun too,' Swift glowered. He obviously didn't like Sinclair any more than I did.

'It was a nasty trick, but that's all it was.' Sinclair sipped his whisky, watching us over the rim of the glass. He put the drink down in one quick movement and assembled a smile. 'Peace, gentlemen. I don't mind the pretence, I sincerely hope for a happy outcome.'

'This isn't a pretence.' I was stung at being taken for a lovelorn sap. 'Someone murdered Monroe.'

His eyes narrowed. 'Can you prove it?'

I sat back. 'Not yet.'

His lips curled with contempt. 'Then don't take me for a bloody fool.'

I wasn't going to be intimidated. 'Why did the gun unsettle you?'

'Because the packaging had Alaskan stamps,' he

replied. 'Even you must realise the implications. Randolph St George died there.'

'And you were with him at the time,' I added.

He sat upright in his seat, regarding us coldly. 'I was in Alaska, but I wasn't anywhere near him. If I had been, I'd have died too.'

There was an aura of absolute confidence about Sinclair. He was in control and afraid of nothing, or so it appeared.

'How did it happen?' Swift asked curtly.

'I imagine he cut the fuse too short.' Sinclair shrugged. 'He was blasting with dynamite, it was a common way to remove boulders from a buried seam. He must have been too close when it went off and was blown into the river along with the rubble. The body was never found.'

I watched him closely, his expression and tone were devoid of emotion. It sounded as though the tale had been repeated often and his answers were almost mechanical.

'Was there an investigation?' Swift continued.

'Of course there was,' Sinclair replied, then suddenly gave a bark of laughter. 'You really are determined to play the detective. Very well, gentlemen, if you want to embark on a wild goose chase, I have nothing to hide.'

'What invention had Randolph devised?' Swift questioned.

'It was a mechanism to search for gold. Rather clever actually, but then Randolph was a clever man.' Sinclair took a swig of whisky.

'You just said he blew himself up,' I remarked.

Sinclair's brows drew together.

'How did the mechanism work?' Swift carried on.

'It was a variation on George Hopkins' Induction Balance for detecting metal.' Sinclair resumed an indifferent manner. 'Randolph found a way to make it more sensitive to gold. The theory was to exclude other metals and save time. It wasn't as useful as we'd hoped, the gold was in river beds or buried deep in the ground.'

'Did Randolph patent his work?' I asked.

'No, it was merely an improvement on an existing design.' He leaned back in self-satisfied ease. 'I've been fortunate to live through a new age of invention and it moves very quickly, gentlemen. These are exciting times, there is much to be made from it.'

'What were Monroe's duties?' Swift switched tack, attempting to throw Sinclair off balance.

'He was my chauffeur.'

'And your bodyguard?' I added, recalling St George's words when he told us that Monroe went everywhere with Sinclair.

Sinclair shrugged, he seemed bored by the conversation. 'He was a military man and I travel in dangerous places. I always took Monroe with me.'

'Have you ever been attacked?' I asked.

'No.' He picked up his glass. 'I take precautions, just as anyone in my business would.'

He was too complacent, so I sought to rattle him. 'Who do you think pulled the trick with the gun?'

'Bertram St George, of course.' Irritation rasped in his

voice as his temper broke. 'I saved this house. I gave his entire family a roof over their heads. I succeeded where he failed and he's never forgiven me for it.' He stopped abruptly. 'Enough of that. My wife has given you permission to play your game, I'll give you one more day, then you leave my house.'

It seems we were dismissed.

'Fine.' I stood up.

Swift was less inclined to go quietly. 'Where were you at five thirty on Sunday evening?'

I thought Sinclair would explode with anger, but he snapped an answer. 'I was here, you impertinent oaf. Now get out.'

We left without another word.

CHAPTER 6

'Sir.' An elderly footman hailed us. He'd been standing near Sinclair's office door. 'I was asked to intercept you.'

'What is it?' Swift asked.

'Lady Penelope would like a private word.' He was a dignified chap with kindly eyes under bushy white brows and a white moustache. He probably wasn't as old as the white hair suggested as he was trim and upright with a resolute air. 'May I escort you?'

Swift didn't bother seeking my agreement. 'Lead on.'

We walked the length of the very long corridor, then rounded a corner and went on some more. The house was huge, with portals and passageways going off to who knows where.

The elderly footman stopped to tap at a door; it was probably as far away from Sinclair's office as it was possible to get.

'Come,' Lady Penelope called.

She looked up as we were ushered in. There was a chap with her, they were seated in the window seat, lit by a weak sun trying to break through the storm clouds.

'M'lady.' The footman bowed stiffly.

'Thank you, Mullins.' Lady Penelope rose to greet us.

'Hey there.' The young man came with her. He spoke with an American accent.

'Greetings,' I replied and bowed over Lady Penelope's hand. Swift followed suit.

'This is Finn.''Finn Patrick, a Yank abroad, at your service.' He was good looking, confident and breezy with red gold hair brushed back from an open face.

'Chief Inspector Swift.' Swift was courteous. 'Retired,' he added.

'Lennox.' I mentioned out of politeness.

Finn Patrick grinned at me. 'You're the guy Lydia was talking about, she said you'd come to act the sleuth and win back your fair maiden.'

'Now, Finn.' Lady Penelope scolded him.

'Nonsense,' I was becoming less amused. 'We're investigating Monroe's murder.'

'Sure you are.' He laughed, unabashed. 'Well, I hope you get your gal. I'll see you all at dinner.' He gave a casual wave of the hand and strolled from the room.

I swore under my breath; I was sick of being taken for a bloody chump.

'Should I bring tea, m'lady?' Mullins stepped into the breach.

'No, we won't be long,' she replied, then became flustered. 'Unless you gentlemen would like something?'

'No, thank you,' Swift replied without asking me.

She showed us to a sofa near the fire. We were in a

pretty day room elegantly decorated in feminine fashion in pale blue and cream. I suspect she spent quite a lot of time in it.

'Please do sit down.'

We sat.

'We've just had an interview with your husband,' Swift began.

'Yes, I am aware.' A frown creased her forehead. 'Was he reasonable?'

'He thinks we're here on a romantic ploy,' I replied, trying and failing, to keep the anger from my voice. 'So does everyone else, apparently.'

She glanced at me, but didn't digress. 'Did he order you to leave?' 'He gave us until tomorrow,' Swift answered.

'Will that be enough?' she asked.

'I'm afraid not,' Swift continued. 'We haven't even spoken to the local police yet or taken statements, or…'

I cut in because he was becoming obsessed with details. 'Do you believe the accident was caused deliberately?'

She paused before replying. 'I really don't know, but it has made me uneasy.'

'Can you tell us anything about it, or what happened that day?' Swift moved into investigative mode.

'I'm afraid not. Mullins came to inform me that Monroe had been killed. The police arrived sometime later.' She seemed distracted.

'Who is that American fellow, Finn Patrick?' I asked her.

Colour rose in her fine cheekbones. 'He is my husband's illegitimate son.'

That brought a hush to the room.

'He's obviously accepted here,' Swift remarked.

'Finn was born while Sinclair was in America. He was adopted, but I…we have kept in contact.' She was choosing her words carefully. 'I don't think this has any bearing on Monroe's death.'

That put us in our place. I was wondering why she'd asked to see us.

'Do you think there's a threat to your husband?' I asked the question.

Some moments passed before she spoke. 'It's possible. First the gun, then Monroe's death… he was my husband's bodyguard.'

'Yes, we know,' I replied. 'But if someone wanted to kill Sinclair, why not just do it, why start with his bodyguard?'

'I… I don't know.' She lowered her eyes. 'Do you think I'm being ridiculous?'

'Of course not, it's a very understandable concern,' Swift was quick to reassure her.

'Well, thank you.' She stood up, a sign that the interview was over. 'I look forward to seeing you both at dinner.'

We were on our feet.

'Yes, and thank you.' Swift gave a bow.

Mullins escorted us into the passage and closed the door behind us.

'What the devil was all that about?' I said to Swift as we trotted downstairs and through the grand hall.

'She was sounding us out.' He didn't seem perturbed by it.

We made our way towards the old wing. 'She was worried that her husband's life was in danger. Do you think it is?'

'Time will tell, won't it,' he replied with equanimity.

Running feet were heard behind us and we both swung around to look. It was the spotty hall boy.

'Sirs, I've been searching for you.' He was breathless. 'The police are here. They're gathering everyone in the servants' hall.'

Swift perked up. 'The police?'

'Yes, sir,' the boy replied. 'Mr Trent said to come and get you, I've been looking everywhere. Then I just bumped into Mr Mullins and he said you'd been up with her lady-ship, and you might be going back to the old wing, and I told him that was where I started off.' He took another breath. 'Been running round in circles, I have.'

He was a lot more talkative here than he had been in the hall.

'Right, we're comin,' Swift announced. 'Lennox?'

I was in need of some quiet time in the fresh air with my little dog.

'I think I'll take a walk, Swift. It doesn't take two of us to talk to the police.'

'But someone may have vital information,' he argued.

'Don't think they do, sir,' the boy answered. 'It's all anyone's talked about since the accident, but no-one saw a thing.'

'There you go, Swift. No need to go at all,' I told him.

'We must co-ordinate with the local force.' He

hesitated. 'But you could have a look for the source of the evidence…'

'You found evidence!' The boy was agog.

'It isn't actual evidence and you're not to repeat a word,' Swift told him firmly, then marched him off.

I carried on to the old wing and entered the kitchen; no-one was about. Foggy was keen to go, and I picked up my little cat to place him in the pocket of my shooting jacket. It was a bit of a squeeze as he'd grown rather fat. We left by the back door to enter a rambling garden. I'd barely noticed it when we'd dashed through in the rain earlier. It faced north and was encompassed by brick built walls containing orchards, flowers and vegetable patches. I followed a stony path, passing shrubs and saplings, while Foggy scouted ahead with his nose to the ground.

I was keen to gain a spot of solitude, my mind turning over the events of the day, who was who and what they'd said. I recalled Lady Millicent mentioning the name Finn earlier. It was a surprise to learn he was Sinclair's by-blow and I wondered what his ambitions may be.

A picket gate in the wall gave onto the formal grounds of the mansion. Foggy and I cut a diagonal through the parterres, rose arbours, knot gardens, fountains, statues and the like. I came to an ancient yew hedge almost ten feet high, thickly grown and perfectly trimmed. I strolled alongside it to a pair of fancy iron gates and stopped in my tracks.

A vista of pastoral perfection stretched down towards the lake. Single specimens of oak, elm and cedar stood amid gently sloping lawns; belts of woodland framed the scene leading the eye down to the shimmering expanse of water. A folly stood in line of sight, a few yards from the water's edge; it was white and in the same Palladian style as the house. It was built on a broad circular plinth about twenty feet across, curved marble walls supporting slender pillars reaching up to a dome topped with a golden pinnacle. I could see movement, someone was there. I followed the slope down to see who it was.

'Oh, you've caught me in my sinful habit.' Lydia laughed. She was smoking, lounging on a seat in a restful pose. She'd changed into warmer clothes, slacks – which were becoming quite the fashion – and a velvet-trimmed jacket over a white blouse.

'Greetings.' I gave her my best grin. Foggy remembered her from our morning arrival and leaped about, yipping for attention.

'He's such an adorable little doggie.' She tossed her cigarette over the folly wall and bent down to fondle his ears. He was ecstatic, but then spotted ducks and raced off to the lake's edge. 'What's he called?'

'Fogg. He's easily distracted,' I replied as we watched him go.

'Do you smoke?' she asked.

I hesitated, thinking that I could very easily be tempted. 'No, I've given them up.'

'Oh, it's quite the rage, you know. And the inhalations are said to protect against influenza.' She adopted an artless air, but there was intelligence in her dark eyes.

I extracted Tubbs from my pocket, causing another bout of delighted laughter from Lydia.

'He needed some fresh air,' I explained and looked around. 'I thought the castle was here?'

'It's beyond the trees.' She indicated a thickly planted copse.'

I gazed at the vista. 'It's bigger than I thought.'

'Yes, the lake is simply huge, Sinclair had it dredged and extended into the quarry. He even had an island built.'

I nodded. It was barely visible in the distance, a dot in the expanse of water.

She leaned back, the better to see me against the waning light. 'Can I call you Heathcliff? It's such a romantic name.'

'I'm not keen on Heathcliff,' I answered without babbling. I had a habit of lapsing into idiocy when talking to pretty girls. I'd given it some thought and decided that if I treated them like suspects and asked questions, I might be able to avoid making a complete fool of myself. I cleared my throat to put the plan into action. 'Where were you when the accident took place?'

She laughed. 'Am I suspect?'

'No, I'm just asking everyone. It's detecting.'

'Well, I was right here, and Jerome was with me. We didn't see or hear a dicky bird.' She picked up Tubbs, who'd toddled over to investigate the wind-blown leaves around her feet.

'Oh…' I tried to think of another question. 'Why was Jerome with you?'

'Because he's my fiancé,' she replied, stroking Tubbs under his chin.

'Really?' That was a surprise. Although I'd noticed she wore a large diamond ring on her finger, so I suppose it shouldn't have been.

'Lennox you simply must rekindle the flame with Persi, it's such a ridiculous way to go on.'

'What? I mean, it's… I wasn't…' I shut up abruptly – things weren't going to plan.

'We've invited her to dinner tonight. We're all going to be there, except Grandpa and Grandma, of course. They never go anywhere.'

'P… Persi's coming to dinner?' I stuttered.

'Yes,' she laughed. 'I just said so. I telephoned her, it's all arranged.'

That caught me by surprise. I sat down on a marble seat, then straightened up as the penny dropped.

'It was you! You rang my house, didn't you?' I threw the accusation at her. 'You pretended to be Persi. I couldn't believe it was her; she's refused to speak to me since… erm.'

'Since you walked out on her.' She finished the sentence for me.

'It was you, wasn't it?' I persisted. 'You didn't find Fogg by chance and come downstairs, you were watching out for us from the windows.'

She hugged Tubbs to her chest. 'Yes, of course.' She laughed. 'I thought you'd be onto me in an instant. Anyway, it worked. You're here and Persi is coming tonight, so voila!'

'Lydia, it isn't funny, I've been made to look like an absolute idiot.' I was furious and it must have been apparent by my expression because she cast me an anxious glance.

'But it will be worth it, really it will.' She tried to placate me.

I wasn't remotely placated. 'What about the accident and the parcel? Was that part of the ruse?'

'No, it's all true,' she insisted.

Damn it, I swore under my breath. I was on my feet, in half a mind to walk away.

'You won't leave, will you?' She looked worried.

'You've dragged me and Swift here...' I suddenly thought about that. 'Why did you telegram Swift?'

'Because I truly think there is something wrong and I wanted you both to come.' She'd given up the silly girl act altogether and was quite serious. 'Everyone has been behaving so strangely... and I'm frightened.'

'Lydia,' I sat down again. 'You'd better explain.'

'It's been quite tense. I...I can't really describe it.' She took a breath. 'When Sinclair opened the parcel, and there was the gun inside, it was such a shock. He threw it away and told Trent to burn the package. Afterwards nobody said anything, but Mama was upset and now she's anxious. And Max was stunned, and since then he's been snapping at everyone.'

'Was this before Monroe was killed?' I asked.

'Yes, and I'm convinced there's a connection. The police couldn't find anything, or wouldn't, so I thought of you. I knew Sinclair would forbid it; that's why I pretended it was to bring you and Persi together.' A smile trembled on her lips. 'And I really do want you to get together, so it was an awfully good plan, don't you think.'

I tried to calm down and make sense of it. 'Why didn't you tell me?'

'I haven't had chance, and… I wasn't sure if you'd become angry and leave.'

'I'm…' I began, then stopped and decided I'd better start acting the detective. 'Right, tell me what you know – and start at the beginning.'

'Oh, thank heavens! Someone who will listen to me.' She suddenly beamed. 'It was Sinclair's birthday, his six-tieth, and he wanted a big party. He'd invited his cronies and their wives, and all the usual hangers on. Trent and Jerome organised it, but they couldn't decide if it should be indoors or out because of the weather.'

'When was the party?' I cut in.

'Five days ago. The sun smiled, so it was held out here.' She waved a hand towards the lake. 'They set tables and chairs along the lawn and the servants ran about with trays of hors d'oeuvres and bubbly on ice. We put on the glitz, it was all terribly glamorous. There were stacks of presents for Sinclair. They'd been piled up in here.' She indicated the folly. 'As the afternoon went on, he decided to open them. Trent carried them out a few at a time while Sinclair and Mama sat beside the lake. Everyone was chatting and drinking. He unwrapped watches and cufflinks – you know the sort of things people buy – and then there was a box. It looked very plain, not at all as a gift should be presented.' She paused to put Tubbs on the floor as he'd been eyeing the skittering leaves.

I waited for her to continue, but her gaze had turned back to Foggy by the lake. 'The gun?'

'Yes.' She brushed a strand of dark hair away from her face. 'Wrapped in old brown paper. There were stamps on the paper, it had been opened a long time ago and torn apart. In the middle of it all was the revolver. Sinclair's face turned white, his mouth fell open and he stared as though he'd seen a ghost. Everybody stopped talking and watched. Then he walked to the edge of the lake and threw the gun as far as he could.'

I was beginning to wish I'd brought a notebook. 'What type of gun was it?'

'An Enfield.' She probably knew quite a lot about guns, given the nature of the household.

'The parcel was from Alaska?'

'No, silly. Someone had taken it from Papa's old rooms.'

'Ah, so it hadn't actually been sent from Alaska.' I'd been puzzling over why Sinclair had thought Bertram St George was behind it.

'Of course not, all Papa's belongings were returned to Lanscombe after he died.'

Well, that was one minor mystery solved. I wondered how sensitive she'd be to the subject of Randolph St George.

'But your father died in Alaska.'

She nodded. 'Papa had some wild dream of finding gold and Sinclair was determined to make his fortune. He wanted to exploit one of Papa's inventions, but they didn't find very much gold. Sinclair went to Boston after Papa was killed,' she continued. 'He died when I was a baby, but Grandma keeps his memory alive. I... I still feel close to him.' She laughed suddenly. 'I'm being quite ridiculous, aren't I.'

I returned a smile. 'Does your mother speak of him?'

'No, she says it's all in the past.' Her smile wavered. 'I've asked her... actually, I used to plague her about it. Whenever I was home from boarding school, I would pretend to be a detective, uncovering the mystery of who Papa was and how he died. It made Sinclair so angry, and that made me even more determined.'

'Why do you dislike Sinclair so much?' I asked.

'He's manipulative and ruthless and he doesn't care about anyone but himself.' Her face fell, all animation died away.

'And he took your father's place?'

'It's not just that...' Her eyes caught mine. 'Did you find a sixpence on the floor in his office?'

'Yes,' I replied. 'I put it on his desk.'

'It was a test, to see how honest you are. He does it to everyone. If someone keeps it, he says they can be bought cheaply. If they give it back to him, they'll be more expensive, or maybe they have to be exploited in some other way.'

'Not very subtle.'

She laughed without humour. 'He doesn't need to be.'

Foggy began barking again.

'Lydia?' A voice called out. 'What is this dog doing here?'

'Oh, it's Jerome.' She jumped to her feet. 'He's called Fogg, he's with us,' she called.

'Wait.' Questions were churning in my mind, but it was too late.

'Hello, you here, Lennox.' Jerome greeted me in the same friendly manner as before.

He turned to address Lydia. 'Are you going to dinner in that get up, darling? You look like you're ready for a hike in the woods.'

She laughed, her good humour restored. 'I could. What do you think? Will they send me to my room without supper?'

He returned her amusement, his eyes seeking hers. 'No, you know they won't, but it would upset your mother.'

'Oh, I was only teasing.' She turned to me. 'Heathcliff, we'll see you later.'

Jerome hesitated and said. 'Just a word of warning, old man. Sinclair doesn't like animals. Keep it in mind, would you.'

'Oh, yes, I should have mentioned it.' Lydia smiled and took her fiancé's proffered arm.

'What were you talking about?' Jerome asked.

'Papa, and the package...'

'You really mustn't worry about it, Lydia,' he replied.

'Oh, but I do.' She looked up at him as they walked away together.

'Fogg,' I called. He came to me, tail wagging happily. The sun touched the horizon to wash storm-laden clouds with violent colour; purple, black and a shimmer of deep red reflected in the still waters of the lake.

I stooped to pick up Tubbs as the first spots of rain began to fall. It was too late to find the castle now and besides, I needed to dress for dinner, ready to meet Persi again. Which was when I realised that it would be in front of everyone in the house...

CHAPTER 7

'Lydia sent the telegram to Braeburn!' Swift was incredulous. I'd told him the details about the gun and Sinclair's party, but Lydia's piece of mischief seemed to excite him more.

'Yes, and she telephoned Ashton Steeple pretending to be Persi.'

We were in my room. I was trying to dress for dinner in the hope of making a good impression. Greggs had been helping, but he'd made such a fuss that I sent him downstairs.

'Damn it, Lennox, why didn't she just tell us?' He was already togged in smart evening wear.

I was searching through my bedside drawer. 'Where would Greggs put cufflinks?'

'I have no idea.' Swift sounded exasperated. 'All this pretext about Persi and...'

'I've borne the brunt of that one, Swift,' I reminded him, although he wasn't listening.

'It took me the best part of an hour to convince the sergeant that the accident could be malicious. Now he's preparing another search of the site and the wreckage.' He was more concerned about his standing with the police.

I found the cufflinks! They were in a leather case in the tall boy. It was a bit of a fiddle to fit them. 'Did you mention the stick?'

'It was a stick in a forest, Lennox.' He was acerbic for no good reason. 'No, of course I didn't mention it. We need concrete evidence.'

'The laboratory might provide it,' I said.

'Evidence which I contaminated myself,' Swift muttered.

'What about the statements? Was anyone missing at the time Monroe was killed?'

'It wasn't a murder enquiry, so they didn't take statements. And none of the staff was missing long enough to have gone to the Dell and back.'

The mirror was too mottled to see very much in it. I straightened my tie, combed fingers through my hair and stuffed a clean handkerchief in my top pocket.

'Not even Trent?' I persisted.

'No, no-one.'

I paused to regard him. 'But if none of the staff was missing, then it could only be one of the family.'

He returned my gaze. 'I know.'

'Hell.' I thought about it. 'I doubt Lydia considered that when she tricked us into coming here.'

'No, and let's hope she doesn't come to regret it. Come on, Lennox.' He made for the door.

'Right... Swift, wait. My bowtie isn't...?'

I was too late, he was already trotting down the stairs. I picked up Fogg and Tubbs to take them to the warm kitchen. Greggs was stirring something in a pot under Lady Millicent's direction. I greeted them with a grin and put the little duo down.

Greggs paused, ladle in hand. 'May I wish you good luck, sir.'

'It's just dinner...' I began.

'Oh, don't be silly.' Lady Millicent came to me and reached on tiptoe to kiss me on the cheek. 'Now, remember, faint heart never won fair maiden.'

St George had been sitting at the table with his nose in a book. He got up and shuffled over to slap me on the back. 'Courage!' He ordered. 'Off you go, my lad.'

Swift was waiting and we set off at a fast pace to arrive in the grand hall. A sentinel footman pointed us in the direction of the drawing room, which proved to be upstairs and only a short distance from Sinclair's office.

The place was even more splendid than the other state-rooms. Tall windows draped with gold damask ran the length of one wall. Persian rugs carefully placed on polished parquet, sofas arranged in informal groups, a grand piano, gilt and white wall panelling hung with gilded mirrors and portraits of ladies and gentlemen in magnificent attire. It was all brightly lit by two huge electric chandeliers hanging from the lofty ceiling.

Lydia greeted us as we walked in. She wore a rose-hued silk frock with pearls. 'Oh, do come and have some champagne. We've already started.'

Jerome was behind her in formal evening dress, a smooth smile on his face.

Trent was on duty. He stood near the open double doors, directing footmen. He nodded briskly to a servant, who took the hint and stepped forward with a tray of flutes filled with bubbly. I'm not usually keen on champagne but one sip changed my mind; it was superb.

Sinclair strode in behind us. 'So, the ardent knight arrives with his trusty squire.' He laughed without amusement.

I didn't think it was funny. Neither did Swift judging by his face.

Jerome sidestepped us to address Sinclair. 'Sir, could I discuss the latest figures…' He indicated he had something of importance to impart. They detached themselves and went into a huddle near the piano. Trent hissed instructions to his minions, then discreetly crossed the room to place himself within hailing distance of his Lordship.

'Persi is with Mama.' Lydia slipped her hand under my arm. She tried to tug me to the other end of the room, where a collection of high-backed sofas were grouped around a blazing fire.

'Just a moment.' I downed my champagne and grabbed another from a passing footman.

'Lydia, I want to talk to you about…' Swift began.

'No, I'm not saying a word until Heathcliff has come to say hello.' She pulled at my arm again.

I finished the champagne, smoothed my jacket and followed her across the room.

'Oh, Lennox, there you are.' Lady Penelope stood to greet us. 'And Inspector Swift.'

'I... erm, greetings,' I stuttered.

Persi was sitting on a sofa. She didn't say a word, she didn't even glance up. She looked stunning, her blonde hair gleaming, a cameo around her neck and the same green silk gown she'd worn when we'd been in Damascus together. My throat was suddenly dry, I'd been waiting... wanting to see her again...

'What?'

'I said, do please sit down,' Lady Penelope repeated, giving me a smile of encouragement.

Persi still hadn't deigned to turn in my direction, so I took a sofa of my own. Swift went to sit next to her; she gave him a tight smile.

Lydia had waited until we'd positioned ourselves then perched next to me. More champagne was offered, I downed it. It really was jolly good stuff, and I was feeling distinctly light headed. I was just about to risk a greeting to Persi, when Lydia leaned forward.

'Persi's thinking of going back to Egypt,' she announced.

'What?' That was a shock. 'I... are you really going?'

'Yes,' Persi replied calmly. 'The team think they're close to a discovery, they've asked me to return and I've agreed.'

'No... I mean, don't. Persi, you... you can't.' I spoke without thinking.

'Why?' She turned her lovely face to gaze at me, her grey-blue eyes glittering with what looked awfully like anger.

'Because… Because, it's not… I…' I was on the tip of babbling and stopped, closing my mouth shut. That didn't help, and she looked away.

'Sorry, I'm late.' Max strode in, smart in evening wear, although his dark hair was uncombed. He dropped onto a sofa opposite us. 'So, how goes the romantic intrigue?'

'Do try to be discreet, darling,' Lady Penelope admonished him.

I saw colour flush in Persi's cheeks.

'Max, you're such a twit,' Lydia hissed, which didn't help.

'Oh, for heaven's sake,' Max sighed in exasperation.

I watched the interplay, aware that one of them could have planned Monroe's death, although I admit, my attention was mostly taken with Persi.

Footmen continued the rounds with champagne trays, I took another glass, so did everyone else. Sinclair and Jerome remained on the other side of the room, deep in conversation.

'Are you really going to return to Egypt?' Swift asked Persi.

She gave a strained smile and nodded mutely. My heart sank, I tried to think of something to say.

'I heard the police were here again today. Have they uncovered signs of dastardly deeds?' Max said, his questions apparently casual, but I saw a muscle tic in his jaw.

Swift answered in a professional manner. 'I asked them to make another search of the site.'

Max directed his taunting at me. 'What did you find in the Dell, Major Sleuth?'

'A stick,' I replied.

He frowned, but didn't let up. 'Well, that about sums up your enquiries. Raking over a simple tragedy for nothing but...'

'Max,' Lady Penelope raised her voice. 'That's enough. Stop antagonising our guests.'

'What is wrong with you, Max?' Lydia objected. 'You're being simply beastly.'

'Ha, Max being beastly, I can't imagine it.' Jerome had strolled over and came to sit next to Lydia. He said something quietly to her. It must have been amusing as she giggled. They looked genuinely happy together. I looked away. Sinclair had gone off somewhere and Trent was missing too. I glanced at Persi, who'd leaned over to talk to Swift. By the soppy smile on his face it was probably about his new baby.

'Hey folks, any bubbly left? I've just struck a deal and I'm in the mood to celebrate.' Finn sauntered in. He took one glance at Persi and switched tack to head in her direction.

'Oh, Finn,' Lydia called to him. 'You really must learn to arrive on time, Sinclair becomes so irritable if we're late.'

'Ha,' Finn laughed at the comment, but his eyes hadn't left Persi. 'The old man knows business comes first.'

'We have guests,' Lady Penelope reminded him.

'Hey guys.' He waved in our general direction, then bowed extravagantly in front of Persi. 'And hello to you, my lovely lady.' He reached for her hand and raised it to his lips. She didn't protest.

The room suddenly fell very quiet and everyone looked from Finn and Persi, to me.

'I must apologise for my stepson's lapse in manners,' Lady Penelope broke in. 'Finn came for his father's birthday party, and is staying for the season.'

'Yeah, that's right.' Finn sat down next to Persi. 'I came over on the cruise liner. Wasn't going to miss my Pop's birthday bash and I have business in London.'

'You've visited before?' Swift questioned while I considered hitting the American.

'I came to look my British family up a few years back, we got on so well I spent every last fall here. Ain't that right, Mom,' he grinned at Lady Penelope, then addressed us. 'This lady here is the best stepmom in the world. Made sure I was cared for as a kid, then gathered me to the family bosom when I found my way to these shores. She's a genuine saint.'

'Finn, would you please come and sit by me,' Lady Penelope ordered him.

'Sure. Hey, Heathcliff, sorry, old man, was I in your place?' He jumped to his feet. 'Here, it's all yours.' He waved a hand towards the spot he'd vacated next to Persi.

Her eyes flashed a warning, so I stayed where I was.

Finn shrugged and resumed his post. It did him no good. Persi stared at the fire, so he turned to chat to Max and they both laughed about something. I watched Persi, she seemed forlorn. I wanted to talk to her, to take her hand and explain, but couldn't, not in front of such a crowd.

'Finn, you're late.' Sinclair came back into the room

and joined the group. He was clutching a large tumbler of whisky and sat down next to Lady Penelope. Trent had also returned and began harassing the footmen.

'Hey Pop, that deal I told you about went off. Got me a corker.' Finn was served a glass of champagne, he was as effervescent as the bubbly.

'Well done, Finn. Chase down the detail, that's where the money is,' Sinclair replied approvingly.

'Along with the devil,' Finn laughed.

Sinclair turned to Jerome. 'You've got to send that telegraph to New York before eight.'

'I'll go before dinner...' Jerome pulled his sleeve back to check his gold wristwatch.

'Good, make sure of it. Can't risk missing this one, there's a small fortune involved.'

'Oh, please leave business for a moment, Sinclair,' Lady Penelope offered a mild reprimand.

Sinclair could have brushed the remark off, but his cheeks flushed with anger. 'Who's going to pay for all your pretty baubles, lady? And this house? I work night and day and not one of you is grateful for what I've done.' He finished his whisky in one gulp, Trent was instantly at his side with a replacement.

Silence fell. I could hear the drumbeat of rain on the window panes. I had my eyes on Persi who had averted her gaze and was looking distinctly uncomfortable. Lydia was upset, her hand gripping Jerome's.

I'd had enough, I stood up. 'You're a bully and a boor, Sinclair.'

His head whipped around in fury. 'Who the hell do you think you're talking to?'

'Lennox,' Lady Penelope cautioned. 'Thank you, but I am quite capable of handling my husband.'

'You shouldn't have to, Penelope. Heathcliff is right,' Persi rejoined in anger. I grinned, that was more like my fearless girl.

'No-one talks to me like that. Get out, you...' Sinclair yelled, then stopped mid-threat as the chandeliers flickered off and on. 'God damn it, Trent. Don't let the power fail...'

The bulbs flickered again, then shut off. The room fell dark, with nothing but the blazing fire to light us.

'Please remain seated.' Trent's voice came from a distance. 'I will change the fuse, my Lord. It will only take an instant.'

'Hell and damnation,' Sinclair swore. 'I pay through the nose for the best electrical installations in the country and the bloody lights go out every time there's a storm.'

'Sinclair, it will only be a moment.' Lady Penelope sought to calm him. 'And it's an exaggeration to say it happens every time.'

'Will you stop lecturing me...' Sinclair started another tirade.

'Leave her alone,' Max yelled. I could see his face in the firelight, there was fury in him and it looked as if it were about to be unleashed.

'No Max, please...' Lydia begged.

'Help.' A shout rang out. 'Help. Come quickly.' A man's voice yelled from the distant darkness. 'I think he's dead.'

CHAPTER 8

'Who has a torch?' Swift was on his feet in an instant.

'Nobody carries a torch to dinner,' Max snapped.

'Where are the candles?' Lady Penelope had risen too, Lydia joined her.

'Jerome, that telegraph has to go to New York,' Sinclair growled. 'Get the power back on.'

'Somebody needs help. Come on, Lennox.' Swift was already moving towards the door. I made to join him with Jerome on my heels.

'I'm coming,' Persi called, I turned and waited for her to reach my side. I gave her a grin but she probably couldn't see it in the darkness.

'I'm right behind you, little lady,' Finn called.

'No, you stay with the family,' Swift shouted back at him.

'They don't need me...' he argued.

Sinclair bellowed out orders. 'Finn, come back here. Jerome, hurry up and switch the damned power back on.'

We passed as quickly as we could through the dimly

lit drawing room – knocking into furniture and cursing quietly – then out into the dark passageway.

I realised Max was behind us.

'Hop, hop, old man,' he needled Jerome.

Jerome turned to frown at him, he didn't say anything but I could sense his irritation.

We carried on down the corridor towards the grand hall and stopped on the landing. The ceiling above us was in total blackness but the floor below showed a glimmer of light.

'Who's there?' Swift leaned over the bannisters to peer down. A lamp appeared from under the stairs and moved towards the centre, throwing shadows across the chequered tiles.

'It's me, Billie,' the hall boy called up. 'Something happened to Mr Trent. They said he's dead.'

'Has anyone called the police?' Swift demanded.

'Or an ambulance?' I added.

'The telephones don't work, sir, nothing works without the electric.' His voice shook with shock.

'Damn,' Swift muttered. He led the way quickly downstairs, we crossed the hall and formed a ring around Billie.

'Why aren't the lights back on?' Jerome demanded.

Billie looked close to tears. 'I don't know, sir.'

'Jerome, he just said Trent is dead,' Persi rebuked him.

'Billie, where is Trent?' Swift asked.

'By the Fuse Room, sir, they dared not move him.' His voice cracked.

'Come on, show us the way,' Swift ordered.

'Aye, sir.' Billie took us to a discreet door leading to a

set of stairs. We went down and entered a long corridor below ground. The floor was flagged with stone, the walls unadorned brick, typical of many of the large, old houses I'd been in. Doors and passages led off, shrouded in darkness. There were more lights ahead and a huddle of figures were silhouetted beneath.

'Trent?' Jerome called.

'He's been electrocuted,' a voice replied.

Two footmen were standing with lanterns held aloft and three others were kneeling beside a prone figure in the centre. Trent lay deathly pale, his short hair awry, his mouth contorted into a rictus snarl, eyes wide and bulging beneath a deeply furrowed brow. He looked shocked, which in the circumstances was to be expected, I suppose.

'Good lord, so he really is...' Max uttered.

'Persi, perhaps you'd rather not...' I began.

'Heathcliff, I specialise in corpses.'

'Long dead ones,' I replied, knowing her passion for forensic archaeology. 'And not Heathcliff, old stick.' I reminded her, then thought better of it. 'Erm... unless...'

She wasn't listening, she had bent to examine the corpse with a professional eye.

'What do you think?' Swift asked her.

'He died instantly,' Persi said quietly. 'It must have been a powerful current.'

Swift muttered something under his breath, then strode over to the fuse room.

I grabbed Billie's storm lantern out of his hands. 'Swift, don't touch anything.' I caught up with him.

'I'm not an idiot, Lennox, I'm going to lock it.' He'd tugged out his handkerchief to reach for the brass doorknob.

I raised the lantern. The fuse box was the standard black metal board with copper dials and wires, dominated by the long handle of the power-switch. The floor was covered by a thin layer of water, something gleamed under the slick surface. I'd hardly registered it when Swift yanked the door closed and turned the key in the lock.

Jerome pushed past the men to reach us. 'Stop. You can't. We have to isolate the fuse and turn the electricity back on.'

'No-one is to enter this room, the police need to search it,' Swift declared.

'I must insist you open the door,' Jerome sounded panicked.

'No.' Swift wasn't intimidated. He put the key in his jacket pocket.

'Mr Jerome, you mustn't, it's too dangerous.' One of the younger footmen came forward to join us. 'Sorry, to speak out, sir, but there are live cables in there. No-one should risk going in before daylight.'

'He's right,' Max spoke up. 'Of course, you could make the attempt, Jerome. If you think it's worth it.'

Jerome hesitated, no doubt weighing Sinclair's wrath against the consequences of a wrong move in the fuse room. 'That stock transaction was worth a fortune,' he muttered.

'Did anyone see what happened?' Swift's interest lay in the dead man.

'I was with him on the occasion, sir.' It was Mullins, the footman who'd attended Lady Penelope.

'Oh hell!' Jerome suddenly called out. 'If the electricity remains off, the alarms won't be working. We must secure the building, get back to your posts. All the security lights will be out. Make sure the windows and doors are locked and guarded.'

'Wait, I need to question this man,' Swift indicated to Mullins.

'Right, the rest of you must go. You too, Billie,' Jerome told them. 'Come on, hurry up.'

They left at a run, their footsteps thudding along the corridor. We waited until the noise died away.

Max had been watching in the shadows. 'There's no point staying here. Are you coming, Persi? Dinner will be off, but Mama will have ordered cold cuts around the fire.'

'No,' Persi replied sharply. 'This man's dead, and all you're thinking about is your own comfort.'

'Exactly, he's dead,' Max replied. 'Why not leave it to the detectives while we care for the living?'

'I'd rather stay.' She looked from me to Swift. 'If I may?'

'Yes, please do,' Swift replied with enthusiasm.

'Suit yourself,' Max retorted and walked off into the darkness.

Swift turned to the footman. 'Why were you here, Mullins?'

'I am senior footman, sir. I came to assist Mr Trent.

I held the lantern as he entered the fuse room.' Mullins spoke slowly, as though measuring his words.

'What did you see?' I asked.

I observed Mr Trent reach for the handle of the power-switch to pull it down into the off position. But…' He frowned, white brows drawn together. 'But, as he grasped the handle there was a flash and a bang, and he was thrown bodily through the doorway. He cried out, it was most unlike him. I hastened to drag him away as it was quite evident the situation was dangerous. I'm afraid it was too late, he was dead.'

We gazed at him for a moment.

'Right, well done, old chap. Very brave of you,' I commended.

He gave a modest bow of the head. 'It was my duty, sir.'

'Was there anyone else down here?' Swift questioned.

'There was not, it was merely he and I,' Mullins replied. He had a way of speaking which was quite old fashioned to our ears.

'We'll examine the body.' Swift shifted into action. He knelt down and carefully turned Trent's head to check if there was blood or any injury. Suspicious as ever, he never accepted the obvious.

Persi picked up Trent's right hand for a better look at the glove. I held the lamp above her, her blonde hair burnished in the light. I could smell her perfume, it was faint and flowery like a… 'What?'

'I said the fabric is charred.' She pointed to a black hole in the white cotton.

'Oh yes, right, I see,' I said, trying to concentrate. I decided I should stick to my questioning strategy to avoid babbling. 'What do you think?'

'It must have been the point of contact.'

'He doesn't smell,' I mentioned. 'I don't think he was erm...' I was about to say fried, but thought better of it.

'Cooked?' Persi said bluntly. 'No, his heart was stopped.'

'The floor of the fuse room was wet.' Swift was matter of fact. 'Trent wore leather shoes. Once he touched a live wire, the current would have passed through his body.'

I glanced at Trent's polished black brogues and the tan soles, which were dark with water stains.

'He was most particular about his shoes,' Mullins mentioned.

'You said he grasped the power-switch handle.' I stood up. 'Why would it be live?'

'I could not elucidate, sir.' Mullins sounded apologetic.

'We can't answer that until we search the fuse room in daylight.' Swift was checking the body, going through pockets, Persi was helping; they were quite systematic. I wondered if Greggs had saved any supper.

'A set of keys,' Swift held up a number of keys on a chain. 'That's all there is.'

'Mr Trent did not like to carry items of bulk upon his person. He believed it spoiled the line of the uniform,' Mullins explained.

'Have you known Trent long?' I asked him.

'We were in the army together, sir, in India with the

Royal Artillery. I was colour sergeant and Mr Trent was the sergeant major. He was a hard man and quite fearsome in battle,' Mullins recounted in his measured manner. 'He was struck by a sword thrust to the skull, fortunately his was thick, or the blow would have finished him. Nevertheless, the army forced retirement upon him and Lord Sinclair offered him a post.'

'Was Monroe in the same regiment?' I asked.

'He was, sir. He was a corporal,' Mullins replied.

'There was bad blood between them?' I added.

Mullins nodded. 'Once we took our posts at Lanscombe Park, Mr Trent maintained order according to our ranks. Mr Monroe refused to kowtow and, as he was close to his Lordship, there was little Mr Trent could do. However, it was not a cause for violence, sir. It was mere pettifoggery.'

'Right. Well thank you, old chap.' I thought him a venerable fellow with the dignity and courage typical of a colour sergeant.

'May we take him upstairs, sir?' Mullins asked.

I thought Swift was about to refuse, but he nodded. 'Yes, very well, but keep him somewhere cool.'

'Without electricity, the house will prove very cool, sir.' Mullins raised the lantern in his gloved hand. 'May I be of further assistance?'

'No, you've been most helpful,' Swift replied graciously.

'Then I will leave you and find some men to aid in Mr Trent's removal.' He went off along the corridor.

Persi was shivering with the cold in her silk frock.

'We should go.' Swift had noticed too.

'Just a moment,' I'd been waiting for Mullins to move out of earshot. 'Swift, open the door.'

'What? No. There's a live power cable in there,' Swift baulked.

I whipped off my bowtie. 'Give me the key, I'll open it.'

'Lennox...' Persi cautioned.

'Swift,' I pressured him.

'I hope you know what you're doing.' He pulled the key out and unlocked the door.

'Persi, hold the lantern.' I handed it to her. She raised it up as I looped my bowtie around the handle of the power-switch and jerked it down into the off position.

Nobody said anything for a moment.

'That was really dangerous,' Swift muttered.

Persi laughed quietly. 'And brave.'

'Look,' I bent down to retrieve the cause of the glimmer I'd spotted.

'What is it?' Persi asked.

I held up a long narrow piece of copper. 'It's the murder weapon.'

Swift peered at it, then pulled out his handkerchief to take it from me. He suddenly grinned. 'Well spotted, Lennox.'

'You're becoming quite the detective.' Persi looked up at me.

'At times.' I gazed at her. 'Could I have the lantern?'

She returned it with a smile. I smiled back.

'How do you think it was done?' She asked.

'I'm not sure…'

'Lennox,' Swift brought me back to reality.

I stopped gazing at Persi and held the lantern up.

Swift leaned in to scrutinise the controls. 'There are scratches.' He pointed to the inner side of the black box surrounding the fuses. 'The copper strip must have been forced into the gap where the power-switch is attached to the panel, it would have sent the current through it.'

'Yes, and the strip would have been positioned to run alongside the handle,' I was thinking as I talked. 'Trent wouldn't have been able to see it.'

Swift nodded in agreement. 'When he reached up to pull it down, he'd have touched the copper.'

'It would have killed him instantly,' Persi said and turned around to glance at Trent's cold dead body lying a short way from us.

'The window has been left open.' Swift pointed. 'Which explains the puddle on the floor.'

I glanced up. We were below ground, there was a small window set high in the wall, someone had pulled it open a notch and allowed the rain to seep in.

'Clever,' Swift muttered.

'And very simple,' I added.

'The killer is going to come back for the strip, aren't they?' Persi said.

'We'll ask Mullins to place a guard at the end of the passageway,' Swift replied.

'Come on,' I could see how cold poor Persi was. 'Let's go upstairs.'

Swift locked the door again and we turned to leave. I offered Persi my hand as she stepped over Trent and she took it. It was quite romantic, apart from the corpse that is.

We returned to the grand hall, the servants had been busy, there were lanterns in every niche and corner, bathing the place in flickering lamplight.

'I'll find Mullins,' Swift declared and went off.

That left just the two of us alone together.

'I should go and say something to the family,' Persi began.

'Right, I'll erm… I'll escort you.' We walked upstairs in silence.

'Heathcliff.' She stopped on the landing near Sinclair's office. 'I was so angry.'

I leaned against the bannister; pools of flickering lamplight lit us from below.

'I'm sorry, Persi.'

'How could you do it to me?'

'I wrote to you any number of times to explain why. You didn't even reply.'

'Yes, I did.' Her tone was sharp.

'You returned the ring I gave you. That hardly constitutes a reply.'

She was standing beside me, her hands on the bannister rail, her face illuminated by the distant lamplight. 'Lennox, after you walked out, I sat amongst my family with an empty chair beside me.'

I heard the catch in her voice. I scrambled my mind to think of something to say. 'Didn't anyone come and sit next to you?'

'Lydia did.'

'Well, it wasn't empty then.'

That didn't appear to be the right answer. Her eyes flashed. 'It wasn't just the humiliation. I realised I couldn't rely on you. I couldn't trust you to be there to support me.'

That stung. 'That's not true. I went all the way to Damascus for you, I even helped get your idiot ex-fiancé out of jail. Not to mention the trip to Egypt, which was appalling…'

'And then you abandoned me in my parents' dining room.' She retorted. 'What sort of future do we have if you can't face my family? I couldn't even trust you to turn up at our wedding.'

She had a point there.

'We could elope.'

That wasn't the right reply either.

'Lennox,' she blazed.

'Persi,' I faced her, thinking to reason with her, but realised that probably wasn't going to work either. I switched tack. 'Will you help with the investigation?'

She glared at me, opened her mouth, then shut it again.

'You know this place and these people. There is a murderer here.'

'It might be a member of my own family.'

I decided not to mention that it almost certainly was. 'One of them might be the next victim.'

She chewed her lip. 'But Monroe's death sounded like an accident, Lydia called me about it just after it happened.'

'But the gun in the parcel frightened Sinclair, didn't that make you suspicious?'

'I haven't heard anything about a gun.' She frowned.

'Didn't Lydia tell you?'

'Tell me what?' At least she'd stopped yelling.

'You mean, you don't know about Lydia calling me and...' I laughed. Then I told her all that had happened and how we'd been tricked into coming to Lanscombe.

'She didn't even tell me you were here when she invited me to dinner tonight.' She was incensed.

'But she was right, there is a killer here.' I'd been watching her face, the mix of surprise and anger. She really was bewitchingly beautiful.

She leaned forward to place her elbows on the rail, the silk of her dress rippling as she moved. 'It's a terrible thought, Lennox. Why would anyone kill Sinclair's men?'

I shrugged. 'We don't know.'

Her brow furrowed. 'What time was Monroe's accident?'

'Half-past five on Sunday evening.'

'Where was everyone?'

'Lydia and Jerome were at the folly, Sinclair was in his office, Lady Penelope was in her room. We don't know where Max and Finn were yet.'

She was looking down at the chequered tiles in the hall below. 'You don't seem to have learned very much.'

'I...' I was about to protest, thinking of all the events in what had been a very long day. 'Well, we've only just started.'

'There are already two dead men.'

'And a very clever killer,' I returned.

'Like in Damascus,' she said and suddenly smiled up at me, then her face fell again. 'But what if it is one of the family...'

'What do you know of Finn?' I thought I'd better divert her.

She sighed. 'Very little. I've heard about him, but tonight was the first time I've met him. He was raised in America.'

'It must have caused quite the scandal.'

She shrugged. 'It was years ago, my mother told me about it. Penelope was heroic. Once she learned Finn had been placed for adoption, she arranged for money to be sent out. She's extraordinary, the whole family adore her.'

'Where was Finn born?'

'In Alaska.'

'At the time Sinclair and Randolph were there?'

'I suppose so, I've never given it any thought.'

'Persi,' Lydia called down from above. 'Is that you?'

'Yes.' Persi turned towards the stairs.

Lydia came down holding a candle. She stopped to glance from one to the other of us.

'Oh how wonderful! You're talking again.' She came to join us.

'Lydia, you have some explaining to do,' Persi warned.

Lydia wasn't daunted. 'Well, we can go upstairs and I'll tell you everything.'

'No, I must leave,' Persi argued.

'Oh, you can't! It's terribly late, it's after ten o'clock.'

'It's only nine thirty.' Persi looked at her watch. 'What happened to your lovely gold watch?'

'It's broken, Jerome is having it mended. Please, come, I've gone to so much trouble,' Lydia pleaded. 'We've had a bed made up for you, there's a roaring fire in your room and tons of blankets. You'll be as snug as a bug in a rug.'

'My car's outside.' Persi wasn't so easily diverted.

'Please, Persi.' Lydia looked close to tears. 'Everyone's terribly upset about Trent, and Monroe. I'd like you to stay.'

'The police will be here in the morning, Persi,' I told her. 'They'll want to interview everyone.'

Her eyes met mine as she realised the full implications. 'Oh, very well.'

That brought an instant change in Lydia. Her smile returned and she tugged at Persi's arm. 'Oh, how marvellous. Come on, we'll make hot chocolate over the fire and munch biscuits.'

'Yes, Lydia, and you can explain why you telephoned Heathcliff pretending to be me...'

I returned to the old wing with a spring in my step. The kitchen proved devoid of life which was a blow; it seemed I'd have to go hungry. I headed upstairs and entered my room; the fire was alight, my little dog and cat were on the bed, and a covered tray of game pie, relish, apple, bread and butter and a glass of claret awaited me on the desk. Good old Greggs, ever a stalwart soldier in time of need.

Foggy sat at my feet, Tubbs on my lap and I ate in contented silence. Persi was just as I remembered, her extensive family were a bit of a millstone though, and it didn't help that I would probably have to finger one of them as a killer...

CHAPTER 9

'Lennox?' Swift arrived with the dawn, holding a lantern.

'Bit early for breakfast, Swift.' I'd only just dressed and Greggs hadn't even brought a cup of tea in yet. 'Why are you up so early?'

'I thought we'd go and see if Mullins has caught anyone.' Keen as ever, he wore his overcoat, scarf and gloves. 'And the police will be here soon.'

I didn't share his enthusiasm, but found my shoes and pulled on my shooting jacket. I told my little duo to stay where they were. They didn't take much persuading, they barely opened their eyes as we left. ''There are plenty of ex-soldiers in this place, Swift. If they had caught someone they'd keep a tight hold of them.'

'Yes, but we should examine the crime scene as well.' Swift was trotting down the pine stairs. 'Did you bring a torch?'

'It's in my pocket.'

We made our way through the St Georges' old wing. It was entirely vacant, which was hardly a surprise given the ridiculously early hour.

He stopped abruptly. 'Have you got your magnifying glass?'

'Swift, stop fussing will you.'

We passed through a procession of state rooms where misty morning sunlight was sending feeble rays through tall windows. Tired looking footmen were standing about doing nothing in particular.

'Lennox.'

'What?'

'Did you speak to Persi last night?'

'Yes, I asked her to help with the investigation.'

'What?' He stopped again. 'She can't, she's related to most of the suspects.'

'She hasn't agreed to do it, yet.' I walked on. I was in no mood to argue, particularly before breakfast.

We entered the grand hall.

'Hello? What are you doing here?' Jerome had been in conversation with Mullins, but turned abruptly when he heard our footsteps on the tiles.

Swift ignored him and addressed Mullins. 'Was anyone caught?'

'There was nobody, sir,' Mullins replied. The poor chap looked as though he'd barely slept. 'A guard was maintained all through the night.'

Jerome was polite but clearly rattled. 'Inspector Swift, I do wish you'd asked me first.'

Swift wasn't interested in Jerome's complaints. 'Have you sent for the police?'

'Yes, I sent one of the men down to the village.' Jerome

shifted his stance. 'Look, I... erm. I was up an hour ago, this dreadful episode has been terribly unsettling. I instructed a couple of men to check the... well, I'll show you.'

'What is it?' Swift asked sharply.

'Come with me, please.' He trotted up the stairs, talking as he went. 'Sinclair is raging about getting the power on.'

'Trent is dead,' Swift snapped. 'And all Sinclair can do is complain about the inconvenience.'

'I'm not excusing him, I'm merely explaining.' He led on up the next flight of stairs.

The upper storey had a less formal air to it, although still sumptuous with gracious portraits, marble sculptures and the like.

'I've had to step in you see, with Trent gone.' Jerome was still talking, Swift was listening, his eyes dark and narrowed, looking very like the dogged policeman he still was at heart.

'Mullins seems capable,' I remarked.

'He's always been Lady Penelope's man.' Jerome explained.

'Hum.' I was quite aware of the vagaries of big house factions and allegiances so I understood what he meant.

'I thought last night's incident was probably caused by water leaking into one of the outside lights,' Jerome explained as we walked. 'Whenever there's a bad storm, the leak can be sufficient to blow a fuse. Trent would switch off the power, change the fuse and all would be well.'

'Your men have checked the outside lights?' Swift asked.

'Yes,' Jerome replied. 'They found the cause, it's in

here,' Jerome opened a door into a formal bedroom. The window was wide open, the sun filtering through the mist. Two liveried footmen stood silently to one side.

'Whose room is this?' Swift asked.

'It's just for guests.' Jerome walked straight over to the window and leaned over the sill. 'That lamp down there, look.'

We looked. About two feet below the window was a large lantern fixed to the stone wall by a metal arm. The bulb was encased in a sealed unit consisting of glass panels. One of the top panels was smashed and open to the elements. We stared at it.

'How was it broken?' I asked.

'We don't know,' Jerome replied. 'I'll have the men remove it for examination, but I thought you should see it first.'

'Why is the lid made of glass?' I asked. I was more familiar with traditional lamps with metal covers.

'It's a security light, it's supposed to shine up onto these windows as well as down onto the lower levels.'

I could see there were a few inches of water in the bottom of the lamp slowly dripping away through the glass base.

'There's enough water inside to blow the bulb,' Swift surmised.

'Yes, which would have caused the short in the fuse,' Jerome confirmed. 'Usually the leaks are around the panel joints. I've never seen a pane break before, they're made of toughened glass.'

'Sinclair said the power always went out in a storm,' Swift reminded him.

'He was exaggerating, he does that when he's angry. The power has only failed a handful of times in the six years I've been working here.'

'You've been with him for six years?' I turned to face him. 'So you weren't in the war?'

'Sinclair's work was imperative to the war effort,' Jerome reddened. 'As his personal assistant I was given an exemption.'

'Let's focus on the investigation.' Swift glanced at us both, then returned to the broken lantern. 'Someone dropped something on it, or reached out to smash it with a sharp object.'

'Possibly.' Jerome twisted around to look up towards the roof. 'Or something fell, a stone or tile.'

Neither of us was convinced by that, particularly after finding the copper strip.

Swift leaned further over the sill. 'An umbrella, or a cane would easily reach it.'

'Sinclair doesn't want anyone to mention this to the police.' Jerome sounded anxious. 'He wants us to say we thought it was an accident.'

'Why?' Swift demanded.

'He doesn't want the interference. It would be completely disruptive.' He glanced at the two silent footmen and said, sotto voce, 'And he said they're only servants.'

I could see by Swift's face he was furious. 'I will be talking to the police and giving them all the assistance I can.'

'You should do whatever you think right, Inspector,' Jerome replied. 'But I must warn you that Sinclair is vindictive. There will be repercussions.'

'I will not be intimidated.'

'Swift,' I cut in. 'We can talk about that later. Let's get on with it.'

Jerome supervised the two footmen, who leaned out to remove the lantern and bring it inside. Swift watched like a hawk. I wandered about, looking for an umbrella or cane. There wasn't anything so I pulled out drawers, peered under the bed and poked around in this and that. There was nothing out of the ordinary, not even a pan of ash in the fireplace.

'Is this room kept locked?' I asked.

'No,' Jerome replied. 'Only the ground floor is kept secured. We don't want it to feel like a prison.'

I notice he said 'we'.

The men had laid the lantern on the hearthrug and Swift knelt down to study it with his magnifying glass. I walked over to watch.

'There's nothing.' He stood up.

'Are you going to dust for fingerprints?' Jerome asked.

'No, it was too far for anyone to reach by hand,' Swift replied.

'How many bedrooms are there in the house?' I asked.

'I'm not sure, I'll ask Trent…' Jerome began, then shut up when he remembered the man was dead.

'What time were the security lights switched on?' Swift turned to Jerome.

'They're automatic. They're set to come on at seven thirty every evening in autumn and winter.'

'Really?' I'd never heard of such a thing.

'Where is the timer set?' Swift asked.

'In the control room downstairs,' Jerome told him.

'Show us,' Swift replied briskly.

'Yes, of course.' Jerome wavered for a moment, his eyes on the broken lantern, then turned and led us out.

I followed them downstairs at my own pace with my hands in my pockets, wondering what Persi was doing, and where she was. And what was for breakfast.

'It's the old butler's pantry, but Trent called it the control room,' Jerome explained. It was a plainly decorated office, discreetly located behind the grand hall. 'It's Trent's centre of operations.' Jerome showed us a bank of small light bulbs and speakers, each labelled with the name of a room. There were other contraptions; telephones and buzzers, a typewriter, an automated brass calendar and the like.

'Which is the timer?' Swift asked.

'Here.' Jerome pointed to a large silver dial attached to a brass box on the wall. I could hear it ticking. 'It is quite easy to use, when the hands come around to a set time, the switch is triggered to either on or off.'

'Swift,' I said.

'What?' He was still peering at the timer.

'I'm going for breakfast.' I'd had enough of detecting on an empty stomach.

He decided to come with me, although he left detailed instructions for what to do when the police arrived. We retraced our steps back to the old wing. The aroma of bacon, eggs, fried bread and black pudding met us at the kitchen door.

'Ah, sir, I have prepared breakfast,' Greggs made the welcome announcement.

There was no sign of the elderly St Georges but Persi was spreading a cloth on the table. Her blonde hair was caught back in a neat knot, she wore country clothes; beige slacks, a cream blouse with a tweed waistcoat. I suppose it was one of Lydia's outfits; it looked stunning on Persi.

Foggy jumped around my feet, as though I'd been away for weeks, then went to leap up at Swift, who bent to scratch his head.

'Hello,' Persi called out.

I gave her my best grin. She offered a smile before turning to arrange cups and saucers and the usual whatnots.

Swift tugged off his coat and scarf and threw them over the back of a chair. 'Persi, I... um, good morning... I hope you slept well?'

'I did, thank you.' She smiled at him too.

'Persi, I know Lennox said you can help with the investigation, but I have to tell you, you can't.'

'Tactful as ever, Swift,' I said, and sat down.

'Yes, I can.' She handed him a cup of tea.

'But you're related...'

'I can find out where everyone was on the day Monroe died,' she told him. 'And I know this house far better than you do.'

'What if the killer really is one of your family?' Swift wasn't backing down.

'Swift's right,' I admitted. 'I'm sorry, Persi, I shouldn't have involved you.'

'Nonsense, I don't think it was one of the family.' She looked from Swift to me.

'Why?' I asked.

'Because the family wouldn't need to resort to murder. They could just dismiss the servants, they wouldn't have to kill them.'

'Sinclair has complete control of the place. |Do you think Max or Lydia could persuade him to dismiss staff?' Swift wasn't convinced.

'Through Penelope, they probably could,' Persi replied.

I thought it was a jolly good point. Greggs had just placed brimming plates of breakfast on the table.

'So it's Finn or Jerome,' I declared, which suited me just fine.

'Jerome was with Lydia at the time of Monroe's accident,' she reminded me. 'You told me so yourself.'

Lydia didn't wear a watch, so I wasn't sure about that, but decided against mentioning it yet.

Swift shifted tack. 'Persi, what do you know of Randolph? He was your cousin, wasn't he.'

'Yes, although he was much older than me.' She stopped eating to reply. 'He died when I was a child. Lady Millicent took it very badly at first, and then she began to pretend he was still alive. We love her dearly, but she can be quite bats.'

I half expected Swift to make notes, but he carried on eating.

'What happened to Penelope and the twins after Randolph died?' I asked.

'Heathcliff, will you wait until I've finished breakfast!' she admonished.

I was on my second cup of tea by the time she was ready to talk.

'Randolph left for Alaska in the summer of 1896,' she began. 'At the beginning of the Klondike gold rush.'

'You would have been about two, then?' I mentioned.

'Yes, which is why I don't remember any of it,' she replied. 'The twins had just been born and everybody here was utterly penniless. Randolph believed he was going to make a fortune and save Lanscombe.'

'Sinclair said Randolph had developed a machine to detect gold?' Swift asked as he picked up his tea cup.

'Something like that. I don't know if it worked, but Sinclair had approached Randolph and suggested they go together.'

'How did they know each other?' I asked.

'I have no idea. Sinclair grew up nearby, so he had family in the district. He served in the Royal Artillery for a time.' She paused in thought. 'He would have learned about guns and machines while there, before he left to begin dealing in weapons.'

'Mullins said, he, Trent and Monroe had been in the Royal Artillery,' I mentioned.

'Perhaps they knew each other?' Persi suggested.

Swift didn't want to be diverted. 'How old was Randolph when he went to Alaska?'

'Twenty two, or three.' A flicker of uncertainty crossed her brow. 'Sinclair was quite a lot older than him, I'm not sure how old…'

'He's just had his sixtieth birthday.' I recalled my conversation with Lydia. 'He would have been thirty-four at the time.'

'Oh, yes, of course.' She nodded. 'Anyway, they went to Liverpool and crossed the Atlantic, then overland to Alaska. A few months later, the family received a telegram saying Randolph had been killed. It was a terrible blow.' Her smile faded. 'Sinclair remained in America for five or six years before returning to England, then he set out to win Penelope. He's dominated Lanscombe Park ever since.'

'What state was this house in before Sinclair took control?' Swift said between sips of tea.

'Dreadful, but tremendous fun. Or it was for us children anyway. Aunt and Uncle St George lived in this wing; the rest of the place was an absolute wreck.' Her smile returned with the memories. 'The main roof was full of holes; there were bats, birds and even a fox living in the ruins. Penelope and the twins lived upstairs.' She pointed upwards, indicating the rooms allocated to Swift and me. 'Penelope would invite everyone over for a picnic and we children would play with Max and Lydia. We spent hours exploring the old rooms and making dens with the furniture. It was always an adventure.'

'Presumably that changed when Sinclair married Penelope?' Swift asked.

'It did,' she nodded. 'He took Penelope and the twins to London while the house was rebuilt. The grandiose style led to some strong words among the rest of the family, but Sinclair never cared. Uncle Bertie and Aunt Millie bunkered down here, refusing to allow any changes to this wing.' She paused to regard us. 'I know everyone dislikes Sinclair, but he isn't all bad. He's done everything that he can for Penelope and, if she hadn't married him, the estate would have been lost.'

I wasn't sure I liked the sentiment. 'But at what cost to her, Persi?'

'Lennox, I'm not saying Penelope sold herself to save the estate… or that I approve.' She sounded offended. 'I'm simply stating the facts.'

'I wasn't implying…' I responded sharply.

'Yes, you were.' Her eyes flashed.

'Nonsense, I was merely saying…'

'You should try thinking before you speak,' she retorted and stood up and walked out.

We watched her go.

'Lennox.' Swift put down his cup with a bang. 'You are an absolute idiot.'

CHAPTER 10

'Lord Sinclair has requested your and Inspector Swift's presence, sir.' Greggs was at his most formal.

Apparently, while I was making rash remarks to Persi, young Billie had come to the door and passed on the message.

'Very well.' Swift was on his feet. 'Lennox.'

I wasn't in the mood for any more chat, so trailed behind with my hands in my pockets, a habit when disconsolate. We trod the now familiar route from the old wing, to arrive at Sinclair's gleaming office door. A footman stepped smartly forward and rapped on our behalf.

'Come.'

We were bowed in, Sinclair was seated behind his desk. A shaft of sunlight fell onto the portrait of the grizzled soldier, illuminating the eyes beneath the iron helmet.

'Someone murdered my butler.'

We sat down.

'We know.' Swift was businesslike.

Sinclair let out an exasperated sigh. His silver hair was

ruffled, his dark suit crumpled. He looked as though he'd dressed in the dark. 'Two of my best men. It's aimed at me, someone is trying to kill me.'

'Why kill Monroe and Trent if you're the intended victim?' Swift drew out his notebook and pen as he spoke.

'I can take notes, Swift.' I wouldn't usually offer, but I was still irritable after the tiff with Persi, and needed the distraction.

He raised his brows at me and slid the book and pen over. He should have dried the nib first because a drop of ink fell onto the open page. I leaned over to grab Sinclair's silver handled blotter, thumped it onto the ink spot and put it back. Then I wrote the date, tugged out my pocket watch to note the time, shook it because it had stopped again, and waited for them to get on with it.

Sinclair gave me a narrow stare, then turned to Swift. 'It's a pattern. First Monroe and now Trent. It's to intimidate me, or for revenge. I'm the best in this business; nobody gets to be the best by being nice. I have enemies and they're closing in.'

I wrote *Sinclair thinks everyone wants to kill him. (with good reason).*

Swift watched Sinclair. 'Why would your business rivals send you a gun?'

That rattled him. 'They... it was...' He banged the desk. 'That was a trick. Whoever killed my men must have heard about it. They might even have been at my party and seen it. Now I've put the house on full alert, the men are armed and they're watching every move.

No-one's going to get near me. I want you to investigate this, Swift, I want the culprit caught.'

'Scotland Yard will be here as soon as the local police report it,' Swift remarked coolly.

'No, I won't allow it.' Sinclair's face was florid. 'They'll dig about in my private affairs, I won't have it. You and Lennox can investigate. I made enquiries the day you arrived, you've got a good reputation. You can get to work.'

That made me look up. 'Work?'

Swift said. 'Lennox, could you just write, please?'

I wrote *Find killer for Sinclair.*

'What have you discovered so far?' Sinclair demanded. Swift told him our thoughts on how Monroe's accident could have been caused. Then he explained Trent's death including the details of the broken security lamp and the copper strip. He took the strip out of his jacket to place on the black desk.

'It's proof.'

Sinclair stared at the gleaming metal. 'Where did it come from?'

'The fuse room.' Swift picked it up and slipped it back into his pocket.

'That's bloody obvious,' Sinclair retorted. 'Who put it there?

'If we knew that, we'd have arrested them,' Swift replied calmly.

'I expect you to find out, not make bloody stupid statements,' Sinclair barked.

He hadn't once spoken a word in sympathy for the dead men.

Swift wasn't intimidated. 'Monroe was your bodyguard.'

'What of it?'

'Trent was too,' Swift continued.

'He was a highly trained soldier, that's why I took him on.' Sinclair looked down at his clenched hands on the desk.

Killer is stalking Sinclair, removing his closest men first, I noted.

'Who's your valet?' Swift asked.

'No-one, I'm perfectly capable of dressing myself.'

'Mullins was in the Royal Artillery, so were you and so were the dead men,' Swift stated, proving he had noted the fact.

'What of it? I knew Trent and when he was invalided out of the army, he came to me. He brought his best men with him.'

'Would you write that down, Lennox,' Swift asked, because I'd been thinking about other things. Such as why did Persi think Penelope was better off with Sinclair than living in poverty?

'Right.' I noted, *Is Mullins in danger? Or is he the murderer?*

I decided to join the conversation. Finn was top of my suspect list.

'Finn was born in Alaska,' I began.

'He was a mistake,' Sinclair instantly replied.

'You put him in an orphanage,' Swift stated.

'I did not, his mother put him up for adoption. Penelope found out and contacted me about it. She's a good woman.' Colour suffused across Sinclair's fleshy cheeks. 'She puts up with me... Look, I'm short tempered, and last night I was under pressure. I shout, but she forgives me. I do my best.'

I think he was trying to apologise for his boorish behaviour. Perhaps Persi was right, he was a difficult and complex man, but he wasn't evil, well not entirely anyway.

'Who was Finn's mother?' Swift was more interested in facts.

'She was a streetwalker. I was never sure he was mine, but she pinned the blame on me to try to extort money. I refused to pay the woman.'

'Where did this happen?' Swift asked quietly.

'Dawson City,' Sinclair replied.

'Dawson's in Canada,' I remarked.

'I know,' Sinclair snapped.

I recalled reading about the Klondike gold rush; there must have been a thousand men for every woman in Dawson City. 'Why would she try to pin it on you amongst so many?'

'Because I had money.'

'Did you strike gold?' Swift continued.

'I found some, yes,' Sinclair admitted. 'It was after Randolph died. I began trading tools and guns in Dawson, it was more profitable than digging in frozen ground.'

'But you already had a business trading weapons in

England. Why did you go to Alaska?' I recalled the story Persi had told us.

'Because I fell afoul of the bloody establishment, that's why,' Sinclair suddenly shouted. 'I wasn't one of them; the toffs! I was a boy from a backwater in Sussex. When they saw how well I was doing, they cut me out and stole my trade. I went to Alaska because there were opportunities there – it wasn't like this damn country. Then the gold began to dry up, so I moved to Boston. It was a good place for trade. I worked until I had enough money to stand up to the establishment and came back here. I bested the lot, they even gave me a seat in the House of Lords.' He ended on a tone of triumph.

I jotted *Sinclair made a toff.*

'What about Finn?' Swift asked.

'I told you, his mother thought I'd be fool enough to fall for blackmail. I soon put her right on that score, she was nothing but an Irish bog hopper.'

Well, that explained Finn's red-blond hair.

'Is she still alive?' Swift asked.

'How the hell would I know,' he barked back.

Swift wasn't intimidated, he continued fact finding. 'How did Penelope hear about your son?'

'Is this really necessary?' His patience had long run thin.

'Yes,' Swift replied calmly.

'It was after I left Dawson.' Sinclair began twisting his watch round his wrist. 'The woman must have run short of money, she didn't know where I'd gone and she pestered the immigration service for my British address.

Randolph and I had registered Lanscombe Park as our domicile, so that's where she sent her threats.'

Swift nodded, his face thoughtful. 'Penelope must have believed the mother?'

'She doesn't know the world as I do.' He calmed down. 'She wrote to me, I'd stayed in contact after Randolph died, so she knew my address in Boston. She was incensed that I'd abandoned the child. I replied, trying to explain, but she declared she was sending money.' Sinclair shrugged. 'I knew she didn't have any. After some fairly terse exchanges, I agreed to support him. The boy was eventually adopted, he never went short.'

'Were you always in contact with him?' Swift asked.

'Penelope kept in touch, sending him Christmas cards and pocket money. Then, when he was twenty-one, he came here all the way from New York on his own. He walked up to the front door and knocked on it. And you know what?' Sinclair leaned forward. 'He's one of the brightest young men I've met. I've no idea if he is my son, but he's got business in his blood.'

Did Sinclair kill Randolph to woo Penelope? I wrote, as an afterthought.

'How long did you remain in Boston?' Swift probably had the same thought.

'Six years. That's how long it took me to make my first million. I swore I wouldn't return to England until I'd made a fortune.' He grunted in satisfaction.

Swift was still thoughtful. 'And you came here?'

'No.' Sinclair was abrupt. 'I lived in London for a few

months. Then I heard Lanscombe Park was coming up for sale and I decided to have a look. Penelope was here with the twins, they were living like paupers. I renewed my acquaintance, realised what a fine woman she was, and married her.'

'Lanscombe Park was for sale?' I sat up. Nobody had mentioned that before.

'The family had nothing,' Sinclair railed. 'Generation after generation had squandered the finances. This place was a wreck, you couldn't even call it a house. I bought it, I could have thrown them all out. As you can see, I didn't.'

I drew a line through my last note. Did Sinclair kill Randolph to woo Penelope? Six years waiting to win over Randolph's widow hardly spoke of a passion fervent enough to kill for. I added, *Sinclair bought Lanscombe Park and everybody in it.*

Swift rose from his chair and turned to me. 'Lennox.'

'Right.' I passed him the notebook, he read the few lines I'd written, and the crossing out, frowned and slipped it into his inside pocket.

'Don't forget what I told you.' Sinclair pointed a warning finger. 'Not a word to the police. No-one is to cooperate with them, I've already given instructions to the men. It's an unfortunate spate of accidents, that's the line. And you'd better find who did it.'

We left without a backward glance.

'What do you think?' I asked Swift as we trod down the stairs to the grand hall.

'I think Scotland Yard should investigate.'

'Really?' That surprised me. 'Why?'

'Many reasons. They have the resources to make a proper search, run forensic tests and check the background of the people here.'

'Including Jerome and Finn.'

'Exactly, we can't just assume they're who they say they are,' Swift said as we reached the grand hall.

'Sinclair would have had them investigated, Swift,' I reminded him. 'He was quick enough to find out about us.'

'Inspector Swift, Major Lennox, sir.' Mullins appeared to have been waiting for us. 'The police have arrived, they are expecting your presence.'

'Right.' Swift cheered up. 'Where are they?'

'They are with Mr Jerome, sir,' Mullins said. 'In the control room.'

The venerable gentleman led off, Swift followed. I hesitated, letting them gain some distance, then turned on my heel and headed in the opposite direction.

I hadn't any particular plan in mind, except to explore and seek out whatever was to be found. I reached the kitchen to collect my little pets. Foggy was all for it, Tubbs had curled up under the kitchen range and refused to move. I told Greggs that I was going to search for clues, hoping it would mollify Swift when he came looking for me.

'Very well, sir.' Greggs had adorned himself with an embroidered apron and was scrubbing a copper pan in the sink. 'Lady Millicent is collecting eggs. We are planning a special dish for lunch.'

'Excellent, old chap,' I replied. 'You don't happen to have seen Persi?'

'I'm afraid not, sir.' He straightened up, paunch to the fore. 'Perhaps you could gather some flowers, or...'

'I think it will require more than that, old chap,' I replied.

'Perhaps a poem, sir? Lady Millicent enjoys Shakespeare.' He raised a hand. 'Shall I compare thee to a summer's day, Thou art more lovely and more temperate: Rough winds do shake the darling buds of May...'

'Greggs, have you been drinking?'

He stiffened. 'I have not sir. Lady Millicent and I merely thought to aid your romantic quest.'

'I'm not on a romantic quest, I'm looking for a damned killer,' I retorted. 'And what's more...' I shouted, then couldn't think of anything suitable to say, so I stomped out.

The mist had lifted to unveil a beautiful day. The air was fresh under a clear blue sky and harboured the scent of autumn; damp leaves, wet earth and woodsmoke. Foggy ran ahead even though he didn't know where we were going. I walked behind my hands in pockets, my mind on Persi and the nonsense Greggs was spouting. Persi wouldn't want poetry, she was a practical girl and down to earth – actually she was usually delving about in it. My mind tumbled over as Foggy and I negotiated the orchard, vegetable plots and whatnots. We didn't spot either Lady Millicent or any chickens, and entered the formal gardens to find it peacefully free of people. There were a few late roses in bloom, I considered plucking some of them, but decided it could wait.

I bypassed the marble folly and headed towards the trees in the direction Lydia had indicated the castle lay.

It was a pretty affair, enclosed by ancient walls with four stone towers; three were stubby and broken, the fourth was intact and stood on rocks jutting into the lake. A thicket of red leafed shrubs almost obscured the entrance of the tumble-down keep, I passed beneath its archway to stand and stare in silence. The curtain wall enclosed an expansive courtyard, where jumbled heaps of fallen stones and roofless buildings clustered around a swathe of green grass.

Foggy caught wind of something and sniffed his way into the largest structure. I followed into what must have been the banqueting hall back in medieval days. Delicate stone frames were cut into walls at least eight feet thick and two storeys high; nothing was left above that level, no roof or rotted joists, just jagged stones, white against the blue sky. My footsteps echoed as I crossed the hall and went to peer into a huge fireplace halfway along the wall. There were piles of twigs and feathers in the old hearth, sure signs of crows nesting in the chimney. Dust encrusted the eroded carving above the mantel; I brushed it away to reveal a dragon writhing and roaring above a weathered sword and shield.

I returned to the central courtyard to gaze at the tallest tower. Steps had been cut into the rock upon which it stood, leading to a door set in an ornately carved surround.

I went to try it, but it was locked or jammed and there didn't seem to be another entrance from the ground. It didn't take long to spy an opening high on the curtain wall.

I discovered the rampart steps beyond the banqueting hall and paced up and onto the battlement running around the top. It took some careful negotiation to pick my way along the worn walkway and reach the chamber at the top of the tower. It proved to be a guardroom with thin arrow-slit windows giving onto the lake, presumably in case of aquatic attack. There was another set of stone steps inside so I carried on climbing to find a flat roof surrounded by a waist-high wall; it was the perfect place to lean out and gaze across the still water.

The lake lay in a long expanse the shape of a lozenge; the island in the distance was coloured by autumnal shrubs and laced with weeping willow. The shore of the lake was formed into shady inlets, perfect for fishing below the lofty trees overhanging the banks.

Some distance over to the right was a boathouse, modern and freshly painted in cream and maroon, built into a deep-cut opening which gave onto the water. Just beyond that was another building marked ancient by its form; narrow and tall under a steeply pitched roof. It looked like an ancient church and lay in a hollow beyond by a copse of sweet chestnut trees. I'd been wanting to find the source of the stick and decided to investigate.

It didn't take long to reach them. Spiky green balls, stuffed with brown chestnuts, hung from thick boughs, and a quick walk amongst them soon revealed the broken stub of a branch. I considered returning to the house to tell Swift, but I thought I may as well take a look about while I was here.

'Come on,' I called Foggy, and he bounded alongside me, ever ready for adventure.

CHAPTER 11

Max was working on a sleek motor boat. Everything in the place was modern and new, a concrete deck surrounding a deep dock perfectly protected a range of tethered craft. A simple rowing boat was tied alongside the motorboat, and four sailing dinghies of different sizes filled the other bays.

The place smelled of fresh paint and wood varnish. Leather buckets, life jackets and coils of rope hung from hooks on the lapped-wood walls. Small fish darted about in the clear water below the boat hulls. I felt a sudden pang of envy for the playthings money can buy.

'What do you want?' Max called out. He had the engine bay of the motorboat open and was wielding a spanner above it.

'Sinclair has asked us to investigate,' I said, just to annoy him.

'He must be desperate.' He put the spanner down and picked up a screwdriver lying in a toolbox on the seat next to him. The engine was in the stern and he was kneeling over it from the cockpit.

'He thinks he's next.'

That resulted in a bark of laughter. 'He would. Everything's about him, even another man's death.'

'There are two deaths,' I reminded him.

'And I'm sorry for them both.' His voice became muffled as he leaned further into the engine.

I walked over for a better look. 'What's wrong with it?'

'She wouldn't start.'

'Not firing?' I admired the engine; someone had kept it in good clean order.

'I've checked the electrics, there's plenty of spark. I think the filters are clogged.'

'Dirty fuel,' I suggested.

'Probably.' He put the screwdriver aside and tugged carefully at a hose.

'I have the same problem with my car.'

'I heard you have a Bentley.' He looked over, a smear of grease on his cheek. 'That's a car I'd like to own. I worked on Bentley's aircraft engines during the war, clever design, the man's a genius.'

'You were an air mechanic?' I asked, knowing the breed well from my days in the Royal Flying Corps.

'Yes, until the last year of the war, then I was upped to an aircraftman when we all became the RAF.'

I laughed, Max couldn't be all bad if he was one of the chaps who kept our kites airborne. 'I flew Sopwith Camels. They had the first Bentley engines.'

'The BR1s.' He gave a grin. 'I wanted to fly, but they wouldn't let me. Eyesight wasn't up to scratch, besides I know how to build engines and they needed mechanics on the ground.'

'Where were you based?'

'Larkhill initially, then out to France. I ended up in Colombey.'

'Near the front line,' I remarked. 'That must have been lively.'

'It was.' He smiled grimly. 'I was roped in with the Yanks, I don't think they knew what hit them, but they were Trojans, took it on the chin. Good men.'

'Yes, I spent time with them in Epiez...' I trailed off, reluctant to go on and switched subject. 'Do you invent, like your father?'

'I try, but it's not as easy as you'd think.' He paused in his tinkering to regard me with intelligent brown eyes.

'Someone said he had a workshop?' I was fishing for information.

'The old church, I use it now.' He indicated the church just beyond the copse. 'You're serious about playing Sherlock?'

'Someone killed those men,' I replied calmly.

'It wasn't me.' He leaned back over the engine bay and resumed his work.

'Where were you when Monroe died?'

'Here, or in the workshop. I wasn't keeping track. It's where I come for peace and quiet, away from the house and the hangers on.'

'Like Jerome?' I suggested. 'Or Finn?'

He sighed. 'They're jockeying for favour with Sinclair.

I understand why, but I think it's demeaning and sometimes I needle them.' He glanced out beyond the bow of the motorboat and into the lake. 'Mama hates it when I do it. Anyway, I come here to let off steam.'

'Jerome's going to be your brother-in-law,' I stated.

'Yes, they get shackled next Easter.' He turned to look at me 'I assume you're still hoping for a happy outcome with Cousin Persi?'

That caught me off guard. 'Erm... I'd like to. I've talked to her, but...'

'Don't worry, I know every shade of the story.' He suddenly grinned. 'Lydia's the great romantic in our family. Never stops talking, or meddling. You'll regret marrying into the St Georges the minute you slip the ring on Persi's finger.'

'If she'll have me.'

'Look Lennox, I've known Persi all my life.' He was suddenly serious. 'She's straight as a die. Just tell her what you feel, she'll understand.'

'I have... it just comes out the wrong way.'

'Well, keep telling her until you get it right.' He returned to the boat engine. 'And try to avoid sending any of her favourite cousins to the gallows.'

I grinned, although it wasn't really funny at all.

I called Foggy and left the boat house. I'd like to explore the old church, or workshop as it had become, but it was mid-morning and Greggs would be serving tea – and Persi might be there.

Max's words reverberated around my mind as I retraced my steps through the trees. I was considering how the evidence might implicate Finn when Fogg suddenly rushed off into the castle grounds. I shouted and whistled but he didn't reappear. I swore to myself and re-entered the courtyard.

The door to the tall tower was ajar, Fogg dashed in, then out again, yipping in delight. He galloped up to run around me twice, with ears flying, then back to the tower. I gathered he wanted me to follow. I strode over to find Lady Penelope barely discernible within the unlit interior.

'Greetings.' I offered a smile from the threshold.

'Hello, Heathcliff, would you like to join me?'

'Um, what?'

'I've come to say prayers for poor Trent.' She waved an elegant hand to indicate a stone altar. 'This is the Lady Chapel. I often pray here.'

'It's...' I walked in. I hadn't been able to see very well from the doorway, but my eyes were quickly adjusting to the faint light. The ceiling extended into darkness, the circular walls depicted faded murals, medieval in design, with haloed saints and winged angels, monks, nuns and a heavenly choir. The altar was little bigger than a coffer, heavily carved from red sandstone and two candles were in place either side of a large brass cross.

'If you pick up your little dog, I will light the candles.' She held a vesta case of matches. I noticed she was dressed for walking, in a hacking jacket and mid-length skirt, her hair tied under a navy scarf.

'He's called Mr Fogg.' I grabbed him. 'If I'm intruding, I'll take him away.'

'No, I'm pleased you're here, and Mr Fogg. We don't have dogs, Sinclair doesn't like them. I've always thought it such a pity.' She sparked the match to light the candles with a steady hand. 'There, isn't that better?'

'Yes, erm, very nice.' The colours in the murals warmed in the candlelight, I could make out the faces of the saints and angels, pink with rosy cheeks and golden haloes. The tower had thick walls, typical of a defensive structure, the interior was around twelve feet across and reached up about twenty feet into what looked like the interior of a steeple, painted in blue with gilded stars.

She followed my line of sight. 'It's a tromp l'oeil, the ceiling is actually flat.'

'It's enchanting.'

'Will you kneel?' She sank to her knees on the dark-tiled floor.

I knelt down beside her as she raised her hands in prayer. I found it more difficult whilst holding a dog, but managed as best I could.

She murmured the Lord's Prayer. I joined in, then she asked God to gather up the dead, including Trent, and begged forgiveness for those who had sinned. She didn't specify who they were, which was a shame because it might have made our detecting easier.

We stayed there some time, my knees grew cold, even Foggy started to shiver. I sent some silent prayers while Lady Penelope whispered hers, then she said 'Amen' and stood up. I put Fogg down and followed suit.

'It was necessary.' She raised her eyes to mine.

'What was?'

'To offer our prayers to the Lord for the sake of the souls.'

'Yes… erm, right.'

'The old church is no longer consecrated so I come here.'

'Ah, yes,' I replied. 'I saw it by the sweet chestnut trees.'

'It was Randolph's workshop.' She was still gazing up at me. 'You have something of his looks, dark blond hair and blue eyes… he was as tall as you, I think. Six foot two.'

'I'm six three.'

She nodded, then blew out the candles. 'It is done.'

'Wait. I'd like to know more about the castle and the history. Could you tell me about it?'

'Oh, of course.' She smiled and led the way back out into the interior courtyard. 'Well, the tall tower holds the Lady Chapel, where the Chatelaine and her maids would say their daily prayers.'

'How old is it?'

'It dates from the Conquest.' She was leading me alongside the roofless banqueting hall. 'The St Georges arrived with William the Conqueror; at first they built a simple castle here of wood and thatch.'

'A motte and bailey,' I added.

'Yes, it was replaced by stone as soon as they could.' She smiled, then asked, 'Do you like to be called Heathcliff?'

'No, it was my mother's idea. How anyone can land their child with such a ridiculous name…' I stopped as she laughed, a delightful musical laugh.

'Oh dear, poor you. Sinclair's first name is Godolphin. He hates it. He won't allow anyone to even whisper it.'

She looked mischievous. 'I call him by it when he's being exasperating. He grows quite red in the face.'

We had arrived at some fallen stones and turned to sit down on the largest. Fogg went off, his nose to the ground. We gazed at the tumble-down buildings, the towers, the keep and the ragged surrounding wall, which kept the wind off and the world out.

Lady Penelope sighed. 'I asked Sinclair not to touch it and he agreed quite readily.'

'So he does have a soul,' I remarked.

'I like to think so.'

I decided that Lord Sinclair had dominated enough of my day and turned the subject to history. 'So, the St Georges have been here since 1066?'

'Yes,' she smiled. 'The land was called Lanscombe even then, I think it was something to do with the type of sheep they bred here.'

'They took up farming?' I returned her smile.

'No, I think they would have been quite hopeless at it. The men were knights, they went off to war and left their wives behind to manage the land and castle.'

'The Chatelaine,' I said, having always liked the term.

'Yes, exactly.' She laughed lightly. 'The lady of the castle.'

'It must have been quite different then?' I prompted her.

'I imagine so. They built the castle alongside the existing lake and excavated a moat. The water was diverted to make the castle into an island.' She pointed at the gateway in the remains of the keep. 'The entrance was protected by a portcullis and drawbridge. They'd always feared an invasion from the Continent, but it was their own king who destroyed them.'

'Really? Which one?'

'King John, he was a terrible man. He inherited the crown from his brother, Richard the Lionheart.'

'Ah, John was the one who persecuted Robin Hood.' That was one of my favourite stories.

'Yes, and was forced to sign Magna Carta. That was in…' she stopped, a slight frown between her brows.

'In 1215.' I was showing off, then admitted, 'Our history teacher drummed dates into us.'

She laughed. 'Yes, that was it, 1215, I'm dreadful with numbers. Everyone hated John and there has never been an English King with that name since.'

I knew that too. 'Why the war?'

'Because the Barons wanted more say in how the King ruled the country. John held absolute power and he was monstrous, he killed with impunity. The Barons made him sign Magna Carta to curtail his authority, but nothing changed, so they decided to be rid of him. They invited Prince Louis from France to reign in John's stead…'

I cut in, surprised. 'The English asked a Frenchman to rule the country?'

'I thought you'd studied history?' She raised her brows.

'The interesting bits, mostly.'

'It is interesting,' she assured me. 'Prince Louis came to England with an army and was welcomed, he was even proclaimed King at Old St Paul's in London. John was incensed and began a civil war. I suppose he didn't have any choice, really.'

'He was a tyrant,' I reminded her.

'And acted predictably.' She sighed and resumed the story. 'Sir Parcival St George joined the rebel Barons and was captured and imprisoned by the King's troops. King John swore revenge on the rebels and set about destroying the castles of any who had stood against him. One day he came here.'

'And broke the castle down,' I said.

'He did worse than that.' Her face became solemn. 'There was a village near where the old church stands, John's forces raided at dawn and rounded all the people up. He slaughtered a dozen of them and threw their bodies into the moat. Then he threatened to kill them one by one until Sir Parcival's wife, Lady Rosamond, gave up the castle. She climbed to the top of the keep and held up the Cross of St George. She told King John she would place it in his hands if he gave his word that he and his soldiers would release the villagers and leave.'

'What do you mean by the Cross of St George?' I asked.

'It was a solid gold cross, purportedly the same size and design as the brass one on the altar of the Lady Chapel. There were myths and legends attached to it and it was extremely valuable. I suspect that was the reason why King John had chosen to attack the castle.' Her face darkened, although I think she was enjoying telling the story as much as I enjoyed hearing it.

'The drawbridge and portcullis would have been closed,' I encouraged her.

'Yes, King John couldn't bridge the moat, that's why he began killing the villagers.' She nodded. 'The King agreed to Lady Rosamond's offer and he gave his word of honour that he would depart in exchange for the cross. The drawbridge was lowered and Lady Rosamond walked out with the cross held high. He grabbed her, laughing at his own duplicity, then ordered the castle to be destroyed and everyone in it put to death.'

'What happened to Lady Rosamond?' I asked.

'She fought with him, clawing at his face, he drew a dagger and stabbed her, but she struggled free. Her men came out to defend her and she managed to flee back inside the castle still clutching the cross. There was said to be a hidden place underground, a sanctuary, and she entered it. John's soldiers began the slaughter, they put the guards to the sword and tormented the rest, trying to force out the secret of Lady Rosamond's hiding place. They threw people from the tower, one by one. Nobody knew where the sanctuary was, or wouldn't admit to it. After they'd killed everyone, the King searched for the cross. When it couldn't be found he ordered the place burned down. The fire raged for days until only the stones remained.'

'Did they find her?'

'No, and she was never seen again,' she replied quietly. 'It's believed she's still here somewhere.'

I looked at the ruins and wondered where lay the tomb of the Chatelaine.

CHAPTER 12

'May I escort you to the house?' I asked.

Lady Penelope smiled. 'Thank you.'

'Right…' I offered my arm, then stopped. 'No, wait, I forgot my dog, he's probably chasing ducks.'

This brought a trill of laughter. 'I must go and supervise lunch, will I see you at dinner?'

'Yes, you will.' I returned her smile. 'And I look forward to it.'

She walked briskly away. I exited the castle shouting for Fogg. He was dashing in and out of the lake, ducks were taking to the air, quacking noisily. I picked him up to put under my arm, then returned to Lady Millicent's garden and the back door.

'Lennox, where did you go?' Swift spotted me as I entered the porch. 'Sinclair asked us to investigate and you disappear.'

'I was investigating. I found the source of the stick,' I replied in my own defence. It didn't garner me much.

'The stick doesn't prove anything. The Laboratory sent

the results back, the fibres were all from my coat.' He was tetchy. 'The police were here, we searched Trent's rooms and now they've taken him away. The electrical engineer came and I had to handle all of it myself. You should have told me where you were going.'

'Why?' I said as I pulled my jacket off.

'I... because...' That flummoxed him, he'd never entirely absorbed the fact that I wasn't an underling. 'It looks better, that's all. And... and it's good manners.'

'Yes, sorry.' I apologised as he was right about the manners. 'I interviewed Lady Penelope and Max.'

'Hum,' he didn't seem mollified. 'Where was Max when Monroe was killed?'

'He said he was in the boat house, or possibly the workshop. And Lady Penelope told me about Lady Rosamond and the cross of St George.'

He wasn't exactly thrilled. 'Look, come upstairs, Lennox. I need to make notes.'

I could hear noises from the kitchen and the smell of baking.

'I'll just go and ask about tea...'

'They're in the middle of cooking.' He cut me off. 'It's almost lunchtime.'

We went up to his room, he threw some logs onto the smouldering fire and we sat before it. I told him about the castle, the old church – and the fact it had been Randolph's workshop – repeated what Max had said, which wasn't very much, and finally recounted the tale of Lady Rosamond. He didn't write a word of it down.

'Fine,' he opened his book when I finished. 'I'll tell you about my morning while I write my report. The police examined the fuse room and dusted for fingerprints. They didn't find any of significance. The electrical engineer was asked to examine the fuse box and wiring while the police and I looked on. He concluded that, somehow, a connection had been made between the incoming power source and the handle. The wet floor would have contributed to an unfortunate set of circumstances. There was nothing of note in Trent's rooms.' He wrote all this down as he spoke.

'Did you tell anyone about the strip of copper?' I asked.

Swift stopped writing and admitted. 'No.'

'Why? I thought you said Scotland Yard should be involved.'

He put his pen down. 'I rang my old chief, and he said we're well positioned to deal with this.'

'You mean Scotland Yard wants to leave it in our hands!' That was a feather in our cap.

'When he said *we*, he actually meant *me*.'

'Oh,' I said, deflated. 'But he sanctioned the investigation?'

'Yes, we have official approval,' Swift explained. 'And I can call on the local police force for support if necessary.'

'Marvellous.' I realised he'd soon be insufferable. 'So, why didn't you tell the police about the copper strip?'

'Why do you think?' His eyes narrowed – he was testing me as if I was some sort of novice.

'Swift, just tell me.' I sat back and folded my arms.

He sighed. 'Right, it's because the copper strip is evidence of murder, not evidence of who committed it. And as we already know it's murder, there's no reason to broadcast the fact.'

'And we might use it to trip someone up later,' I added.

'Exactly.' 'Is Sinclair behind this authorisation?'

'He had spoken to the chief before me,' Swift admitted.

I knew what that meant, Sinclair thought he could control us. 'He might be the killer.'

'Well, if he is, we'll make damn sure he hangs for it,' Swift replied tartly.

My mind wasn't entirely on the discussion. 'Have you seen Persi this morning? After she left breakfast, I mean.'

'Yes, she was with Finn in the drawing room.' He frowned. 'We need to stay focused, Lennox.'

'Fine,' I replied, wondering why she thought it was necessary to sit with Finn in the drawing room. 'Do you think he's after Sinclair's fortune?'

'Possibly, although killing two of his men would be a strange way to go about getting it.'

'Why kill them? I can't understand it.'

'No, well that's the mystery, isn't it.' He sounded exasperated.

'What about Mullins? They were all in the army together,' I reminded him.

'Trent said no-one was missing on Sunday afternoon,' Swift argued.

'I think you should add him to the suspect list.'

'Fine.' He wrote it down.

'And Randolph.' I said.

'What?'

'Perhaps he isn't dead after all and he's come back to exact revenge.'

'Lennox, that's the most ridiculous thing you've said all day.' He closed his book with a snap.

The gong rang downstairs. I was off in an instant, not having eaten a thing since breakfast.

Greggs was in the kitchen.

'Oh, there you are,' Lady Millicent said gaily. She held a basket of ripe blackberries and placed it on the sunny windowsill. 'We've had such a time of it. I went to the orchard to gather eggs, then I picked berries from the bushes.' Her face was alight with joy. 'And dear Greggs has prepared lunch.'

'Excellent. Well done, Greggs,' I congratulated him.

He simpered.

'Such a time we've had.' Lady Millicent almost sang.

'Would you be seated, m'lady?' Greggs came to her side and pulled a Windsor chair from the table. He took the napkin from over his sleeve, and flicked it across the seat, then helped her settle with a plump cushion at her back.

'Oh,' she sighed happily.

We sat too, though without any cushions or help from my butler.

'I have prepared a dish to her ladyship's own recipe.' Greggs sounded very pleased with himself. 'A little *je ne sais quoi.*'

Good Lord, now he was spouting French.

'What is it?' Swift asked.

'A surprise, sir,' he replied.

Bertram St George shuffled in and came to join us at the kitchen table. He was attired once more in the thick dressing gown and slippers, but without the deerstalker. He banged a spoon on the table-top. 'What's all this about, eh? First Monroe, now Trent, what is it, a madman on the loose?'

'Yes,' I replied.

'What?' St George's mouth fell open.

'It's nothing to worry about.' Swift frowned at me.

'Ladies and gentlemen,' Greggs announced as he advanced slowly upon the table holding a steaming dish between two thick serving gloves. 'Cheese soufflé!'

'Bravo.' Lady Millicent clapped her hands.

Greggs placed the dish with the surging soufflé on the table, where it promptly sank.

We all groaned.

'Cheese pancake it is then, Greggs,' I remarked and picked up my knife and fork.

It was chewy, but tasty and I was starving.

'Come along, tell me about Trent,' St George demanded between mouthfuls. 'Didn't like the man but didn't expect him dead.'

'He was electrocuted,' Swift told him.

'I know that, young Billie came with the tale. They're saying someone did it deliberately. Can't have it,' he boomed. 'Killing men, what's it all about?'

'It may have been an accident,' Swift lied.

Lady Millicent wasn't in the least perturbed. 'I'm sure it was, Bertie, and they always come in threes, you know.'

'I had a look around the castle.' I attempted to divert the conversation.

'Oh, Lady Rosamund,' Lady Millicent said. 'Poor soul.'.

'Dead, all King John's doing. The knave.' St George banged the table. 'Burned the village and the castle, killed everyone. Bad show. Family abandoned it! Moved away to Cornwall, had land there, lost it.' He became animated. 'No brains for commerce the St Georges. Soldiers, that's what they were! Brave and loyal to a man. Old Simon St George joined the battle against the Spanish Armada for Queen Elizabeth. 1588 it was. Simon saw those blasted foreigners off, fought alongside Drake himself. Good Queen Bess was generous. Handed over bags of gold, silver and what have you. Simon came back to Lanscombe, built this house and lived like a king.'

'He didn't build it in its present style.' I waved towards the Palladian splendour beyond the corridor.

'He did not, it was a proper house in those days, not this modern nonsense of Sinclair's.'

I didn't like to mention that everything was modern at some time.

'Persi said it was in need of some work.' Swift was more tactful.

We'd finished the rubbery soufflé and Greggs was serving tea with macaroons. I had a particular penchant for macaroons.

'Nonsense, it was just like this, perfectly comfortable,' St George blustered.

Lady Millicent laughed. 'It was not! The roof had gone and we lived here, it's the old servants wing. There was just us and Randolph, it was such a happy time.' She sighed.

'And did Randolph and Penelope settle here when they married?' Swift was eyeing the tiered cake dish, as was I.

'They were in Bath for a short while, that's where Penelope comes from. He met her there on an outing,' Lady Millicent continued, seemingly quite willing to talk about her dead son. 'They fell head over heels. Always laughing...' She stopped suddenly.

'Now, now Millie.' St George tried comforting words. 'Max will fill the place with children one day, you see if he doesn't.'

'But Sinclair owns Lanscombe.' Swift held a macaroon, poised ready to eat. 'Why would Max have the house?'

'Sinclair doesn't own it, he has a lifetime lease,' St George growled. 'After he's dead, Lanscombe comes back to the family.'

That was news, no-one had mentioned it before.

Swift put the macaroon down. 'Sinclair doesn't own it? But it must have cost a fortune to rebuild...'

'What of it?' St George barked. 'Sinclair and Penelope were engaged and he wanted to buy Lanscombe. I said he couldn't have it. Not going to sell to some Johnny come lately. But he kept banging on about it, and then my man of law proposed a lease. Sinclair jumped at the idea, said he'd put the estate in order, spend money on it.'

He ruminated for a moment, his jaw working. 'I accepted, but only on one condition, it would pass to Max.'

That gave us pause for thought.

'What about Lydia?' I asked.

'Humph, yes, her too.'

'It sounds generous of Sinclair,' Swift remarked.

'Balderdash, he got what he wanted, what would it matter to him once he's dead.'

'Bertie saved Lanscombe for Max and Lydia,' Lady Millicent said. She seemed to have overcome her distress.

'So Max and Lydia inherit jointly?' Swift's lean face had sharpened.

I helped myself to another macaroon from the cake stand. They were jolly good, they even had cherries on top.

'They do. Penelope insisted on it.' St George shook his head. 'She said women are just as capable as men, and so they may be, but I had a clause put in anyway.'

'Which was?' I asked.

'When Lydia marries, she forfeits her claim to the estate,' he replied.

'That's a bit harsh,' Swift said sharply.

'We didn't want any gold diggers after her,' St George growled. 'Seen it before, not having it.'

'Lydia will retain a very generous allowance,' Lady Millicent explained. 'But her husband will not be able to live off her fortune.'

'And now she's engaged to that bounder, Jerome,' St George replied.

Swift fidgeted, probably itching to write this down in his notebook.

There was something else on my mind 'What about Finn? Wouldn't Sinclair want him to inherit?'

'Too late now,' St George replied. 'All tied up when Sinclair took on the lease.'

I wondered if that were true.

'Lydia mentioned Randolph's rooms are upstairs.' Swift turned the subject.

'Yes, we keep everything ready for him,' Lady Millicent beamed.

'Could we go and see it?' Swift asked.

'Yes, of course you may, my dear.' She smiled, her eyes bright. 'But finish your tea first.'

'We will,' I promised.

'And you won't move anything?' she continued.

'No, of course not,' Swift replied.

'Someone stole his gun…' her voice faltered.

'Don't worry yourself, Millie.' St George patted her hand.

'Do you know who?' Swift was ever the policeman.

Lady Millicent shook her head mutely.

'Are any of Sinclair's servants allowed in here, or upstairs?' I asked St George.

'No, already said so, didn't I? Not allowed,' he rumbled. 'Can't have people running willy-nilly about the place.'

'But the family can come and go as they please?' Swift continued.

'We have always encouraged the children,' Lady Millicent seemed keen to talk about the family. 'The twins bring their friends.'

'Which friends?' Swift asked.

'All of them. They came to tea not long ago.' She turned to her husband. 'When was it, Bertie?'

'Few days, might be more. Every day's the same, unless someone dies,' St George mumbled through a macaroon.

'Was it about a week ago?' I asked. 'Around Sinclair's birthday?'

'Oh, you are quite right. It was the day before. Well done.' Lady Millicent smiled.

'That was it.' St George was suddenly animated. 'Came for afternoon tea and Millie baked a chocolate cake. Six eggs, and they were all brown.'

'All brown,' Lady Millicent repeated.

'You must make it again,' St George told his wife.

'I will, and dear Greggs will help.' She turned to him. He was pottering about but paused to give a soppy grin.

'Who came?' Swift was chasing facts.

Lady Millicent thought about it. 'The twins, dear Penelope, Jerome and the young man, Finn. He was quite the jester; he made us all laugh. And then Lydia showed them the rooms. She likes to tell stories about her Papa.'

'Does Sinclair ever come?' Swift continued.

'No. Not having him in here.' St George stiffened. 'The bounder, the...'

'Now dear, do calm down.' Lady Millicent stroked his arm, or rather the sleeve of his dressing gown. 'Have another macaroon, I baked them especially for you.' She leaned towards the plate. 'Oh, they've all gone!'

'Right.' I decided it was time to be off.

'Thank you for lunch.' Swift pushed his chair back, the legs scraping on the tiles.

'Excellent macaroons,' I added.

We made our escape and headed for the stairs. It was three flights to the very top of the house, and we arrived in the attics to find a poorly lit corridor. The place held an air of disuse, cobwebs in corners, dust layered over the panes of a small dormer window and sill. There were two doors leading off the passage.

Swift tried the first, it was unlocked, we entered and stepped back in time. Paper maps were stuck on walls, carefully constructed drawings of steam driven engines and locomotives were pinned between, as were schematics of various mechanical devices. A model balloon, formed from brightly painted strips of tin, hung in a dark corner. Books were piled on shelves, along with models fabricated from wood, metal and even matchsticks. The bed was made and the curtains drawn, it was as cluttered as the St Georges' drawing room, although with a melancholy air of abandonment.

I pulled open the curtains.

Swift went to the desk and picked up a card. 'It's a postcard from New York. 'Arrived safe and well. Onward to the West Coast. We are full of hope for a good outcome. Yours as ever, Randolph'.'

'Could I see?'

'It's a picture of the SS Umbria.' He handed it over. 'They must have travelled across the Atlantic on it.'

I took a long look at the photograph of the steam ship, being interested in that sort of thing. Then observed the stamp on the reverse. It had a picture of the Statue of Liberty on it. Randolph had written in block letters, the ink faded to brown.

Swift picked up a yellowed paper. 'A telegram. 'Arrived Alaska. STOP. Cold, hard place, but v excited. STOP. Miss you, but it is all for the best. Be home soon. STOP. Randolph'.'

'What's the date?' I asked.

He turned it over. 'May 22nd 1896.'

'They must have had a terrible journey,' I remarked. 'The snow and ice would have barely melted.' One of my favourite books from the era was Jack London's 'Call of the Wild', set in the frenzy of the Klondike gold rush. It's about a heroic dog called Buck, who is abducted and forced to fight for his life, and the prospectors had to endure some pretty grim conditions too.

Swift was still searching the desk. 'Here's one dated a month later. 'Tomorrow we depart for the gold fields. STOP. We have made all preparations. STOP. Will be out of contact for some time. STOP. My thoughts are with you, Randolph. STOP'.' He gazed at it. 'It's hardly sentimental.'

'Nobody puts anything private in a telegram,' I reminded him. 'Are there any written letters?'

'Yes, here.' He leafed through grubby pages written in

a schoolboy hand. 'But they're from his time in boarding school. There doesn't appear to be any more from Alaska.'

I shoved my hands in my pockets and gazed about.

Swift was in police mode, he opened a cupboard door; flakes of paint fell away as he rooted around in it. 'Nothing, just English country clothing. He'd have taken furs or padded leather to Alaska.' He turned to survey the room again. 'There must be legal papers. He and Sinclair would have gained licences and staked out plots of land, their claims had to be registered.' It seemed Swift had some knowledge of the gold rush after all.

'I'll try the other door,' I told him and went back out to the corridor.

It opened into a cupboard and produced a bonanza. Brown paper parcels bearing stamps from Alaska, were neatly stacked on six shelves.

'Swift,' I called him, he was quick to arrive.

'So, this is where they are.' He pulled a magnifying glass from his inside pocket and carefully scrutinised the packages. All were open and had been left loosely bundled. They were mostly clothes, musty and lightly layered with mould. One parcel contained pocket instruments; a brass compass, green with verdigris, an ivory rule, tin scales with small lead weights, a hammer and other tools wrapped in a rotting leather case. 'There's no gap, nothing apparently missing...' Swift said.

'They only had to rearrange the parcels to cover up the theft of the gun.' I was considering it. 'But it's not what is here, it's what isn't here.'

'What do you mean?'

'As you said, papers, claims, letters. Nor any photo-graphs – there's nothing personal from Alaska at all.'

'They may not have been returned,' he considered. 'Or he had them on him when he died.'

'Possibly.' I looked again at the cupboard. 'How do you think the gun and package were smuggled out of here?'

'I don't know, but I think we need to ask a few perti-nent questions,' Swift said and turned on his heel.

CHAPTER 13

'Of course no-one removed the gun while I was there,' Lydia replied.

'Could they have gone back shortly afterwards?' Swift wasn't giving up.

'We all left together, we came back here and played a silly game until it was time to change for dinner.'

We were in the drawing room of the mansion, sitting on the sofas. It was bright, with sunshine falling through the tall windows. We'd gone through to the house and found Billie to send him off in search of Lydia. She was supposed to come alone, but Persi had been with her when the message was delivered and had refused to take no for an answer. I was pleased to see her, but she remained aloof.

'Did Finn act strangely?' I asked.

'No, he made us all laugh; it was fun.' She was enjoying herself despite our questioning.

Persi added, 'I asked him where he was at the time of Monroe's accident and he said he was in his room, making calculations.'

'Can he prove that?' I asked.

'He said Trent had seen him,' Persi answered.

'Very convenient,' I remarked.

'Lennox, just because you don't like him, doesn't mean he's a murderer,' Persi retorted.

I decided to shut up.

'Lydia, who arranged for the parcels to be sent back from Alaska?' Swift continued.

'And when?' I added.

'It was Sinclair.' Lydia regarded us. 'I only realised it was him when I was older and recognised his writing. Mama said he packed up the belongings after Papa was killed and returned them to her.'

Swift paused at that, as did I. It made sense, and it was probably one of the reasons why Lydia had begun her childhood detecting.

'Do you believe Sinclair killed Randolph?' I asked her outright.

Her silliness vanished. 'Yes, I think he could have.'

'Lydia, you've been plaguing everyone with this nonsense for years.' Persi was exasperated. 'If Sinclair had killed your papa, why would he send his belongings back? Why would he even have come here? He'd have tried everything possible to distance himself from it.'

'Papa's death never meant anything to him, he only returned the belongings because Mama wrote to ask him.'

'At least he did return them,' Persi retorted.

Lydia's brows suddenly snapped together. 'Persi, you've

always supported Sinclair. Just because he helped your parents pay for your school fees.'

'That's a ridiculous thing to say.' Persi seemed shocked.

'No, it isn't, everyone makes excuses for him,' Lydia rebutted.

Persi retaliated. 'Your mother would hardly have stayed with him if he were so dreadful.'

'That has nothing to do with it. Sinclair gets away with anything he wants. He throws a handful of money at someone and they just buckle. He buys people, and I thought you were better than that.' She looked close to tears and suddenly got up and ran out, which brought the interview to an abrupt end.

'What was all that about?' I asked.

Persi looked downcast. 'My parents had a financial embarrassment and he loaned them money. They paid it back... Look, I don't like Sinclair and I don't admire his tactics, but he was prepared to help when no-one else would.'

'Do Lydia's suspicions about Sinclair have any basis in fact?' Swift asked.

'I've never heard any proof.' Persi looked away and then back again. 'She's always disliked him, but now she positively seems to hate him. She's becoming quite extreme. I haven't been to Lanscombe for such a while, and...' Her face dropped. 'There's so much tension here. I felt it when I arrived. It's almost tangible and now these deaths...'

I wondered if I should take her hand or something.

'I think it really could be one of them...' She blinked away tears. 'Lennox, I've promised to stay for dinner, but then I'm going home. I really shouldn't have become involved.' She got up and walked out.

'That went well.' Swift remarked.

I assumed he was being sarcastic.

The sun slipped behind a cloud and the room dimmed as a result. 'This isn't helping my attempts to win her back, Swift.'

He let out a sigh. 'No… Look, all we can do is solve the case and you'll just have to deal with whatever falls from it.'

'That's very reassuring.' It was my turn to be sarcastic.

'Come on. We won't achieve anything sitting here.' He leapt to his feet.

'Where are we going?' I stood up.

'To question Jerome.' He strode off.

It took some time to find him. He was writing at his desk in the ticker room, which apparently doubled as his office.

'What…? What are you doing here?' He looked up in shock as we entered, then hastily closed the leather-bound file he'd been working on. There was an empty coffee cup on the smooth surface of the desk-top.

'I'd like some coffee,' I said, as we sat down and looked about. It was a workaday place, three plain oak cupboards and a long table under a bare window. It supported a typewriter, blotter, ink stands, box files and notebooks. There were deep-sided postal trays, two labelled 'In', three labelled 'Out', and various complicated looking bits of office equipment. One of the machines suddenly sprang to life and started ticking as though someone were typing in a frenzy. A line of paper, about half an inch wide, began to reel out of the machine. Jerome dashed to it and tore off the extruding tape.

'Ah, excellent.' He returned to his chair behind the desk.

I could see letters and numbers printed in grey ink, AS 3.29, USG 1.22, EV 0.78. I assumed they were stocks or shares or whatever, I'd heard of such things, but this was my first sighting of one.

Jerome placed the tape into the leather folder and closed it again.

'Sinclair was being blackmailed,' Swift lied with conviction.

That threw Jerome off balance. 'No… what… what do you mean?'

'Monroe was blackmailing him. What has Sinclair done?' Swift continued matter-of-factly.

'No… it's not true… how could…?' Jerome stuttered, then burst into peeved affront. 'This is out of order, gentlemen. Sinclair has instructed you to investigate these deaths, you can't make accusations like this.'

'We're not employed by Sinclair.' Swift's tone turned cold.

'And we'd like some coffee,' I added.

Swift frowned at me. Jerome stared in confusion then got up and went to a contraption attached to the wall near the window. He raised an earpiece and spoke into a black transmitter. I could hear a tinny response.

'Coffee for three, my office,' he ordered and put the earpiece back on its hook. He noticed my interest. 'It's an intercommunication device.'

'Ah.' I thought it the most useful invention I'd seen in the whole house.

'Was Trent working with Monroe?' Swift carried on.

Jerome had composed himself. 'I understand you must explore every avenue, gentlemen, but you really cannot think Monroe and Trent were killed because of some sort of scheme revolving around Lord Sinclair.'

'Why?' Swift wasn't giving up.

'They were devoted to him, all the men at Lanscombe are.' Jerome maintained a smooth diplomatic deftness.

I decided to join in. 'If anyone were blackmailing Sinclair, you wouldn't necessarily know about it.'

'Of course I would.' Colour rose in Jerome's cheeks. 'I run the company accounts, nothing goes in or out without my seeing it.'

'Sinclair must have private accounts.' Swift didn't believe him. 'He wouldn't share everything with you.'

'Yes, he does.' Jerome leaned back and smiled. 'You haven't learned anything, have you?'

'What do you mean?' I asked.

'The company will belong to me one day.' He tried, and failed, to keep the smugness from his tone. 'Sinclair has promised. The transfer begins on my marriage.'

'Who else knows this?' Swift demanded.

'Everyone, I imagine,' he replied with a shrug. 'It isn't a secret.'

'Then perhaps it's you who's being blackmailed,' I retaliated.

Jerome's brows creased. He was saved by a knock at the door. Mullins entered with a pack of letters tied with string and a tray of coffee and biscuits.

'The post, sir,' he intoned, as he poured three cups of strong-smelling coffee.

'Thank you, leave it on the table.' Jerome waved towards the post trays.

'As you wish, sir.' Mullins did as requested and left the room on quiet feet.

'Inspector, these implications are ludicrous.' Jerome leaned forward to put his elbows on the desk. 'I showed you the broken security light, I'd hardly have done that if I was involved in anything untoward.'

'You'd look doubly guilty if we'd found out from someone else,' Swift replied.

'And you can't prove where you were when Monroe was killed,' I tossed in.

'What?' He jerked upright. 'I was with Lydia, you know I was.'

'She doesn't wear a watch, how did she know what time it was?' I countered.

'I… I told her, but that doesn't mean… Are you implying I'm lying?' he stuttered in outrage.

'Yes,' Swift replied.

I ate a biscuit.

Jerome sighed in exasperation. 'You're supposed to be helping, not interrogating me, or Sinclair. We're running a complex business worth millions of pounds and we can't have our time wasted with these minor matters.'

'Two murders are hardly minor matters,' I retorted.

Jerome twitched with suppressed anger.

Swift cut in. 'What does Sinclair actually do?'

'He buys inventions and patents them.' Jerome settled down again, obviously more comfortable discussing business. 'He has the weapons developed into working prototypes. Those that prove commercially viable are sold to armament manufacturers.'

Swift continued. 'Where are these weapons developed?'

'In Wiltshire. Sinclair is head of a consortium. They own a research facility located at the military base there.'

'Does he control this consortium?' I asked.

'Yes, he's the majority shareholder.'

'And you'll get his shares,' I stated.

'I've already told you this.' Jerome was becoming rattled again.

Swift finished his coffee and put the delicate porcelain cup onto Jerome's desk-top. 'Thank you. Come on, Lennox.'

'Right, erm...' I emptied my cup in a gulp. 'Jolly good coffee,' I told Jerome and gave him a cheery wave. He didn't say anything, just looked relieved we were leaving.

'That was illuminating, Swift,' I remarked as we trotted downstairs.

'Yes, St George has miscalculated.'

'Well, he said the family didn't have any brains for commerce,' I reminded him.

'Max may inherit Lanscombe Park when Sinclair dies, but there won't be any funds to go with it,' he said.

'Exactly, Sinclair's fortune isn't tied to the lease. He can leave it to whoever he wants to.' We were walking back through the house towards the old wing.

'Surely St George must have realised that?' Swift shook his head in disbelief.

'He's hardly worldly, Swift. I doubt it ever occurred to him.'

'Well, I suspect it's occurred to everybody else,' he replied tartly.

CHAPTER 14

'We need to change for dinner,' Swift remarked.

We were returning to the old wing, our minds occupied with the revelation and how significant it may be.

Greggs was in the kitchen. He was sitting by the range with a glass of dark red wine in his hand, staring at the wall.

'I'll see you shortly,' Swift said and parted for his room. 'I'm going to write to Florence before I get dressed.'

'Greggs?'

He jerked upright. 'Sir?'

'Are you all right?'

'Yes, sir.' He looked up at me with eyes vaguely out of focus. There was a dusty bottle at his elbow. 'Sir Bertram has granted me the key to the cellar, sir,' he replied ponderously. 'He has foresworn liquor on account of the gout.'

I picked up the bottle and wiped dust from the label and read Beaune des Aigrots, 1915. 'Is it any good?'

He blinked. 'It is outstanding, sir.'

I took a sniff of his glass, it had a tempting whiff.

He snatched it off me, then the bottle, and held it to his chest. 'Mine.'

I knew better than to come between Greggs and good liquor. 'Not going to break into poetry, or French are you?'

I knew what he was like once he'd started drinking.

'If I so wish, I will,' he replied with dignity, only marred by a slight slur.

'Right, I'm off to change.' I left him to it.

I went to my room, realising I should make a few notes before dinner as my mind was a jumble of thoughts. My notebook was brand new, with dark green leather and thick cream pages. I found it in the desk drawer and rummaged about for my pen, it was in my jacket pocket. The room felt damp, so I moved to the fireside and sat poised over a pristine page. Fogg and Tubbs had come upstairs with me and they cuddled on the hearth rug together.

Swift had a habit of lecturing me on proper detecting methods. I tried to remember what he'd said. Motive, method and opportunity, I think? He should have mentioned suspects too, because that was the most important part.

I wrote: *Sinclair, Jerome, Max, Finn, Lydia, Penelope, Mullins...* I hesitated then added *St George and Lady Millicent.*

Lydia triggered the investigation, pretending to be Persi. Lydia's suspicion is anchored in a childhood obsession and further aggravated by the gun and package sent to Sinclair on his sixtieth birthday. The package was from Randolph's rooms. All suspects could have accessed the rooms...

How? I thought about it. *When the St Georges were taking a nap.*

Sinclair couldn't get into Randolph's rooms, well I suppose he could sneak in at night, but it was hardly in his nature… Damn, we should have considered that earlier.

Maybe not Sinclair, I wrote, sighed and decided to push on.

Both killings were thought out and carefully constructed to appear as accidents. The killer knew the men's habits; Monroe would buy liquor on Sunday and Trent would reset the electricity when it failed. The stick was taken from the woods near the lake, tests on the fibres didn't prove anything.

I stopped to refill my pen. It took the usual fiddling about with ink pot and blotting paper. Tubbs jumped up to help, he batted my pen, then sat on the open book. I'd noticed he had a habit of sitting between me and whatever I was trying to look at. I admonished him to his sooty face, he yawned, not in the least contrite. I put him down with Foggy and carried on.

A strip of copper was used to connect the power to the handle. It's a secret. Only Sinclair knows about it, along with us and the killer.

I paused, trying to think how it was set up.

Method: The killer would have worn gloves, rubber ones probably. They pushed the copper strip into the gap next to the handle of the power-switch. Then they opened the window to let the rain in. They broke the glass on the lantern below a guest room window and poured water into it, sometime during the day.

Whoever did it had a good knowledge of the house and electrical system – which makes it less likely to be Finn.

It seems I'd just discounted Finn and Sinclair, which was a grave disappointment. Should I remove them from my suspect list? No, the killer was clever and sneaky, and they were the two cleverest and sneakiest people in the whole house.

What about opportunity?

Monroe's accident happened at 5.30pm. The servants were taking their own meal before preparing and serving the family's dinner. Lydia had gone to the folly for a cigarette, Jerome said he was with her, but he could have lied about the time. So he may have gone to the Dell and back, and he knows the intricacies of the household.

Max said he was at the boathouse or his workshop, but can't prove it. He was vague, and he's also bound to know about the electricity.

Sinclair was in his office.

Finn was in his room – Trent was a witness (conveniently dead).

Penelope was in her room.

Where were the St Georges? They say they never go anywhere, but Lady Millicent goes into her gardens and orchard.

I stopped to consider my notes and Swift's detecting advice. Method and opportunity were all very well, but without understanding the motive we were hunting in the dark.

I wrote...

Reason and logic are vital to an investigation.

And I underlined it because it was true.

I cleaned excess ink from my nib while I thought about why someone would have wanted to murder Monroe and Trent.

Sinclair? Blackmail?

Jerome? Perhaps he did it under Sinclair's orders, or maybe Jerome was being blackmailed because he'd done something wicked – betrayed Lydia with a femme fatale? (interesting, but unlikely).

Swift said the police had searched the dead men's rooms and nothing had been found. If they'd committed blackmail, wouldn't there be some evidence of it.

We should probably give up the idea of blackmail.

Max is behaving badly according to the family, why?

Persi said there's tension in the house.

That gave me pause for thought, but I couldn't add to it, so carried on.

Lydia? She loathes Sinclair, but killing his servants is a bit obtuse.

Penelope? No, or at least I sincerely hope not.

I had more questions than answers. I put my pen down and leaned back in my chair. Jerome would be given control of Sinclair's business. It must be a bitter blow for Max, but was it relevant unless Sinclair was the victim…?

Swift walked in, breaking into my meandering. 'Are you going to dinner?'

'Yes.'

'Like that?' He was smartly turned out in his city suit with his hair combed and shoes polished.

'I'm going to change, I was just making notes.' I put my pen and book on the hearth.

He sat down in the chair opposite. 'Here,' he handed over his silver flask.

I shook it; it was full. 'I thought we'd emptied this?'

'Emergency supply.' He gave a grin. His missive home must have cheered him up.

I found a couple of tumblers and poured one each. We raised our glasses and took a mouthful.

'That's the best I've tasted, Swift.' It was superb.

'It's our oldest malt, I was going to save it to celebrate you and Persi getting back together.'

I stopped drinking. 'What?'

'But as you're making such a hash of it, I decided we'd better just drink it.' He watched me over the top of his glass.

'I'm not… look, it isn't…' I had another sip. 'I'll talk to her tonight.'

He laughed and leaned back in the chair, his legs crossed. 'Can I see your notes?' He nodded towards my book.

'Here.' I passed it over.

He read through it, it took him less than two minutes. 'You've barely written anything.'

'I haven't finished.'

He handed it back. 'I agree with you about Sinclair, I don't think he's behind it.'

'No, but what the hell is it all about?'

'I wish I knew.' He finished his whisky and put the glass down. 'What did you think about Jerome's revelation?'

'It's not relevant to the case, but it might explain why Max is so angry.'

He nodded. 'Yes, he'll inherit Lanscombe Park without any funds to support it.'

'Lydia comes out well,' I remarked.

'You mean Jerome comes out well. He'll have the controlling hand.'

'Yes, and it's a nasty twist of the knife. I suspect Sinclair did it deliberately.' I sipped the whisky slowly, savouring it. 'He's stuck to the lease, but thwarted the principle.'

'And St George would never have considered it when he agreed to the details,' Swift replied.

'I wonder what Penelope makes of it all,' I mused.

'If you'd spent less time talking about ancient tombs and more about the case, you might have found out.'

'I didn't know about it then,' I said in my defence.

He threw me a sideways look.

'Do you think Finn could be Randolph's son?' I asked a question that had been niggling me.

'Randolph's? Not Sinclair's?' He thought about it. 'I suppose it's possible.' He picked up the flask and slipped it into his pocket. 'You'd better change, Lennox. Drinks will be served shortly.'

I dressed in quick time and we left to make our way towards the drawing room. Persi had said she was coming to dinner, and then she would leave. How was I going to find a way to persuade her to stay?

We spotted her on the upper landing as we made our way to the drawing room. She looked enchanting, her blonde hair shimmering under the chandeliers and she was wearing the same green frock as last evening.

'Hello, Persi,' Swift called.

'Oh, hello.' She came to join us.

'Greetings, old stick.' I decided to go for broke and gave her a peck on the cheek.

She didn't object, actually she didn't take much notice. 'Heathcliff?'

'What?' I smiled down at her.

'I'm not sure if I should come to dinner.'

'Of course you should.' Swift tried to jolly her along. 'Come on.'

We took a few steps and she stopped again.

'Have you made your peace with Lydia?' I offered my arm.

She took it. 'Not really... and there's something I've just discovered. It's... well, it's quite disturbing.'

'Sinclair's going to hand over the reins to Jerome,' I guessed.

'You knew?' She stopped and glared at me. 'Why on earth didn't you tell me?'

'We only found out this afternoon,' Swift explained.

'Oh... But don't you see, it's all going to be lost after all. Max won't be able to afford to keep Lanscombe. He doesn't have any money.' She looked upset.

'He might marry an heiress.' I tried a cheery note. It didn't help.

'That's not a plan,' she replied, and finally walked with us along the corridor.

Champagne was offered as we entered the drawing room. I decided against. The place was almost exactly as it had been last night; servants bustled about, the family were togged out in elegant evening wear, a fire blazing in the hearth. Nothing had changed apart from the expiration of Trent.

Persi spotted Max and went to join him while Swift headed in the direction of Lydia, no doubt to interrogate her further. Finn watched with an amused grin on his face. He was smart in a tuxedo, his red-gold hair neatly combed above his pleasant features.

'Good evening, sir.' Mullins bowed, he was on duty by the sideboard, where I'd noticed Burgundy was available.

'Greetings, old chap.' I pointed at the bottle. 'I'll have one of those.'

'Certainly, sir.' He poured it himself with white-gloved hands. He was looking particularly spruce; moustache and sideburns fluffed, snowy hair brushed back and his red and black uniform in very smart order. He sported a black armband, as did all the staff.

'You haven't donned the butlering garb yet?'

'Ah, no, sir.' His moustache drooped. 'I'm afraid his Lordship has deemed my years rather too advanced to step into Mr Trent's shoes. In fact, he has decreed that tomorrow must be my last day at Lanscombe.'

'What! That's unfair,' I exclaimed. 'Does Lady Penelope know?'

'She does, and is upset. But alas, she has not yet been able to convince his Lordship to amend his decision.'

'What are you going to do?' I asked.

He gave a faint sigh. 'I hope to find some employ for which my military training has prepared me, sir.'

He handed me a glass generously full of rich red wine. 'And what's that?'

'Sharpshooter, sir,' he replied and turned away to supervise the drinks tray.

That made me raise my brows.

Lady Penelope was sitting with the group around the fire, I strolled over, thinking to ask some question of relevance. I didn't get very far.

'I want dinner now.' Sinclair bulldozed in with Jerome on his heels.

'Sinclair, please. It's barely past seven.' Penelope rose to her feet.

'Jerome, go and tell chef. Get on with it,' Sinclair ordered.

Jerome left, almost at a run.

'Godolphin, I really don't…' Penelope tried again.

'Don't argue.' Sinclair wasn't listening. 'We missed selling stock on the American market last night thanks to Trent and that bloody fiasco, we're not missing it tonight. We'll be working until the early hours and I want dinner now.'

Lady Penelope's eyes blazed with anger for a second, then she took a breath and calmed herself. 'Very well. I suggest we move to the dining room.'

'Where the hell do you think I'm going,' Sinclair snapped and stalked off, leaving his wife standing.

I stepped forward and offered my arm.

Her lip trembled, then she sighed. 'Thank you, Heathcliff.'

She paused to ask Mullins to make the announcement and we waited for him to lead us through to the dining room in formal style.

It proved to be the most sumptuous of all the rooms I'd seen in the house. A double-height ceiling, three glittering chandeliers, walnut panelling and a table set with monogrammed linen, silver bowls, crystal goblets, porcelain dishes and gilded cutlery. It was lavish and splendid, and rather wasted on such a small party of people.

Mullins fussed over us, spreading napkins, arranging glasses and all the usual whatnots. I was seated next to Persi, Finn bagged the chair next to her and immediately started chatting.

Sinclair was at the head of table. 'Have you found him?'

I realised he was talking to me. 'What?'

'Don't play the fool, man.'

I lowered my voice. 'If you mean the murderer, no, we haven't.'

'Well, you'd better get on with it. It's my life at stake, it's a damn good thing I've got men about me. Twenty-four hours, that's all I'm giving you, then you're finished.' He had a glass of red wine in his large hand. 'And when I say finished, I mean I'll destroy your reputation, both of you.' He glowered at Swift, then knocked his drink back.

Swift glanced up and frowned. I emptied my own glass then turned to Sinclair.

'We don't work for you and I don't give a damn about your threats.'

He spluttered into his wine. Lady Penelope suddenly let out a peal of laughter and everyone turned to stare.

'Lennox, you're a brave man,' Finn shouted, with glee in his voice.

'He's a fool,' Jerome said.

'Right, you bloody upstart. Get out of my house.' Sinclair snarled in my direction.

'It's not your house,' I goaded him. 'You only have a lease.'

He turned puce. 'It's mine as long as I live and I'll bloody well decide who stays here and who doesn't.'

'Hey, Pop,' Finn shouted over. 'Enough already, this guy has guts. You need a private dick, and him and his sidekick are on the scene.'

The ladies raised their brows and stared at him.

'A private *what*?' Sinclair almost exploded.

'He means a detective,' Max informed him dryly.

Lydia giggled, Persi smiled, as did Penelope. Swift didn't look amused; he probably objected to being called a sidekick.

Soup was placed in front of us, which shifted attention. Sinclair glared at me again, then picked up a bread roll and began tearing it into pieces.

'What sort of electrical appliances do you import?' Persi suddenly asked Finn.

I stared, then realised she must have found this out earlier in the day.

'Wireless sets, gramophones, refrigerators, vacuum cleaners.' Finn was full of enthusiasm. 'I'll bring in whatever sells. This country can't get enough of American inventions.'

'Where do you find them?' Swift leaned forward to ask.

'There are factories springing up all over the States, I go check 'em out.' Finn replied as he spooned his soup.

'Do you know how they work?' Swift continued.

'I sure do,' Finn grinned. 'I got my college degree in electrical engineering.'

'And he's got a business brain to go with it,' Sinclair added with a semblance of pride.

The soup course was cleared away. I drank another glass of Burgundy.

'Pop has been good enough to back my import and export enterprise.' Finn was in fine form. 'I'm goin' to pay him back a hundred-fold.'

'What do you export?' I asked.

'Liquor, as much as I can get a hold of.'

'Liquor?' Swift's attention suddenly focused. 'But there's prohibition in America.'

Finn laughed. 'Which makes it all the more valuable.'

'Gosh, Finn, are you a rum runner?' Lydia asked with an excited giggle.

'It's illegal,' Jerome said. 'That makes you a criminal.'

'Now, hold your horses.' Finn put a hand up. 'There are plenty of legal ways to import spirits into the States. I have a licence to supply the pharmacies.'

Succulent beef, with small roasted potatoes, carrots and some greenery was served with gravy. It was absolutely first rate and I tucked in while the rest indulged in chit chat.

'You mean brandy?' Swift asked.

'Brandy, sherry, port, whisky.' Finn was enthusiastic. 'If you have the right licence, it's all considered medicinal.'

'You mean American pharmacies are licensed to supply alcohol?' Swift wasn't giving up.

'Yeah, sure. A tame doctor writes the prescription, for a price.' Finn winked. 'And the pharmacist supplies the medicine. It's all legal and above board.'

'Swift produces whisky,' Persi said. I kicked her, she turned to look at me. 'Why...?'

'You do?' Finn was all ears. 'What brand?'

'Braeburn Malt,' Swift replied.

'No! You don't say.' Finn leaned in his direction. 'That's the bees' knees, that is. Nothing beats Braeburn, that's the one that everybody wants. I gotta make a deal with you. Pop, did you hear that? This guy is Braeburn whisky.'

'I thought he was a detective,' Sinclair growled. 'Jerome, did you know about this?'

'His wife's family produces whisky,' Jerome replied with a slight shrug. 'It's highly rated in America.'

'Darn sure it is.' Finn leaned further across the table to point a fork at Swift. 'And I bet those London chisellers are paying you no more than two bits for it. Every one of them liquor merchants sends spirits to the Bahamas and by hook or by crook they get it across the Florida Straits. They're pocketing a packet.'

'You mean people are smuggling Braeburn whisky into America?' Swift was aghast. 'In contravention of the Prohibition laws?'

Persi had stopped eating to watch. In fact everyone seemed to be taking a great interest in the conversation.

'They sure are, but if you sell it to me, I'll pay you a fair price and make it all legit.' Finn grinned.

'What… wait… you mean…' Swift was almost dumbstruck. 'But, I have an exclusive contract with the London merchants.' He turned to face me. 'Lennox, your cousin set it up. You said it was going to gentlemen's clubs in London.' He raised his voice for no good reason.

'Well, the thing is Swift…' I began.

His brows lowered. 'You're not trying to tell me that you knew about this?'

'I… erm… Look, once it's sold, it could go anywhere,' I tried to explain.

'No, it could not.' He was becoming quite angry. 'We had an understanding.'

'Well, it wasn't the same understanding, was it?' I replied, with a retort he'd aimed at me once.

He simmered.

I had another drink. Pudding was brought in.

'Treacle sponge and custard for dessert.' Lady Penelope smiled at her husband.

He nodded, mollified and patted her hand. 'You arranged it.'

'Yes, I wanted you to have all of your favourites.' She spoke quietly. 'I know you're upset about Trent.'

'Trent was good at his job. He made sure everything was done for me. He was always nearby…' They were talking quietly between themselves, as any husband and wife would. I ate my dessert, trying not to eavesdrop.

'Persi,' I put my spoon down and leaned towards her. 'You're not going home tonight.'

She was just tucking in. 'Yes, I am.'

'I…' Damn it, what should I say? 'You did well to find out about Finn's electrical knowhow,' I congratulated her.

'Perhaps.' She laughed. 'But I had no idea about Swift's whisky.'

I grinned. 'I don't know why he's so priggish. Everyone's smuggling liquor into the States.'

She finished the last spoonful of treacle sponge. 'Is Finn a suspect?'

'Yes… no.' I had another drink. 'I really have no idea. The case is a complete mystery.'

'If it is, Lennox, you're sacked,' Sinclair had been listening.

'I thought you'd already sacked us,' I countered.

'My wife thinks I should give you a second chance.' Sinclair pointed at me then Swift. 'Two days, that's what she asked me to give you. I've agreed, but I want the name on my desk in forty-eight hours, or you're finished.' He stood up abruptly and nodded to Jerome. They marched out together without another word.

The party broke up after that, everyone strolling from the room, chatting quietly, except Finn who was laughing with Lydia.

Swift was fuming. 'Lennox…'

'I'll be a moment, Swift.' I remained seated with my hand over Persi's on the table.

He looked from one to the other of us and decided on a tactful retreat.

'Persi, can I say…'

'No, please don't, Heathcliff.' She sighed. 'I'm the one who should apologise. I've made a hash of things, Lydia gave me a terrible dressing down this afternoon and I didn't appreciate it, but… well, she was right.' She bit her lips.

'You mean about Sinclair?'

'No, about me.' She was staring down at the table. 'My attitude, my… my intransigence. She said I sabotaged my relationships, which I thought was nonsense, but she insisted. She said I set unrealistic expectations and then become angry when people don't live up to them. And I'm self-reliant because I don't trust anyone and…She said I'm going to end up an old maid and I have only myself to blame…' She stopped talking and sniffed.

'Nonsense, you're just rather forthright and…'

She raised her eyes. 'You could sound more convincing.'

'I admire your self-reliance and I think it's good that you have strong opinions.'

'So you think I'm opinionated too?' Her eyes flashed.

'No…'

'Lydia said I was, have you been talking to her about me?'

'Yes, I mean no, not in…' I was beginning to babble so shut up.

She waited but I couldn't think of anything to say.

'I'm leaving.' She made to rise.

'No.' I said, quite loudly. 'Persi, just wait a moment, will you'

She stayed where she was, staring at the damask table-cloth in front of her.

'Look, Lydia was talking absolute rot. I was in the wrong and you are right to be angry.'

'But I...'

'Come on.' I took her hand before we had any more nonsense.

'What? Where?'

'I don't know, somewhere...' I led her off. We walked along the corridor and found our way back to the drawing room. It was vacant apart from a footman putting logs on the fire. He beat a retreat when we arrived.

'Sit down.' I sat on a sofa.

'Why?' She wouldn't look at me, I tugged her to sit next to me.

I raised my hand to touch her chin and gently turn her face until she was gazing into my eyes. 'Because I love you.'

She blinked a tear away, and gave a tremulous smile.

And then I kissed her.

CHAPTER 15

The scent of breakfast greeted me the next morning as I entered the kitchen.

'Greetings,' I beamed.

'I have fried the sausages in dripping, sir.' Greggs was in charge of a large cast-iron frying pan. 'With black pudding and bacon.'

'Excellent, old chap.' I clapped my hands and strode to the table.

'Lennox…' Swift was already seated, still fuming by the look on his face.

'Can we have breakfast in peace, Swift.' I had slept well and was feeling positively sunny, despite the dense fog clouding the windows.

'Ah, you still here.' St George arrived, togged in nightcap and dressing gown, with a napkin tied under his chin.

He pulled out a chair to join us.

'I saw Randolph this morning.' Lady Millicent had been in the pantry and now returned to the kitchen. She began pulling plates from the dresser shelves. 'It's so misty outside, I doubt he could see a foot in front of himself.'

'What?' We all stared at her.

'I went to pick mushrooms for breakfast,' she sang out. 'He was going to his workshop.'

St George looked at her. 'Now, Millie, old girl…'

'You saw Randolph?' Swift asked, barely disguising his disbelief.

'He always goes to work early. He makes his own breakfast and slips out before we come down.' She came to lay the table. 'But he'll be hungry by lunch, I'll bake a pie, and then we will have his favourite cake.' Her eyes sparkled. 'Did you hear, dear Greggs? We will make chocolate cream cake.'

'Indeed, m'lady.' Greggs was carefully turning sizzling bacon over with a wooden spatula.

'She was up early,' St George said, which didn't explain anything.

'Would fried bread be required?' Greggs created a diversion.

'Yes, please,' came a chorus of replies.

'Lennox about the whisky…' Swift's mood hadn't improved.

'I didn't know it was being smuggled.' I picked up my napkin.

'But our whole production depends on selling…'

'Exactly,' I intervened tersely. 'And nothing has changed.'

He wasn't convinced and I could see he was itching for an argument.

Greggs delivered two plates of steaming bacon, eggs, sausages, mushrooms and fried bread. He served the St Georges first, then returned with two more plates.

I had just taken the first mouthful when there was a loud rapping on the door. Billie appeared without waiting to be called.

'You'd best come, sirs.' His eyes were like saucers, his cheeks flushed as though he'd been running.

'What's happened?' Swift was instantly on his feet, his meal forgotten.

'It's Lord Sinclair. He's missing.' Billie spoke between breaths. 'They're out in the grounds, lookin' for 'im. Everyone's panicking and Miss Persi said to come for you.'

'So, they got him at last,' St George said with satisfaction.

'Now Bertie.' Lady Millicent sounded a mild reprimand before they both carried on eating.

'You were right, old girl. Always comes in threes.'

'Lennox.' Swift was already heading towards the door. 'Come on.'

I hadn't finished breakfast. 'We should take a torch,' I told him between mouthfuls. 'And a magnifying glass.'

'Ah, yes. I'll go up and fetch them. And we'll need Fogg, he might smell him out.' Swift dashed for the stairs.

I gave my little dog a piece of sausage. 'Bit optimistic.'

Swift returned just as I'd cleared my plate. He was wearing his overcoat, scarf and gloves.

'Ready?'

'Yes, Swift.' I stood up.

'Come on.'

Billie was desperate to return to the house, he was almost running as we passed through the state rooms.

'They went out from the east terrace, sirs,' Billie told us when we arrived at the grand hall. We strode across the chequered tiles, our footsteps echoing. A couple of maids were talking animatedly in a corner, but there wasn't a single footman around. The place seemed strangely bereft.

'Through here, sirs.' Billie led us along a corridor to a spacious room. 'It's the orangery.'

It was probably the prettiest room I'd seen in the mansion It was filled with flowers and plants, including small orange trees. French windows overlooked a broad terrace and the formal gardens, and made me realise there was a lot of this house I still hadn't explored.

Lady Penelope was standing at one of the glass doors, peering out into swirling fog. She turned around as she heard us arrive. 'Oh, thank heavens you are here. They're out searching, but it's so misty, no-one can see a thing.' She was dressed in warm tweeds, her shoes were muddy, her dark hair escaping from a carelessly tied scarf.

'When did he go missing?' Swift switched to policeman mode.

'Just after six this morning,' she replied, her face taut and anxious.

'Could you tell us what happened?' I asked.

She bit her lip, trying to retain her composure. 'Jerome came into the breakfast room at eight o'clock asking for Sinclair. None of us had seen him, so he went to look and… and,' she paused to quell a quiver in her voice. 'Finally we questioned the servants. One of the footmen had seen Sinclair walk out from the doors here just as it was becoming light. He thought it strange, but he didn't dare ask him where he was going.'

'Was Sinclair alone?' I tried a gentle tone.

'Yes, entirely alone,' she replied. 'Are you going to join the search?'

'Shortly. We need more information first,' Swift continued in businesslike manner. 'What's his usual routine?'

'Very well.' She looked out of the windows. 'He likes to go to his office early, around six and work until breakfast at eight. He has always done so.'

'What time did the search begin?' Swift asked.

'When we realised he was missing.'

'And you're sure he hasn't simply gone for a walk?' I asked.

'No, he dislikes the mud, he's not a country person at all.' Lady Penelope caught her breath, I could see she was close to tears. 'I can't imagine where he is… but after Trent and Monroe… I'm so fearful.'

I wondered if I should offer comfort somehow. 'Where is everyone?'

'Outside, they have all gone, most of the footmen, Mullins, even Lydia and Persi.' She raised a hand towards the door in a forlorn gesture. 'It's been almost two hours since he disappeared…' Tears ran down her cheeks.

Swift offered a clean handkerchief. 'We've brought a dog.'

We all looked down at Fogg, he was wagging his tail in his bright-eyed, happy manner.

'He's very keen,' I said by way of support.

'We'll start in Sinclair's office,' Swift announced.

'Why? Jerome has already looked in there.' Lady Penelope was confused.

'There's a reason why Sinclair went out so early,' Swift told her. 'His office may hold a clue.'

'Right,' I agreed and turned to Lady Penelope. 'Perhaps you'd like to wait in the drawing room, or...?'

'No... yes, I suppose I should. But you will join the search, won't you?'

'Yes, of course, we will. He has police habits,' I explained, then turned to follow Swift out.

We raced upstairs to Sinclair's office. There was no-one about and the door was unlocked, so we walked straight in.

'He came here first...' Swift stood in the centre and gazed around.

The room was quiet, almost peaceful without Sinclair's restless energy.

'Something, or someone, enticed him out,' I added.

'A message,' Swift replied. He went to the tray of letters on the desk-top and started rifling through them.

'It may have been a telephone call.' I sat in Sinclair's chair; it was large and quite firm. It swivelled, so I pushed myself around. 'Although if Jerome questioned everybody, it would have been mentioned.'

'Unless he were the killer.' Swift had moved to the waste bin and was pulling out crumpled paper.

'You think Sinclair's dead?' I stopped swivelling.

'I think his death was the intention from the start.' He

was unravelling balled-up sheets of paper and laying them in a pile on the desk. I moved to help without making any reply because he was probably right, but I couldn't help feeling we should have done something to stop it.

'There's nothing out of the ordinary, here.' Swift stood back, regarding the waste paper we'd untangled. 'Where would he put a note?'

'In his pocket,' I replied.

'Yes, damn it, why didn't you think about that earlier. This is probably a complete waste of time.' He began pulling open the doors of the drinks cabinet and rooting between the bottles. I've no idea why.

I returned to sit in the swivel chair. Fogg had a sniff around and discovered there wasn't a hint of mouse or biscuits anywhere.

'We'd better go.' Swift stood up and ran fingers through his hair. 'He could be anywhere. The estate is enormous.' His dark eyes suddenly fixed on something. 'Wait, move the chair, Lennox.'

'Why?' I stood up again and pushed it aside. It was heavy, made from steel and padded leather, and rested on small castors that raised it just above the dense pile of the carpet.

'Look.' Swift bent to retrieve a small ball of tightly crumpled paper.

He uncurled it with a delicate touch. It was as thin as onion skin and yellowed with age. It bore a scrawled note that had been written as though in haste. *'Sinclair, I'm at the workshop. Randolph.'*

'Randolph!' The hairs rose on the back of my neck. 'Perhaps Lady Millicent really did see him.'

'Nonsense.' Swift was more prosaic. 'The notepaper must have been taken from his rooms. Someone wrote this message on it to lure Sinclair out.'

'Yes…' I stared at it over his shoulder. Despite Swift's cold logic, it still felt as if a ghost had returned.

'Come on, at least we know where he was going.' He placed the paper carefully in his wallet and headed for the door.

'Direct everyone towards the workshop.' Swift barely broke his stride as he called to Billie, who was standing to attention at the bottom of the staircase.

'What… I mean, pardon sir?' He called. 'Why?'

'Sinclair was meeting someone there,' I told him in passing as we exited the front door with a very excited little dog at our heels. 'Inform Lady Penelope.'

The fog was dense, clammy and cold. Somewhere high above us, the sun was trying to break through, but at ground level we could barely see a yard ahead. It didn't take long to turn the corner of the house and cross the formal gardens to the folly. Grey shadows could be seen moving near the indistinct structure.

'Don't tell anyone about the note,' Swift said sotto voce.

'I wasn't going to,' I hissed back.

'Hello,' Swift called out. A clamour of voices responded.

'We can't find him, it's hopeless,' Lydia replied.

'Oh, thank goodness you're here.' Persi turned towards us, her face as worried as everyone else's.

'Did you bring your dog?' Jerome was with them.

They were on the steps of the folly, all in warm country wear. Even Jerome had changed out of his usual tailored suit and put on wellington boots.

Max stepped forward. 'Could you take your dog along the lakeside? He might find a scent.'

They obviously weren't acquainted with my dog.

'Sinclair was going to the workshop,' Swift announced.

Incredulity showed on their faces.

'How do you know?' Jerome recovered first.

'What on earth for?' Persi asked.

'He was meeting someone.' Swift was calmly taking command. 'Where's Finn, isn't he with you?'

'He usually sleeps until late,' Jerome answered the question. 'We didn't see the point in waking him.'

'You mean, you didn't,' Max retorted.

'Mama will send someone for him,' Lydia added tactfully.

The tension was simmering beneath the surface, fracture lines were already beginning to crack open.

Swift was watching them as closely as I was.

'We'll go to the workshop.' He led off, although I doubt he knew the way.

I hung back to fall in step with Persi.

'Hello, old stick.'

'Hello.' She slipped her hand in mine.

Lydia turned to see us, and smiled.

The workshop was closed up. Early morning cobwebs wove a dew laden lattice across the doors, proof that it hadn't been touched since nightfall.

'We've already searched around here,' Max said.

'Do you have the key?' Swift demanded.

'Yes, but you can see it hasn't been opened today,' Max protested. 'If you want to waste time poking around in there, I'll unlock it.'

'Is there another entrance?' Swift wasn't giving up.

'No.' Max was adamant.

'There isn't, truly,' Lydia called out in support.

Swift gazed at the muddy ground. 'Are these your footprints?'

'Yes,' Jerome replied as everyone looked down at the puddled mess outside the door of the workshop.

'We walked around the perimeter,' Jerome told him.

'Well, now I'll do it.' Swift went off and I went with him. It didn't take long to circle the building and return to the door.

'Find anything?' Max asked.

The look on our faces probably made that plain.

'What about your dog?' Jerome was insistent.

'Right.' I looked down at my little mutt. 'Fogg, phezzie, off you go, find the phezzie,' I ordered him. Phezzie being the word to go and search for something.

He cocked his head, then turned and ran off into the mist. Moments later we heard the sound of splashing and ducks quacking in alarm. I called him back but he didn't come. The quacking continued.

Swift turned to rattle out orders. 'Jerome and Max, you two come with me to the boathouse. Lennox, you go to the castle.'

'Right, come on, Persi, Lydia.'

We walked quickly up through the copse of sweet chestnut trees, their drooping yellowed leaves clinging to dark twigs. Drips fell onto our heads and shoulders as we trod through the mist-shrouded silence.

The castle was at its most beautiful, its towers lost in the white haze.

'Oh, it's such an age since I was here,' Persi exclaimed.

'We should have a picnic when the sun comes out,' Lydia declared.

'Lydia…' I reminded her.

'Oh, yes, Sinclair.' She went off to look inside the banqueting hall.

We searched under bushes and amongst the ruins. I ran up to the ramparts and peered over them; there was no sign of Sinclair. We scouted about for ten more minutes before regrouping in the castle courtyard.

'It sounds as though they've got the boat running.' Persi pointed to the lake where the engine could be faintly heard in the distance.

'And your dog's barking,' Lydia told me.

'He's probably found more ducks.'

'He sounds quite excited,' Lydia continued.

'Fine, we'll go and see.'

We left the castle and walked in the direction of the noise. Foggy was near the boathouse. The mist had begun to thin along the shoreline, but was still dense and swirling beyond the banks. I saw the flash of his golden coat in the reeds.

'Fogg,' I called him. He turned to look at me, and gave a yip.

'I'll go,' Persi volunteered. She was moving towards the high earth bank, which fell steeply away to the waterline.

'No, he's my dog.' I sat down and tucked my trousers into my boots. I stepped onto the tightly grown reed bed, thick black mud oozed up around my soles.

'Be careful,' Lydia called, which didn't help.

I went slowly, searching out firmer spots and sinking in the mire when I took a wrong step.

'Fogg, come here, good boy.' I tried cajoling him, which made no difference. He was balancing on a floating mass of reeds and lilies. I saw what had set him off, it was a man's brown leather shoe. I reached out to grab it, then caught my little dog and squelched back to the bank with him firmly under my arm.

'What is it?' Persi called out.

'Poor little doggie,' Lydia cooed. I'm not sure her mind was really on the search at all.

I put him down and followed him, my boots thick with cloying mud.

'He found a shoe.' I showed them.

'Oh, it's Sinclair's.' Lydia's face suddenly paled as her hands flew to her mouth.

It wasn't a surprise, but it brought a cold shock of reality to the morning. The sound of the motorboat grew louder though I could barely discern it in the dense fog blanketing the water.

'Lydia, is that you?' Jerome's voice called out.

'Lennox?' Swift shouted.

'Yes,' I replied loudly. 'We've found a shoe.'

The boat came closer, emerging from the mist to halt a few yards offshore. I could make out Swift and Jerome in the cockpit, Max was behind the wheel.

'We've found Sinclair,' Swift called.

CHAPTER 16

'Is he dead?' I shouted across the water.

'Yes, of course he is,' Swift retorted.

'Where is he?' Persi asked.

'On the island,' Jerome replied, sounding miserable.

Swift started rapping out orders. 'Persi take Lydia back to the house, and inform the police. Lennox, meet us at the dock.' He ordered Max to return to the boathouse and they motored away.

I turned to Persi. 'Lady Penelope will have to be told.'

Persi's face fell. 'Oh, she'll be devastated.'

'We'll tell her together,' Lydia told her. 'We'll be brave.'

Persi nodded. 'Yes, but it's dreadful.'

'Would you take Foggy?' I asked. 'He hates dead bodies.'

'Oh, can I?' Lydia stooped to pick him up. 'Dear little doggie, perhaps I can have one of my own now.'

I was bemused by her reaction. She may not have liked Sinclair, but his death was a shock if nothing else.

Persi caught my eye and gave her head the briefest of shakes. 'You'd better hurry, Heathcliff.'

I hesitated, thinking to give her a reassuring hug, but she'd turned away, so I set off at a jog. I reached the entrance to the boathouse as Jerome was coming out.

'Make sure they telephone the police the moment you reach the house,' Swift called after him.

'Of course I will,' he replied as he dashed past me to catch up with Lydia and Persi.

Max was holding the boat against the dock, the motor purring quietly. It was a handsome craft and I admired it once again.

'Come on,' Swift called. 'We'll make a proper examination this time.'

'How did he die?' I asked, once I'd clambered aboard.

'We're not sure,' Swift replied as Max steered the boat expertly back out into the misty water. 'We didn't land, it was clear he was dead. I thought it was more important to come and report the news.'

'Was he drowned?' I continued.

'It didn't look like it.' Swift was staring ahead into the fog, then turned to me. 'He was wearing a life jacket.'

'A life jacket,' I exclaimed. 'Why?'

He didn't answer.

Max had increased the boat's speed with a smooth, easy touch; he was evidently skilled in its handling. 'Nearly there,' he said. 'I'll land at the jetty.'

The island emerged in the mist. I'd only seen it from a distance; it was larger than it had appeared from the castle. The jetty was built onto a rocky finger, reaching into deeper water. Max switched off the engine and let the boat drift in to butt gently against a simple dock of wooden planks. He hopped out and tied the bow line neatly to a brass cleat, before fastening the stern. I noticed the rope was wet.

'He's on the south side.' Swift walked along the planking and strode confidently on. I followed, Max brought up the rear. We crossed the wide grassy centre, fringed with cultivated shrubs and weeping willows. It was the perfect spot for a picnic on a sunny day; swimming in the lake, sipping champagne and feasting on tasty delicacies prepared by your own chef. I could imagine how tempting such a life must be.

We arrived at some rocks where a stony path led up to a small plateau overlooking a strip of sandy beach.

'Wait.' Swift turned to Max. 'Stay where you are. Lennox, we need to scan the scene first.'

'Fine,' I agreed, though unsure what he meant.

'Look for footprints or anything out of place.'

I stood and scanned. There was nothing peculiar, apart from the corpse, of course. No footprints, discarded gun, knife or weapon of any sort. The body was lying half in and half out of the water; the sand around him was undisturbed, it looked as though he'd washed up rather than scrambled of his own volition. I climbed down the rocks and walked across the beach. Swift followed, grumbling about making fingertip searches and such nonsense.

We came to a halt beside the earthly remains of Lord Godolphin Sinclair, his bulky form and forceful presence already diminished by death. He was lying on his back, his eyes bulging, his cheeks mottled purple and blue, his mouth pulled back as though he'd been gasping for breath. The tendons on his jaw and neck were tightly clenched and his hands were hooked like claws above his chest.

'What the devil was he doing out on the lake?' I muttered.

Swift wasn't ready for questions. 'We need to pull him up onto the shore.'

'Fine.'

We grabbed him under the arms and heaved until the body was almost clear of the water.

Swift knelt down. He pulled out a magnifying glass and used it to peer at the life jacket. It was made of green canvas and had been pulled up under Sinclair's chin.

'Was he drowned?' Max had followed us and now leaned over Swift's shoulder.

'Please move away,' Swift ordered without looking up.

'Look, I had nothing to do with it,' Max muttered, then stepped back and shoved his hands in his pockets.

Swift put the magnifying glass aside and began carefully untying the fastenings at the front of the life jacket.

'They're tightly knotted.' I watched him closely.

'Yes, more than you'd expect,' he remarked as he patiently fingered them apart.

'He was clawing at it,' I said quietly, so Max couldn't hear. 'There look.' I pointed at scratch marks on the life jacket.

'I saw,' Swift replied.

I bent to prod the wet canvas which was stuffed like a cushion.

'Kapok,' I remarked.

'Cork is more bouyant.'

'It's only a lake, Swift.'

He finally pulled apart the ties on the life jacket and opened it up. I observed Sinclair's sodden navy-blue suit. It was crumpled and wet, like the rest of him.

Swift pushed his fingers into Sinclair's top pocket. 'Just a handkerchief.' He tugged it out and pushed it in again, then flipped the lapels aside. There weren't any signs of injury on the white shirt; no bullet holes, stab wounds or blood. He searched the rest of the pockets and linings.

'A few coins, no wallet – it may have fallen out.' He lifted the hands next. 'He's very cold to the touch.'

'The water's freezing,' Max remarked. He'd moved forward again.

'Yes, but he has no residual body heat,' Swift replied. 'Max, go and wait on the rocks.'

Max went off, muttering under his breath.

'So how long has he been dead?' I asked.

'I don't know, over two hours.' Swift was scrutinising one of Sinclair's hands with the magnifying glass. 'There's mud and fibres under the fingernails.'

'The fibres are probably from the life jacket,' I remarked.

'Yes, or a rope,' he replied quietly.

'There's some blood on his head.' I'd walked around to the other side of the corpse.

Swift peered over. 'Just tip him this way, would you?'

I disliked touching the dead, but rolled Sinclair over to his side anyway. The body was stiffening already.

Swift watched. 'There's no water coming out of his mouth.'

'Does that mean he didn't drown?' I held Sinclair in place. He wobbled a bit.

'It makes it less likely, but only a post-mortem will prove it.' Swift didn't move. 'Just keep him still, would you, Lennox.'

'Right, but hurry up.'

He leaned over to observe the back of Sinclair's skull. 'There's a swelling near the temple and a minor contusion on the crown. Two strikes on the head.' He was lifting portions of Sinclair's wet hair aside with the tip of his pen. 'Most of the blood from the wound has been washed off in the water. It's already congealed, so he must have been alive when it happened.'

I let the body fall back and stood up.

'Both his shoes are missing,' I remarked.

'He must have struggled,' Swift muttered, then turned to shout to Max. 'Could he swim?'

'Yes, he was a strong swimmer,' he called down. He was standing up on the rocks, irritated but calm and not distressed at all.

'You don't think he drowned?' I asked Swift quietly.

'No, I think he had a heart attack.'

'Perhaps he saw a ghost,' I remarked.

'Don't be ridiculous, Lennox.'

I sighed and glanced at the water where Sinclair's stockinged feet were lying. It was crystal clear and free of the black oozing mud on the lakeside. Small fry darted among the stones, the surface was as still as glass, not a ripple or wave disturbing it.

Swift straightened up. 'We'll go back and bring the police over when they arrive.'

We made our way up the rocks to where Max was waiting.

'Someone should stay with him,' Max said. His apparent consideration surprised me.

'If you want to,' Swift replied.

I looked out over the misty lake. It would be a lonely spot with only a corpse for company.

'No,' Max replied coolly. 'But the crows will have him if he's left alone.'

'Yes.' Swift nodded. There weren't any crows to be seen, but cawing cries could be heard somewhere above us. 'Is there a blanket in the boat?'

'There is, we use it for picnics, but he'd be better protected in the changing hut. It's beyond the willow trees.' Max pointed to the other side of the island.

'Fetch the blanket, we'll use it to carry him,' Swift ordered.

Max ran back to the boat and returned with a large tartan rug. We trudged back to the body. Sinclair proved to be as awkward as he was heavy, and his waterlogged clothes didn't help. His passage wasn't elegant, but we managed to heave him across the island. The bathing hut was red roofed and quaintly pretty and it seemed a shame to clutter it up with a sodden corpse. We manoeuvred him inside and laid him on the slatted bench seat running along one wall.

'Right.' I was rather pleased with our efforts. 'Now what?'

'Back to the house,' Swift replied. We made our way to the jetty in silence.

The boat ride only took a few minutes across smooth water. Finn was on the dock when we arrived and Jerome was with him.

'Is it true? He's dead?' Finn shouted as we approached the boathouse.

'Haven't you been told?' Swift called back. He was standing in the cockpit, legs akimbo.

'Yes, but I wanted to hear it from you.' Finn's usual bounce had evaporated, he was angry and upset. He wore a casual outfit in brown and cream and looked as though he'd dressed in a hurry. 'They left me out... I would have helped.'

'It wasn't deliberate, Finn,' Jerome sought to placate him. 'I keep telling you, the search was started quickly.'

'You did it on purpose,' Finn yelled, jabbing a finger at him. 'He was my father.'

Max manoeuvred the boat around to reverse into the dock. He did it calmly and smoothly.

'That's enough,' Swift snapped as he stepped onto the deck. 'Where are the police?'

'I don't know, why don't you ask the big chief here.' Finn flicked a thumb at Jerome. 'He's been giving out orders, throwing his weight around...'

'For God's sake, Finn, what's got into you?' Max switched the engine off.

'Somebody here just killed my father,' he shouted. 'What the hell do you think's got into me?'

That resulted in a fractious argument and it took Swift's sharp temper to shut them up. They finally left, each of them maintaining a hostile silence.

'There's little love lost there,' I remarked, as we walked slowly out of the boathouse.

Swift sighed in exasperation. 'It was only Sinclair holding it all together.'

'You mean his money.'

'Yes, and now it's all going to explode into the open.'

'What was he doing in the water?' I returned to the murder.

Swift was walking with his head down. 'He must have been lured to the boat.'

'Why the life jacket?'

'Lennox, the whole point of an investigation is to find answers to these questions, not just pour them out at random.' He was tetchy.

'Right.' I shoved my hands in my pockets. 'The stern line was wet, did you notice?'

'Yes.' He nodded. 'Lennox, do you think we could have stopped it?'

'No. Every act has been ruthlessly planned and executed, I doubt anyone could have stopped it.'

'But, it was predictable…'

'He was surrounded by his own men, in his own home,' I cut in, then shifted the tone because I wasn't interested in recrimination. 'What about the motive?'

'Money,' he replied instantly.

'But, why such an elaborate series of killings?' I asked.

'I don't know.' He became grimly serious. 'But that murder was vicious. Sinclair didn't die quickly.'

'What do you mean?' I stopped as we were about to enter the formal gardens.

'Think about it. The life jacket was almost throttling him, the knots were pulled tight, he was dragged behind the boat.'

'Ah, yes, that explains the wet stern line. It was used to pull him through the water,' I agreed, then realised the implications. 'He was tortured.'

'Exactly.' Swift nodded.

'But why?'

'Information, I suppose. Why else would you torture someone.' His lean face was drawn in hard lines. 'He knew something.'

I considered that. We were approaching the house, and slowed down to discuss the killing. 'But we just decided it was about the money.'

He stopped and stared up at the serene splendour of the mansion. The sun was breaking through the mist, driving away the wreathing shadows. 'I wonder if they got what they wanted?'

'What do you mean?'

'The heart attack. The killer wanted to force some sort of secret out of Sinclair, but he died suddenly.'

'So it isn't finished?'

'No, there's something more,' he replied. 'Something we don't know about.'

'Right, well we'll have to find out then, won't we.'

CHAPTER 17

We walked around to the front door and it swung open. A small party of elderly people awaited us in the grand hall: Bertram St George, Lady Millicent and my butler.

'Greggs?'

'Ahem.' He gathered himself up and puffed out his chest. 'Sir Bertram has an announcement to make.'

'What?'

He raised an arm and stood aside, his theatrical tendencies getting the better of him. 'Sir Bertram is here to claim his rights.'

St George stepped forward and removed the pipe from his lips. He was still in dressing gown and slippers, he'd shed his napkin and added the deerstalker.

'The sword of justice has swung.' St George was also in dramatic mood; I wondered if they'd been rehearsing. 'I am now master of this house.'

'Are you?' I raised my brows.

Swift lowered his. 'How?'

St George was on fine form. 'As the oldest surviving St George, I inherit Lanscombe Park. Every stick and stone, inside and out, it's all mine. Ha! How do you like that!' He raised a fist towards Sinclair's office.

Swift was in no mood for theatrics. 'This is a matter for the law…'

'Bertram, just a moment, please.' Lady Penelope came down the stairs. She had changed into a simple, dark blue dress. Billie trailed behind her, presumably he'd gone to sound a warning.

'Oh, Penelope, my dear, we are so sorry about Sinclair.' Lady Millicent went to meet her.

'No, we're not,' St George muttered.

'Thank you, the shock is quite…' Lady Penelope raised a hand to her cheek, then gathered her composure. 'We must remain calm.'

'I'm calm and ready for the fray,' St George declared. 'Let no man say I faltered.'

'Yes, Bertram, but under the terms of the lease, it is Max and Lydia who succeed Sinclair,' Lady Penelope reminded him.

'What…?' St George's mouth dropped open. 'But, they're only children.'

'They're twenty-seven years old and perfectly capable of doing their duty.' Lady Penelope spoke quietly. 'Now, could I offer you tea, or…?'

'No, no.' St George was wilting. 'If the youngsters are indeed ready, I must concede.' He stuck his pipe in his mouth and puffed on it.

'But I'm sure they will depend on you for guidance, Bertram,' Lady Penelope added kindly.

'Will they?' That cheered him and he suddenly beamed. 'Ha! They can rely on me. A St George never wavers; steadfast and true. That's our motto.'

'There! I knew you would make things better.' Lady Millicent took her husband's arm. 'Come along, my dear. I have made a cake.'

'Is it chocolate cake?' He asked, as she led him away.

'Yes, dear with cream.'

'Did you make it with brown eggs?' St George asked.

'We did, six brown eggs.' She turned to my old retainer. 'Wasn't he wonderful, Greggs? Quite masterful.'

'Indeed, my lady,' he agreed in stately manner.

We watched them go.

'Oh, I really don't think I can take much more.' Lady Penelope almost buckled, her face creasing with sorrow.

We stepped forward immediately.

'I'll help you to your room,' I offered.

Mullins appeared. 'M'lady,' he said and took her arm. He helped her upstairs.

I was perturbed, and not just by Lady Penelope's distress.

'Swift, come to the drawing room.'

'No, I want to interview the staff.' He was in full police mode.

'You can do it later.' I led the way along the corridor. We arrived in the drawing room to find it as perfect as ever. It could hardly be described as cosy, but with the row of tall, sunlit windows, a blazing fire to ward off the autumnal chill and deep-cushioned sofas, it was probably the most comfortable of all the state rooms.

'Why are we here, Lennox?'

'It's about Max.' I was reluctant to have the discussion where we might be overheard. 'He would have known the boat had been used before he started it for the search.'

Swift frowned. 'Yes, of course. The engine would have been warm.'

'Did he say anything?' I asked.

'No.'

'He was fixing the boat yesterday when I interviewed him.'

He drew out his notebook and began writing in his neat hand. 'Was it just maintenance?'

'No, he said it wouldn't start.' My heart sank as I spoke. Aside from having taken a liking to Max, I knew Persi would be devastated when she found out he was probably the culprit.

'Sinclair was going to hand over the business to Jerome.' Swift continued to write as he spoke.

'He may never have intended leaving anything to Max,' I added.

'We need to know what's in Sinclair's will.' Swift made a note and underlined it.

'There's something else, Swift.'

'What?' He looked up.

'Randolph's rooms…' It had been playing on my mind. 'The note used to lure Sinclair out, Lady Millicent seeing Randolph…'

He cut in sharply. 'Lennox, if you're suggesting he's returned...'

'No, not that. I just wonder if all this is connected to whatever happened to him.'

He stopped writing. 'Lennox, I've been in this business a long time, believe me, it's about the money.'

I was inclined to argue, but let it go for the instant. 'What about Finn?'

'Why would Finn kill Sinclair? He's got nothing to gain.' Swift was dismissive.

'He was in debt to Sinclair,' I reminded him.

'He'd have to be deranged to kill three people just to avoid a debt. Look...' he paused in thought. 'We should bring in the men and interview them all together.'

'Why just the men?'

'Because whoever forced Sinclair into the boat had to be strong,' he retorted.

He was right, I wasn't thinking clearly. 'I'll call Mullins, he can fetch them.'

I decided to try out the contraption I'd seen Jerome use in Sinclair's office, there was bound to be one in there somewhere. I found it near the piano and dinged on the buzzer.

'Sir?' Mullins's voice could be heard on the other end.

'Could you tell Mister Max, Jerome and Finn to come to the drawing room, please?'

'Very well, sir, and there is no need to shout. I can hear you perfectly clearly.'

'Righto.' I placed the receiver back on its hook. 'Ingenious device that, Swift,' I told him, on returning to the fire.

'It's an intercom, Lennox. They're quite common.'

'Where are they common?'

'Offices, police stations. Places like that.'

'Oh...I'll take notes if you like,' I offered.

'Fine.' He handed me his notebook, pen and some blotting paper. 'Try to make them legible.'

Max arrived in short order, followed by Finn and finally Jerome, who had changed back into his city suit.

'Sit down,' Swift ordered.

They took various sofas and chairs at a distance from each other.

'Right,' Swift began. 'Which one of you murdered Sinclair?'

That brought a storm of protest.

'You have no right...' Jerome remonstrated.

Finn's pleasant features were marred with anger. 'This is ridiculous, what are you going to achieve that the cops can't?'

'Lennox.' He frowned at the notebook which I'd left on the low table between us.

'Right.' I made ready with pen and paper. 'Fire away.'

'Where were you all at six o'clock this morning?' Swift demanded.

'Asleep,' Finn answered instantly.

'I was reading a book in bed,' Jerome replied with irritation.

'I was working at my desk in my room,' Max said. 'I had some ideas for modifications to the carburettor and wanted to draw them up before I forgot. I can show you if you like.'

'Not now,' Swift answered before I opened my mouth.

I wrote *sleeping, reading, drawing,* then added, *one of them is lying.*

'Did anyone hear or see anything suspicious?' Swift continued.

'No,' came the predictable answers.

'How is this helping?' Finn asked.

Swift didn't answer, I shut the notebook because Finn was right, we weren't getting anywhere.

The door opened, Lydia and Persi came in with Foggy bounding at their heels.

'We've come to help.' Lydia sat down next to Jerome.

I made room for Persi beside me. I gave her Swift's notebook and whatnots. She smiled, I smiled back. Fogg jumped up and wriggled his way between us.

'Why would someone kill Sinclair?' Persi didn't beat about the bush.

'For his money, of course,' Max replied.

'Are you saying Jerome did it?' Lydia's excitement turned to anger in a flash.

'He's going to get Sinclair's business.' Max remained matter of fact in the face of his sister's wrath.

'Says who?' Finn jumped in.

Jerome had become agitated as the others sniped. 'Sinclair promised to pass the business to me.'

'Yeah, well he promised it to me.' Finn leaned back with his arms folded.

'What?' Jerome twisted around to stare.

'He liked what I did, I'm his son and a real business-man, not some toady bookkeeper,' Finn sneered.

'When did he tell you that?' Lydia demanded.

'Wouldn't you like to know,' he replied, then shut his mouth.

Persi was writing quickly in a neat hand.

'Well done, old stick,' I told her.

A smile crossed her lips, but she didn't look up.

'Why would I kill Sinclair before he'd handed the company to me?' Jerome had regained his diplomatic calm.

'Do you have any proof of Sinclair's intentions?' Swift asked.

'His word was enough,' Jerome replied, his handsome face taut but under control. 'And everyone knew about it.'

'Finn didn't,' I remarked.

'So he says,' Jerome snapped. 'It's obvious he's lying.'

'Sinclair wouldn't leave it to you,' Finn jumped in. 'He was my Pop, blood comes first.'

'Stop,' Lydia shouted. 'Stop now. It's awful. Everyone is squabbling and it's all for nothing. This isn't about Sinclair, it's about Papa. It's about Randolph, don't you see?' She burst into tears.

Silence fell. Jerome placed an arm around her shoulders and drew her to him.

Swift broke the uneasy atmosphere. 'Right, we'll carry out interviews one at a time. All of you stay here and wait to be called.'

'We're not going to sit around at your convenience,' Finn objected.

'Yes, you are.' Swift was on his feet. 'Lennox.'

'Persi, you should come,' I told her.

She closed the notebook and rose to her feet. We followed Swift along the upper landing to the door of Sinclair's office.

'We'll take statements for where they all were and what they were doing at the time of each murder.' He was eager to get to work. He crossed the office to manoeuvre into the swivel chair and sat down. 'Persi can take notes and...'

'Swift,' I interrupted. 'I'll leave you both to it.'

'What...? But, you can't,' Swift objected.

'No, Heathcliff, don't...' Persi protested.

'You don't need me. I'll go and do some rooting about while you've got them all penned up in the drawing room,' I told them and made my escape before they could argue further.

We'd probably got all the information they were going to give, the interviews would be tedious and I had better things to do. Fogg had followed me and I found Billie loitering in the hall.

'Log store?' I asked him.

'Sir?'

'You know where it is?'

'Yes, sir.' His sandy brows drew together.

'Meet me there,' I told him.

'But I ain't supposed...'

His protest came too late, I'd walked off. Fogg trotted behind me back to the kitchen of the old wing where my butler held knowledge pertinent to the case.

'Greggs, where's the wine cellar?' He had a glass at his

elbow and was rubbing saddle soap into the leather binding of an aged tome.

'Access is by invitation only, sir.' He picked the glass up as he spoke.

'Nonsense.'

'Sir Bertram was quite specific that the wine was for confederates only.'

'I'm not after the wine,' I told him. 'Point the way.'

He raised a wobbling finger. 'There is a door leading out of the boot room, sir. It is situated behind the porch.'

I've no idea why I hadn't thought about the cellars before, every big house had them. I found the boot room and the door and trotted downstairs to reach a brick-built cellar full of bottles of every hue and age. It was tempting to stop and pull a vintage Burgundy from the rack, but I stuck to my task and carried on until I came to a heavy door. It opened quite easily and swung back on oiled hinges.

'Aaaagh,' Billie let out a loud squeak.

'What?'

He'd turned pale, his eyes round with fright. 'Sir! You… you never said you was coming through the cellar, I wasn't expecting… Oooh, that made me jump, that did.'

Fogg had come with me, and went sniffing along the stone-tiled floor.

'Why isn't this door locked?'

'I don't know, sir.'

I ran my torch about. The cellars were actually a series of vaulted rooms, reminiscent of dungeons, and were as original as the old wing.

'Are these the fuel stores?' I could see stacks of logs filling one of the bays, others were empty and blackened with coal dust.

'They are sir, but we don't keep coal no more on account of the electric heating.'

'Is there a door to the outside?'

'I reckon so, only been down a couple of times and never on my own. Mr Trent would have logs brought up under his own eye, then he'd lock it all up again. For security you see. He was very careful about locking doors.'

'How did you get down here, then?'

'It weren't locked, which was peculiar...'

'Come on.' I strode off.

'It's a bit scary, sir.' Billie followed me on tiptoe for no good reason.

Our voices echoed in the dark. We found an alcove leading to a passageway. I shone the torch beam around the floor, but there were no signs of footprints or trailing mud. We came to a set of wooden steps leading upwards between two walls.

'I reckon that goes up to all the family's rooms above stairs, sir. In the old days, the maids would have taken coal to light the fires before the family woke up.'

They still did in many of the houses I was familiar with.

I gave the staircase a cursory flick of my torchlight, but was more interested in the door in the corner with sunlight showing under its base.

I went over and pulled the handle. It swung silently open.

'The doors have been oiled, sir,' Billie exclaimed.

225

'Obviously,' I replied.

Stone steps led upwards into an overgrown patch of bushes and trees. We were in Lady Millicent's garden, Fogg spotted a chicken and ran off in chase. I called, but he wouldn't come back.

'Do you reckon someone's been sneaking in and out of here?' Billie looked about at the thick bushes concealing the steps.

'Yes, blast it,' I cursed, we should have found this earlier.

'You mean the person what killed everybody?' Billie's eyes widened.

'Come on, Billie, back inside.'

'I'd rather stay out here, sir.'

'With the murderer?'

He jumped and looked around, then ran back down the steps. I grinned and closed the door with a bang.

'Billie, don't mention this to anyone except Mr Mullins. Go and find him and tell him to lock all of these doors, use padlocks if necessary.'

'Aye, sir.' He dithered for a moment, staring about as though expecting to see someone lurking in the shadows before running off. I heard his footsteps echoing along the passage until they faded away, then I went back to find the wooden stairs leading up to the mansion.

I trotted up and paused. There were more stairs leading ahead. I knew I must be near the drawing room, but decided to investigate properly, so carried on to the very top and stepped out. It opened onto a corner of a remote corridor. I knew where I was; it was right next to the room where the broken lamp had been discovered. Satisfied that duty was done, I wandered back down and found my way to Sinclair's office.

Swift was seated at the desk, looking over his notes.

'Lennox, where the hell have you been?' His mood hadn't improved.

'In the cellars, they run under the whole house, including the old wing. The killer's been using them to sneak out through the orchard.'

'Hell.' His face fell. 'We should have found that earlier.'

'We had enough mysteries to keep our minds occupied,' I replied.

'But we could have secured it…'

'Yes, fine.' I was keen to get on and breakfast felt like a long time ago. 'What did you discover from the interviews?'

'Not very much. I questioned Max about whether the engine was warm when he started the boat – he said it was.'

'He admitted it?' That was unexpected.

'He said he was going to tell us if we asked.' He glanced at me. 'He seemed to think it was some sort of test of our abilities.'

'I hope you gave him a dressing down.'

'Yes, for all the good it did.' Swift's lean face was drawn tight, his confidence flagging. 'Look, we'll go and search Sinclair's bedroom and dust the cellar door for fingerprints.'

'No, the police can do that when they arrive, we need lunch.'

'Now, look Lennox. We've committed to this investigation...'

'Exactly,' I replied. 'And we're not going to solve it by following finicking procedures. This killer is far too clever to leave clues. We need logic, Swift, and I think better on a full stomach.'

He was ready to argue, but I turned to leave, then realised someone was missing. 'Where's Persi?'

'Erm, she had a crisis of conscience,' he admitted sheepishly.

'A what?'

'I might have upset her.'

'Damn it Swift, she's only just started talking to me again. What did you say?'

He sighed. 'We interviewed everyone, then I dictated my morning report, including the discovery of the body, the time, weather conditions, all the relevant facts, and she made an excellent job of writing it all down. Then I listed the suspects, Max being the most likely culprit. She became upset and said that she felt like a traitor, helping to hang one of her own relatives.' He reddened. 'I pointed out that there was some truth in that, and she left.'

'That was tactless.'

'Yes, I know.'

'Should I go and make amends?'

'Actually, I think she might need to cool down first.' He was on his feet. 'Come on.'

We found Mullins and Billie coming up to find us.

'I have questioned the staff about the unlocked doors, sir,' Mullins explained in measured tone. 'Nobody knows anything.'

'It doesn't say much for security, does it,' Swift reasoned.

'I suspect Mr Monroe held a spare key and Mr Trent was privy to the situation, sir,' the old chap remarked. 'It was known Mr Monroe could move about unhindered, but not how.'

'Was a key found on the body?' I asked.

'Not to my knowledge, sir,' Mullins replied.

'There wasn't anything in the police report,' Swift said.

'It could have been taken after he'd crashed the car,' I remarked. It would have taken a cold heart to have searched the corpse, I thought.

'We have a message, don't we, Mr Mullins,' Billie reminded him.

'Ah, indeed. Lady Penelope would like a word, sirs. You will find her in the orangery.'

'She's not having lunch, by any chance?' I enquired.

Mullins smiled beneath the moustache. 'It is quite possible, sir.'

'Excellent.' That put a spring in my step and we headed to the pretty room overlooking the gardens.

CHAPTER 18

'Do please sit down.' Lady Penelope was seated in a wicker chair, encircled by fragrant flowers and perfumed shrubs.

There was a glass-topped table and more wicker seats, cushioned with silken fabrics, grouped around it. We sat as directed.

'Lady Penelope.' Swift was on a mission. 'Where are the police?

She appeared composed, despite the tension in her jaw. 'I ordered the servants not to call them.'

'You… but…' Swift spluttered, almost speechless. 'It's the law.'

'One of the family did it. You must realise that as well as I,' she replied.

'Yes, of course we do.' Swift was terse.

'So…' She searched for her words. 'I would like you to find the culprit, and then we will call the police.'

'No!' Swift reacted instantly.

'Yes,' I cut in. 'We will.'

'Lennox…' he warned.

'You said the local bobbies were out of their depth,' I reminded him.

'Please, Inspector,' Lady Penelope appealed to him. 'Nobody will escape justice, I'm not trying to cover up for anyone. I simply want to avoid tearing my family any further apart.' She stopped and closed her lips tightly, trying not to cry.

'If we can name the culprit and present them to Scotland Yard, we should, Swift.' I was adamant. 'They've already granted us authorisation to investigate. If they come here, you know how they will act. Everything will be picked apart and everyone will be a suspect. And that includes the old folk.'

I let that sink in. He knew it himself; he had a deep respect for the law, but also knew how harsh the turning of its wheels could be.

Mullins arrived which curtailed the debate. He was followed by a phalanx of footmen.

'Lunch, m'lady,' he announced.

'Oh, Mullins, I really couldn't,' Lady Penelope protested.

'The repast is designed for the gentlemen, m'lady, but chef has added a small dish of delicacies for you.' Mullins lifted the silver cover from a china plate. 'It is your favourite, smoked salmon with cream cheese, rolled in garden herbs and a small salad.'

'Thank you, but...' she tried again.

'Lay it all out, Mullins,' I told him. 'We'll help ourselves.'

'Very well, sir.'

He arranged platters of the sort of fancy food the very wealthy have a penchant for. I have to admit it was superb. Slivers of marinaded duck, liver pâté on thin toast, black olives and gooseberries seeped in oil, discs of beef with creamy mustard, crab and cucumber canapés, warm bread rolls with churned butter and a choice of red or white wine for accompaniment. Lady Penelope nibbled some salmon, Swift and I polished off the rest.

'Tea, to follow, or coffee?' Mullins was all attention as footmen dashed in and out with dishes of this and that, rustling the long fronds of tropical plants as they passed through the greenery.

'Coffee, please,' we all agreed.

'Jerome was convinced Sinclair was going to hand him the company...' I began.

'Yes, he had promised it to him,' Lady Penelope replied quietly. 'But Jerome should have realised he couldn't trust Sinclair. He knew what he was like, he played games with people.'

'Finn said it had been promised to him,' Swift stated.

'He was telling the truth,' she admitted. 'Sinclair was very impressed by Finn, he admired his initiative and energy. But no-one could trust Sinclair, what he promised or threatened one day, he would often rescind the next.'

That was true, we'd already witnessed it.

'Did he leave a will?' Swift asked.

The coffee arrived. There were little strawberry tarts and miniature chocolate eclairs.

Lady Penelope took a sip of black coffee before replying.

'No, he refused to write one. He said that if they want his money they can fight for it.'

'What about you?' I asked.

'I have an allowance,' she replied quietly.

Swift nodded, then returned to the subject. 'Sinclair knew when he signed the lease with St George that the funds wouldn't go with it.'

Her eyes flicked away as I spoke.

'You must have realised that,' Swift accused her with soft words.

'Not at first.' She glanced at him. 'Sinclair could be charming and generous, and he was to begin with. I thought we'd become a family, and he'd care for us all… we would be complete again. But his true nature was very different. He didn't understand love and compassion, he acquired people, then he controlled them.'

'Why didn't you leave him?' I asked the question that had niggled at my mind since I'd met her.

She paused to sip her coffee; I ate a few more tarts.

'If I'd left, Sinclair would have forced everyone to leave with me.' She regarded us with a steady gaze. 'We'd all have lost our home. I thought I'd wait until the children were old enough, but then the war came. Max survived, thank the good Lord, and Lydia announced she and Jerome were going to marry. It seemed easier to stay.' She sighed. 'It isn't a terrible life. I was accustomed to Sinclair, I knew what he was like, I think he even loved me in his way… In the end I decided to take the easier path.'

I watched her closely. Colour rose in her cheeks as we probed her private life; I was certain she was telling the truth.

'So Max knew he wouldn't have the funds to support this place,' Swift stated.

'You must understand Max's nature, Inspector,' she replied. 'He doesn't want to run the estate, he'd be happy in a cottage provided it has a workshop attached. He'd like to invent, as his father did. He has no desire to spend his life with this millstone around his neck.'

I caught Swift's eye, I could see he was about to challenge her. I shook my head, and he closed his mouth.

'Did you know Sinclair before you married Randolph?' I asked. 'He was local, wasn't he?'

She looked up at that question. 'He was local, but I wasn't. Randolph didn't know him either. Sinclair approached him because he'd heard about Randolph's invention from some acquaintances.'

'The metal detector, you mean?' I remarked. 'Sinclair said they took it to Alaska with them.'

'Yes, it was meant to detect gold.' A ghost of a smile touched her lips. 'Sinclair said it was inadequate to the geology.'

'Where were you living then?' Swift had finished his coffee and put the little cup down on the table.

'We'd settled in the old wing, but I had a very difficult pregnancy and we moved back to my parents' house in Bath for the birth. The medical care was very good at the local hospital, but even so, I was terribly ill afterwards. I stayed there for some months before I was well enough to move about again.'

'So, you weren't here when Randolph and Sinclair left for Alaska?' Swift prompted her.

'No, none of us were. Millie and Bertie had come to Bath to help. They weren't terribly good with babies, but they dearly wanted to be involved, and Lanscombe was...'

I finished her sentence. 'A wreck.'

'It was dreadful,' she admitted. 'My family were modest people, and when I told them I was going to marry Randolph St George and live at Lanscombe Park, they were terribly impressed. Then they came to visit and their reaction was really quite comical.' She laughed quietly. I could see the young girl in her suddenly – very like Lydia, although more thoughtful.

'Randolph wanted to make your fortunes,' Swift led her back to the topic.

'Yes, he thought it was his duty and it could help his career if the modified detector was a success,' she replied.

'Sinclair said it was merely the development of an existing idea,' I mentioned.

'It was, but it was a sophisticated development. Many people had been trying to create such a refinement and he was the first.'

'Do you have any knowledge of these devices?' I asked.

'Oh yes, that's how Randolph and I met. My father had a small manufactory of instruments and Randolph came to buy tools from us. I helped in the office, but I was fascinated by the technology and when Randolph came to consult my father, he spotted me and asked if I could help him find what he was looking for. We fell in love over slide-rules and electrical transformers.'

'You miss him?' I suggested.

'With all my heart,' she replied with a shake in her voice. I could see she was tired and the shock of Sinclair's murder was taking its toll.

'I'm sorry,' I said.

'And I'd like to express my condolences,' Swift added, then checked his watch. 'We should get back to it, Lennox.'

'Wait.' She raised her dark eyes. 'What is going to happen now?'

'We'll investigate and tell you what we can,' I said, then marched Swift through the greenery before he started another diatribe about the law.

Mullins stepped forward as we were leaving the orangery. 'If you were contemplating a search of his Lordship's rooms, I am available to assist, sir.'

'Yes, fine, show us the way,' Swift replied. 'We need to get a move on.'

'It doesn't take both of us to search a room, Swift,' I argued.

'Yes, you're right. See if you can find Finn. I couldn't get him to open up, you might be able to,' he agreed.

'Right, will do.' I set off to hunt Finn down. He was flicking through a magazine in the drawing room.

'If you've come looking for trouble, you're in the right place,' he warned as I dropped into a sofa near the fire.

I laughed, which didn't help.

'My Pop's dead and you think it's funny,' he growled.

'No, but your posturing is.' I turned serious. 'He didn't leave a will.'

He opened his eyes at that. 'But he promised…'

'His words on the matter were, 'if they want his money they can fight for it'.'

He eyed me coldly. 'I've got a legal birth certificate, it should give me some rights to his fortune.'

I wasn't ready to discuss that and switched tack. 'Finn? Is that short for Godolphin?'

'Yeah, stupid name but my mom chose it – my real mom, I mean.'

'Is she still alive?' I asked with a lighter tone.

'No, she died last year.'

'But you knew her?'

'I did.' He nodded, his green eyes watching me warily. 'I grew up in Seattle, that's where my adoptive parents took me to live. They really cared for me, good church folk who couldn't have children of their own. When I was older, I wanted to know about my birth parents, so I asked them. They didn't hide nothin', they told me all about it. My real mom's name was Kerri and she was still living in Dawson, far as they knew.'

'She remained in Dawson?' That surprised me.

'Yeah, lots of people live there, just not as many as during the gold rush.'

'Did you go and see her?'

'I sure did.' He relaxed and leaned back in the cushions.

'My folks sent me with their blessing. Mom, Kerri, wasn't well. The cold in Dawson eats away at you. I took along blankets and mittens for her, and she sat in a rocking chair and told me about her life.'

'And your father,' I prompted.

'Yeah, I was real curious about this Godolphin I'd been named after. She said she'd fallen in love with him and, well, you know how that can end. Anyway, when she told Sinclair she was gonna have a child, he turned nasty, called her names and denied it was his.' His lips twisted as he spoke. 'He cleared out before I was born and Kerri blessed me with her own surname, Patrick. They all called me Finn Patrick, because no-one had ever heard such a godawful name as Godolphin.'

'Sinclair said she was a street walker,' I said bluntly.

'That's a damn lie,' he swore. 'She worked in a bar; that didn't make her no street walker.'

'She was certain Sinclair was your father?'

'There couldn't be no other. She swore on the Bible in front of the magistrates, not that it did no good.'

'Because Sinclair had already moved to Boston and didn't leave an address?' I knew that Finn's mother had written to Lanscombe Park. 'And then Penelope stepped in?'

'Yeah, I told you, she helped as much as she was able. Kerri was destitute. She'd lost the job with the bar, the gold rush was finished and folk was leaving Dawson in their droves. She was desperate to keep me, her last hope was to get some money out of Sinclair; it didn't work.

Penelope sent what she could, but it wasn't enough and so I was adopted.'

'Do you believe he was your real father?' I asked the question.

'I've no doubt on that, but I take no pride in saying it.'

This was a moment of truth. His friendly relationship with Sinclair had been a sham.

'You understand that you have no rights of inheritance under English law.'

'You mean because I was born out of wedlock.' He gave a grim smile. 'Someone else was at pains to explain that to me.'

'Who?'

'Jerome.'

'Ah, yes, well he would, wouldn't he.' A thought occurred to me. 'Did your real mother, Kerri, ever mention Randolph?'

'No, why would she?'

'When did you first meet her?' I questioned.

'Back in 1918.'

'Six years ago,' I calculated.

'Yeah.'

'You first came here when you were 21?'

'End of 1918, there was a war on before then, I couldn't come.' He frowned. 'What are you getting at?'

I wasn't inclined to answer and was interrupted anyway.

'Heathcliff,' Persi came into the room. 'I've been looking everywhere for you. Will you come?'

CHAPTER 19

Foggy was with her, he ran about yipping in excitement.

'Swift is waiting in the hall,' she told me as we paced along the corridor and reached the stairs.

'What is it?'

'I was upset and went out for some fresh air.' She was breathless. 'I went to the castle, I could see the island from the top of the tower and thought about what Swift had said about how Sinclair died. I decided to take a look in the boathouse, and found blood on the dock wall and I'm certain there's something in the water.'

Swift was in the hall, keen to go. 'Come on, Lennox.'

We headed for the front door, a footman sprang into action and opened it.

We made quick time round to the formal gardens and reached the folly. Lydia was there with Jerome, watching a couple of swans drift by on the water. Lydia threw her cigarette away when she saw us.

'Where are you all going?' She called out.

'I asked you to stay indoors.' Swift went straight on the offensive.

'Really, is there any need for this?' Jerome replied.

'Why shouldn't we be out here?' Lydia objected. 'You are.'

'We're hunting down a murderer,' Swift retorted.

'So you can send one of us to the hangman.' Lydia's tone was cool. 'You too, Persi?'

Persi's cheeks flushed, but she held her tongue.

'That's enough,' I told Lydia.

'Now look here, old man…' Jerome stepped forward.

'Go back to the house and stay there,' Swift requested coldly.

Lydia looked mulish, Jerome stood beside her as though on guard.

'Lydia, please,' Persi pleaded.

'Oh, very well.' An angry flush rose in her face and she turned away. Jerome took her hand and spoke quietly to her.

We waited for them to go before striding through the trees, heading for the boathouse. It seemed dark below the broad roof, probably due to the contrast of bright sunshine outside, although my imagination may have been lingering on the events of this morning.

Persi pushed the stern of the boat aside and knelt on the concrete dock to point towards the waterline. 'Down there on the stonework, look. It's quite clearly blood.'

Swift pulled out his torch and shone it along the wall. 'Yes, I can see. Lennox, do you have any chalk?'

'No, of course I don't.'

'I'll see if I can find some,' Persi offered. There was a cupboard in the corner. She opened it to reveal fishing tackle: rods, baskets, hooks, lines and all the usual whatnots.

I took her place next to Swift. The surface of the dock was concrete, slightly roughened to prevent slipping, the wall below was built of large stones and one of them was smeared dark red about a foot above the water.

Swift was lying flat on the floor, his torch aimed at the stain. 'How did you find it?' His voice was muffled.

Persi returned with some green wax and handed it to me. 'I wondered how anyone could possibly bundle Sinclair into a life jacket? He'd fight back, he was a strong man – a cosh to the temple was an obvious answer. So I came here to have a look, and that's when I saw the blood.'

'A cosh would cause swelling, it wouldn't break the skin,' I said as I marked a large arrow on the dock with the wax.

'No, but I remembered Swift saying there was swelling to the temple and a graze to the skull. I thought that if the life jacket was tied to the stern, then Sinclair would have been dragged from the dock when the boat took off. The back of his head probably struck the side wall and caused the graze.'

I was impressed by her logic, and realised it meant either a man or woman could have done it.

'There could be hairs on it.' Swift had focused his magnifying glass on the bloody mark.

'Was there a priest in the cupboard?' I asked.

'A what?' Swift twisted around to ask.

'It's for killing fish, it looks like a cosh,' Persi told him. 'I think it's down in the water, I was looking for it when I saw the blood on the wall.'

We all leaned over as far as we could.

'Could you find a keep net?' I asked her.

She returned to the cupboard and came back with a long-handled net. 'I'm not a handmaiden, Heathcliff.'

Swift took it from her and dug about in the mud below the boat.

I gave her a grin. 'You're awfully clever, old stick.'

'Got it,' Swift announced. He pulled the net up, it was smeared with mud and weed, and weighted down by the priest.

'Could there be fingerprints?' Persi sounded excited.

'Unlikely.' Swift upended the net to let the priest roll onto the dock. 'It's too wet and the killer's been careful not to leave any clues.'

'Until now,' I reminded him.

Persi raised her brows.

'The life jacket hadn't been removed from Sinclair's body, and he'd been clawing at it,' I told her. 'It clearly marked his death as murder.'

'Oh, of course. I should have thought of that, I was so caught up in the details.' She smiled at me, which gladdened my heart. 'But why didn't they remove it?'

I didn't have the answer to that.

Swift pulled on gloves and picked the priest up. It was

turned from solid ebony, similar in shape to a policeman's truncheon and just as effective.

'The perfect weapon for knocking someone out,' I remarked.

'And the killer didn't even have to bring it down here with them,' Persi added.

Swift dropped it into his pocket. 'They knew where to find it.'

'That's pretty obvious,' I remarked.

We rooted around the boathouse, being much more thorough this time, but nothing else turned up.

'We'll open the workshop, we haven't searched inside there yet.' Swift was in full investigative mode.

'Right,' I agreed. He led the way and Foggy bounded along with us, tail up and tongue out.

'Do you have the key?' Persi asked as we passed below the sweet chestnut trees.

'No, but I have my lock picks.' I jangled them in my pocket, keen to show off my favourite piece of detecting kit.

When we arrived at the workshop, the mud outside was beginning to dry in the sun.

Swift examined the lock then tried the door handle; the door swung on its hinges. 'It's open.'

'Oh.' That pricked my pretensions. We walked in unhindered.

I recalled Lady Penelope's words; it had been built as the village church before the castle was attacked by King John and his army. Despite the horrors of history, it held an atmosphere of peace. Slates covered the roof, the joists looked to be only a few centuries old, windows were cleaned, the frames newly painted. The walls were in their original state and bore faded frescoes in flaking red, yellow and blue paint: St Christopher, a parade of haloed saints, Adam and Eve, a writhing serpent, a host of Angels. A gaunt Christ dominated the whole.

On one side of the church, trestle tables were weighed with mounds of mysterious shapes, hidden under dust covers. The other long wall held similar tables showing signs of frequent use. Tools placed where the hand had left them and models in metal and wood stood between sheets of drawings. There was even a small generator in the corner, rather incongruous next to a stone font carved in simple country style.

'It must be eight hundred years old,' I muttered.

'It is,' Persi replied. 'Or rather, the walls are – the roof and floor were rebuilt in Elizabethan times.'

I kept forgetting she'd been familiar with Lanscombe since childhood.

Fogg discovered something interesting beneath the generator and scrabbled about, raising dust.

Swift sneezed.

Persi went to the opposite wall and pulled aside one of the covers on a nearby trestle table, causing more dust to fly into the air. 'Oh, these are Randolph's drawings.'

I went over to join her.

She traced a finger over one design. It was something complicated with wheels and cogs. 'It's a centrifugal separator.'

'How do you know?' I was impressed.

'It's written here,' she pointed to a line of neat copper-plate script.

'Ah.' I began turning pages over. 'There should be blue-prints for Randolph's metal detector here. That was his last project.'

'What would it look like?' Persi watched me.

'It depends, there are different designs,' I told her. 'There were large ones used to clear minefields in the war, they had round detection plates, like cart wheels suspended on a pole. Smaller types were designed to be held by hand and had a metal cage attached by a cable to a box. The cage could be swung over the ground like a pendulum. We tried one once.'

'Really?' Persi gazed up at me. 'Did you find anything?'

I laughed. 'Yes, horseshoes, spent bullets, and a hob-nailed boot.'

'Where were you?'

'France, one of the aircraft mechanics was keen on new technology. He'd found an article in a magazine on how to manufacture a metal detector and cob-bled one together. We found all sorts of gubbins and then the farmer turned up and threatened us with his shotgun.'

That made her laugh. 'So no buried treasure?'

'Not a bean.' I grinned.

Swift had come to join us. 'These drawings should have been preserved.'

'They are.' Persi turned serious. 'The St Georges had

the place closed up, they refused to let Sinclair touch it when Penelope married him.'

'And it's Max's domain now,' I mentioned.

She glanced over at the other part of the building. 'Yes, but it looks as though he's never disturbed this side.'

Swift was more interested in the investigation. 'If Max did it, there may be something here.'

'Like a strip of copper,' I suggested.

'There's plenty of that.' Swift pointed to a heap of metal scraps.

'Anyone could have come in here and taken it.' Persi turned on him. 'It doesn't mean Max did it.'

'He was fixing the boat yesterday, Persi,' I reminded her.

'That doesn't make him a murderer,' she retaliated.

'No,' I agreed, 'but it makes him a primary suspect.'

'Persi, if you can't remain objective…' Swift cautioned.

She bit her lip. 'But why Max? Why not Jerome, or Finn? Max doesn't inherit his company,' she countered. 'One of them will.'

'No, they won't. If Sinclair died intestate, then Penelope will inherit the company,' I said. 'And she will almost certainly give it to Max. The estate will be saved and the St Georges' fortunes restored.'

I felt a bit of a heel. I knew it upset her, but it had to be said.

She turned pale, though wasn't about to concede. 'That doesn't explain why Monroe and Trent were murdered, or why Sinclair was tortured.'

Which was true, actually, and neither Swift nor I had an answer to that.

'Sir, Inspector Swift, sir.' Billie ran in, his pimply face bright red. 'I've been looking everywhere for you.' He panted for breath.

'What happened?' Swift was instantly alert.

'Nothing actually happened sir, but Mr Mullins found these papers. He said they had to come to you and no-one else. It's dead secret. He even said it was dangerous.'

'What?' I asked as we crowded around him.

'Show me,' Swift demanded.

Billie handed the sheaf of papers to him. 'They were on his Lordship's desk, just as if he'd put them there himself. Mr Mullins went in to lock the office and he saw them, clear as day.'

Swift was unfolding the first page. 'I was in there myself before lunch, I would have seen them.'

'Mr Mullins said they must have been put there after that. The door was shut, but it weren't locked.' Billie was trying to read the papers in Swift's hand. So was I, until Swift realised and folded them over.

'Inform Mr Mullins that we'll take appropriate action.' He stared Billie in the eye and spoke gravely. 'He must not tell anyone, and nor must you. And I mean no-one. Not Sir Bertram, or Lady Millicent or Lady Penelope, not even if you are directly confronted. It's very important that you understand this.'

Billie nodded anxiously. 'I understand, sir. I'll keep out of the way, I'll stay with Mr Mullins, sir.'

'Right, off you go.' Swift dismissed him.

Billie turned and ran as fast as his legs would carry him.

CHAPTER 20

'It's a design which has been lodged with the patent office.' Swift opened the papers out on the nearest trestle table. We looked over his shoulder.

'For what?' I asked.

'A machine devised for the detection of gold.' Swift read out the title, 'An Induction Balance.'

'You mean Randolph's metal detector,' Persi stated the obvious.

Swift handed me the application and scanned the next page. 'It's from America, a lawyer called Sprague, based in New York.'

He carried on reading to himself.

Foggy came bounding up, he'd found an old rag and was shaking it, shedding dust into the air and causing Swift to burst into a fit of sneezing.

'Let's go outside,' I suggested.

They agreed and we walked out to stand in the bright sunshine.

'Here.' Swift handed over the next page between blowing his nose. 'Read it out would you, Lennox.'

'Dear Sinclair…' I skipped the effusive remarks about how honoured he was to be Sinclair's representative and came to the meat of the matter. 'We have continued to renew your Patent numbered US, 387,562 B. May I enquire if you would like the Patent to be extended further? As you know the United States Government is disinclined to allow patents to continue for excessive periods, and any further application may not be successful. Given the age of the original device, I beg your consideration as to the efficacy of renewal…'

'That invention belonged to Randolph.' Persi's eyes flew to mine.

'Sinclair said it was merely a modification and wasn't patented,' I said.

'Here.' Swift passed me another sheet of paper.

'It's a copy of the Patent Certificate. It's in Sinclair's name.' I reread it, checking the number against the one listed in the lawyer's letter.

'Look at the date.' Swift told me.

Persi moved closer to read it with me, I could feel the warmth of her shoulder against my arm, smell the scent of her hair…

'What?'

'I said 'May 1896',' Persi repeated.

'That was the date they arrived in New York to travel over to Alaska,' Swift said.

'Wait,' I turned back to the lawyer's letter. 'This is dated three weeks ago.'

'And there's this…' Swift handed me a sheaf of papers.

'It's a handwritten copy of the second-class passenger list for the SS Umbria, that's the ship they travelled on from Liverpool to New York.'

The list had been supplied by the Cunard company and their letterhead was stamped on the top of each page.

'Is there a letter with it?' I asked.

'No,' Swift replied.

I ran my eye down the lists. There were seven pages written in a tight script. 'What did you find?'

'Godolphin Sinclair had a second-class cabin,' he replied. 'A double cabin, but only his name is listed against it.'

'What about Randolph?' Persi asked.

'His name isn't there,' Swift said coldly.

We both looked at him. 'Not there?'

He shook his head. 'I don't think he went to America.'

'He didn't...' Persi said. 'But where did he go?'

'Possibly nowhere,' Swift said. 'He may never have left this country.'

Finally, it made sense, that's why there weren't any personal letters in Randolph's rooms.

'Sinclair murdered him,' I stated.

We were standing outside the church, the sun streaming through the trees, yellow and orange leaves blanketing the ground and a bird singing somewhere in the distance. A perfect autumn day, but I felt a cold chill run down my spine.

'He murdered Randolph,' Persi stated blankly as the extent of Sinclair's crime sank in. 'And took his wife, his

253

children, his home.' She turned to stare at me. 'He was a monster.'

'Why were these papers left on his desk?' Swift was still fixed on the investigation.

'We need to think this through, Swift,' I told him. I was stunned and I was angry. We'd been running like rats in a maze since we arrived in Lanscombe Park. It felt as though we were being manoeuvred and I wanted to know who the hell was doing it.

'There are some logs by the lake,' Persi commented. 'We can go and sit there.'

'Right,' I grunted.

She led us down to the shore, where a couple of fallen tree trunks had been carefully placed as part of the picturesque design.

Fogg was delighted. He darted to the water's edge and ran straight in.

We watched in silence, each of us with our own thoughts.

'These murders are about Randolph,' I stated. 'Which changes everything.'

'Yes,' Swift muttered. 'It's more likely to be...' He glanced at Persi and shut up.

'Who found out what Sinclair had done?' Persi murmured, gazing into the distance.

'Whoever it was, would have been driven to murderous fury,' I said slowly, my mind turning it over.

'Evidently,' Swift remarked dryly.

'Do you think Randolph is buried here?' Persi asked.

'Possibly, but only Sinclair could have answered that question,' Swift replied.

'That's it, that's why Sinclair was tortured.' Persi suddenly sat up. 'The murderer wanted Sinclair to tell them where he'd buried Randolph's body.'

'And to do that, they had to isolate Sinclair,' Swift realised. 'That's why Monroe and Trent were eliminated.'

'So they could force him the truth out of him,' Persi added.

Swift nodded. 'Yes, it makes sense. Sinclair was coshed, then dragged off the dock with the line hooked onto the life jacket. The killer would have released him in deep water. He probably circled around him in the boat to stop him reaching the shore.'

'And the life jacket would have stopped him drowning,' I added grimly.

'That's rather nasty,' Persi remarked.

'He deserved it,' I muttered.

'But why leave the papers?' Swift could be remarkably pedantic.

'Sinclair had a heart attack,' I answered. 'He must have died before he divulged where the body is buried.'

'Are you saying the killer wants us to find Randolph?' Persi continued.

'Yes,' I replied. 'Why else leave the papers for us to find.'

'You didn't find them,' Persi pointed out. 'Mullins did.'

'Someone would have given them to us,' Swift asserted. 'That's why they were left in the office.'

I wondered if it were Mullins acting on Lady Penelope's orders, but decided not to say anything. It was already confusing enough.

'Why not look for the body themselves?' Swift persisted.

'Because it would give the game away. They may as well admit they killed Sinclair and his men,' I replied, thinking it was pretty obvious.

'Hum.' He didn't seem entirely convinced.

'We must find Randolph,' Persi said.

We both looked at her.

'It's like looking for a needle in a haystack,' Swift replied. 'And we need to identify the murderer. Searching for Randolph won't achieve that.'

'I think it could,' I disagreed. 'If we find the body, we can use the information to lure the killer out.'

'Yes, you must see that, Jonathan,' Persi insisted.

'We can't waste what little time we have.' Swift had become obstinate. 'We should be able to outwit the murderer.'

'Well, we haven't done so far,' I remarked.

'What about the passenger list?' Persi suggested. 'Who-ever requested it would have had to give their name and address. We could question the staff, one of them may know something.'

'Yes.' Swift was impressed. 'Would you do that, Persi?'

'Yes, I will.' She was on her feet.

'Persi…' I stood to face her.

She gave me a reassuring smile. 'No-one's going to harm me.'

'No.' I was sure she was right. 'But we're about to kick over a hornet's nest. It will be traumatic.'

Her smile faded. 'Yes, I know… but I'm going to do it, nobody can be allowed to get away with three cold-blooded murders.' She gave me a kiss on the cheek, turned and walked back towards the house.

'She's plucky,' Swift remarked.

'Hum,' I sighed. 'Right, the killer wants Randolph found.' I looked about at the rolling acres of gardens, woodland, fields and lake. 'Hell, where do we begin?'

'Consider the facts.' Swift moved into detecting mode. 'Sinclair had the lake dredged and extended, he wouldn't have risked doing that if there was a body in it.'

'That leaves about a thousand acres of land to dig up then,' I replied.

'Not necessarily.' Swift had his hand to his chin. 'Bodies are heavy, it's unlikely he'd have gone very far.'

'Yes, but where do you think he was killed?' I replied.

He eyed me. 'Good question. Either the house, or workshop.'

'The house has been completely renovated,' I mooted. 'It must be the workshop,'

'Is there a crypt underneath?' He asked.

I considered it. 'Doubtful, it's in a hollow and would be prone to flooding.'

'What about outside?' He stood up. 'Is there anywhere Sinclair left untouched?'

'The castle,' I replied. 'Lady Penelope said Sinclair never made any changes there.'

'Right.' He brightened up. 'We need spades.'

'Just a moment.' I held a hand up because I'd thought of something. 'Randolph would have been wearing a belt with a buckle or possibly had coins in his pocket.'

Swift was quick to catch on. 'You mean we should use the metal detector?'

I nodded. 'That patent letter in your hand has the design attached.'

'We can't make one.' He turned the pages over to stare at the drawing.

'No, but there's probably prototypes in the workshop. Come on.'

We headed back inside and went straight to the trestle tables that bore Randolph's old inventions. The covers seemed to have lain untouched for years and were thick with dust. We both sneezed as we removed them to uncover jumbled wires, coils, cogs, various rods of copper, rusted iron, brass and bronze. There were wooden forms supporting small engines, pistons, a crude amplifier and devices that I could only guess the use of. I thought I'd be able to identify a simple metal detector, but now I wasn't so sure.

'Lennox,' Swift called. 'What's this?'

I went over. 'That's something like it.' I felt a spark of excitement.

Swift held up a makeshift model. 'It looks like the drawing.'

'It's too rudimentary. Let's find one that works.' I began moving the tangle of parts.

'Wouldn't he have taken it with him?' Swift was having doubts.

'Well, Randolph didn't, but Sinclair might have,' I remarked dryly. 'It doesn't matter, there would be more than one.'

He turned back to rummage some more.

I picked up a small metal cage and discovered it had a cable attached to a wooden box. 'This could be it.' I pushed aside a mess of wires.

Swift looked dubious. 'Are you sure?'

'Yes,' I told him. There was a grimy gauge fixed to the side of the box. I opened the lid. It held the usual copper coils and connectors. 'All of the electrics are in there, but there's no battery.'

'What size does it take?'

'Six volts, I think.'

'Fine.' He went over to Max's side of the building and started a search, returning in short order with a battery. 'Here.'

I took it from him. 'And some paraffin.'

He muttered under his breath and went back again. Max had equipped his section of the workshop with plenty of up-to-date tools and whatnots. It didn't take Swift long to find what was needed.

'A wire brush,' I mentioned.

He stalked off again, returning moments later. 'Lennox, I'm not a damned handmaiden, either.'

I laughed and set about cleaning the corroded workings. The copper terminals had grown verdigris and I had to chip the encrustation off with my knife and brush them away with a spot of paraffin. Then I rubbed the dust from the gauge and attached the battery with cables. It let out a faint fizz of energy.

Swift grinned. 'I've never used one of these before.'

'They're pretty erratic,' I replied, almost as excited as he was. The case sported a leather strap, I slung it over my shoulder and carefully lowered the metal cage on its cable until it was suspended an inch or so from the ground. It looked rather like a lantern case on a long wire which was attached to a bulky box. The one I'd used in France had been more modern, with a disc on a pole rather than the cage on a cable. The method was the same though, the sensor had to be swung in an arc over the ground in the hope of detecting metal.

'We should test it,' I said.

We walked back outside into the bright sunshine.

'Right.' Swift pulled a handful of coins from his pocket, took a silver sixpence and threw it into the distance. 'Let's see what it can do.'

CHAPTER 21

We'd walked to the area where he'd thrown the coin.

'How deep can it penetrate?' He was beside me, his eyes fixed on the gauge screwed to the outside of the box.

'I have no idea.' I was moving very slowly, swinging the metal cage in an arc in front of me, but the gauge hadn't so much as flickered.

'How does it work?' He was full of questions.

'Does it matter?'

'Hum.' He shoved his hands in his pockets. 'Will it be able to find the sixpence?'

I didn't deign a reply. I was already becoming frustrated and turned another circle, lowering the metal cage until it was skimming the ground. The grass was long and still wet despite the sunshine throwing rays of warmth through the trees. 'Where the devil did it land...'

'Look,' he cut in, excitement in his voice. 'It moved, the gauge went right across the dial. Stop Lennox.'

I had already stopped. He was eager as a schoolboy.

'Wait.' I twirled the metal cage in small circles, trying to get the best signal.

He bent down, rummaged in the grass and lifted the sixpence in triumph. 'Found it!' He grinned.

'Ha!' I was impressed. 'Randolph must have been a good inventor.'

'Right.' He clapped his hands. 'We need to be organised, we should make a grid from string and pegs, if we start at the far end of the castle we can…' He was still pointing to a distant spot when I walked off and went over to the edge of the ruined keep.

I began moving the metal cage, one swinging arc with each step forward. 'Come and watch the dial.'

He sulked for a moment, hands on hips, then came to join me. 'I can take over if you like.'

'I'll go as far as the rocks, then you can do it,' I told him.

Fogg came to see what we were doing. He sniffed about, nose to the ground, stopping at the occasional pile of rabbit droppings.

Nothing happened for ages. We walked, I swung the cage, Swift watched the dial. It was all rather tedious.

'Stop,' Swift shouted. 'It moved.'

'Really?' I stepped backwards and swung it again.

'There.' He pointed to the ground.

'Spade, Swift.'

'Oh, damn it.' He turned and ran back to the workshop. As detectors go, I think we'd just failed the basics.

I'd pulled out my clasp knife and by the time he

returned I'd scraped some grass and soil aside. Fogg kept pushing his nose in to see what I'd discovered.

'Let me.' Swift drove the point of the spade into the ground and carried on with enthusiasm.

'Wait.' I stopped him as the soil flew. 'Let me try the cage again.'

I couldn't find the signal as I swung it over the black earth. 'Where...' I muttered, then saw the gauge flick over the dial. I bent over and picked up a bent nail.

Swift's face fell. 'Oh.'

I grinned, I'd done this before. 'It's not going to be easy.'

'No.' He left the spade sticking out of the ground and we carried on.

More nails, a horseshoe, spent cartridges, bullets from the distant past and a wire rabbit trap were our total haul by the time we reached the stone base of the curtain wall.

'Oh, you found one.' Persi called as she came up the hill. 'Clever you. I thought all the electrics would be corroded away.'

'Hello, old stick.' I gave her a grin. She smiled back and I wondered if I should offer a peck on the cheek.

'We aren't getting very far.' Swift showed her the haul.

'Can I help?' Persi was keen. 'You know, this would be rather marvellous in the field. Particularly in Egypt; I'm amazed the team hasn't thought to buy one.'

'Did you find anything at the house?' Swift hadn't forgotten the investigation.

'Yes.' Her face clouded. 'One of the footmen recalled

seeing a letter from Liverpool, he comes from there. It was addressed to Sinclair.'

'Sinclair?' That was unexpected.

She pushed a strand of blonde hair back from her face. 'It was taken to Trent's office, he received the mail. I thought Jerome might know more, but I decided I'd better leave it to you to question him.'

'Trent…' Swift's brows lowered.

'When did it arrive?' I asked.

'The footman wasn't sure, but he thought it was about a week before Sinclair's party.'

That was food for thought. Trent probably sorted all the mail, which made it easy for him to intercept anything before Sinclair or anyone else in the house saw it.

'We can ask questions later,' I said and handed the box and cable over. 'Your turn, Swift.'

'You can watch the dial,' he told me. 'Unless you'd like to Persi?'

'I'd love to,' she volunteered.

I gave her another grin, she was standing very near me, the sunlight playing on her hair and face…

Swift cleared his throat. 'Ready?'

'Yes.' She laughed. 'We might even find buried treasure!'

I suppose archaeologists always expect to find buried treasure, or dead bodies. I followed behind with my hands in pockets until boredom set in.

'Just going to stretch my legs,' I told them, then cleared off. I made for the tower where the view across the water tugged at my soul. At home in Ashton Steeple, I had a small lake fed by a meandering brook, and there was nothing more entrancing than casting a fly into the rippling shallows on an autumn evening. I gazed at the island, the roof of the wooden hut showing as a smudge of red amongst the foliage. Sinclair would have hardly imagined when he woke up that morning that his day would end in such an ignominious fashion. I mused along the lines of how the mighty had fallen, then moved to more relevant matters, like who the devil had killed him.

Discovering that it was about Randolph blew a hole straight through our theories surrounding the inheritance. Someone discovered the truth about Randolph. The lawyer's letter about the patent must have set them on the trail. Could it be Lydia? Was she really a cold-blooded murderer? She had always suspected Sinclair and must have been a constant thorn in his side. I'd thought her campaign against him had been born of resentment; he had usurped her father's place, and she had never forgiven him for it. But once she'd been proven right – what would her reaction be?

Max was still top of the suspect list. He'd resented us and our investigation, and could have interfered in ways we wouldn't even know about. Had he done that to protect himself, or someone else, like his mother?

Lady Penelope had been kind, helpful and gracious, but she gave very little of herself away. Had she really married Sinclair to save the estate? Sacrificed herself to ensure the future fortunes of her children? How would she have reacted when she discovered her sacrifice was to the monster who'd murdered her husband?

She would surely want to know where Randolph was buried – as would the St Georges. Randolph was their beloved only child, killed at the hands of the man who'd taken everything which had been his. But then they couldn't possibly have found the lawyer's letter, or written to the shipping company, not without help in the house. So, who would help them out…

'Lennox,' Swift called from the castle courtyard.

'What?'

'I think we've found something.'

'Right.' I was down the steps of the tower in an instant and paced quickly along the battlement. I joined them just beyond the ruins of the great hall.

They'd left the metal detector on a low wall. Broken stones lay on top of a black earth mound. Fogg had caught the excitement and was frantically digging his own hole nearby.

'There was a building here once, it's just rubble now.' Persi pointed a torch to shine a beam down at a hole in the ground. 'But look what we found.'

It was knee deep and Swift was busy brushing soil aside with his hands. 'We had a really strong signal here….' He felt carefully with long fingers, then suddenly lifted something free of the dirt.

'What is it?' I was leaning shoulder to shoulder with Persi.

He moved aside to let us see. 'It's iron, it could be a handle.'

'Is it attached to anything?' Persi reached a hand down to grasp the metal. It was caked with clinging soil and rust.

'Yes.' Swift made to scramble out of the hole. 'But we need to be careful not to break the fastening.'

Persi took over, reverting to her role as forensic archaeologist. She pulled a magnifying glass from her jacket pocket and examined the loop. She rubbed dirt away with a thumb, then let the iron handle down carefully and wiped the soil from the boss holding it in place. 'It's early medieval in style. It could have been made when the castle was first built.'

'What's it attached to?' I asked.

'Stone, it's a trapdoor,' she called back, still engrossed with brushing earth from around the iron boss.

'Can we lift it?' Images of treasure and the lost tomb of the Chatelaine rose in my mind.

'If you can find a rope, I think I can clear the edges enough to try,' Persi told me.

'Right.' I was off like a shot. I ran back to the boathouse, grabbed the nearest line and raced back again. Foggy came with me, barking as we went, thinking it all marvellous fun. I handed the rope to Persi, who'd cleared out the sides of the hole.

'The metal looks strong enough to take the strain.' She tied it expertly around the hoop and passed it to Swift.

'We'll need to use the spade as leverage,' he told me.

I didn't argue, just grabbed it. I could feel it slip into a gap between the trapdoor and its surround. The slab of stone was visible now. It was rectangular in shape, about two feet by three and roughly hewn, as though hacked rather than saw cut. The metal hoop was fixed in about two-thirds of the way up, held by a thick cast iron pin driven through the stone.

I gave Persi my hand to help her up to ground level. She was laughing, back in her element and evidently enjoying herself.

'We need a strong, steady pull,' she told Swift.

They both took the rope and I pried the spade back. Nothing happened, they tugged, I pushed the spade, then the stone shifted a fraction.

Swift started shouting. 'When I say heave, we all heave.'

I shoved the spade deeper.

'Heave,' Swift ordered. 'Heave.'

The stone lifted, a smell rose from the ground, damp and very old, with the tang of decay.

'Pull it right out.' Swift was still in command. I let the spade fall and went to haul on the rope. We levered the stone upright and then back to let it fall over the mound of soil until it was entirely free of the opening.

We paused, breathless, then moved to peer down into the blackness below.

CHAPTER 22

There were steps. They looked to be almost unused, with no sign of wear.

'Man made,' Swift stated as he aimed his torch downwards.

'Obviously.' I was following the beam of light. The walls were green and black with mould, the opening only shoulder wide. The bottom was lost in darkness.

'I'll go first.' Persi was already lowering herself inside.

'No.' I put my hand on her shoulder.

'I've been in far worse places,' she reminded me.

I recalled Damascus, and the snakes and scorpions, which hadn't bothered her a jot. 'I know, but I don't want any harm to come to you.'

She laughed and went down the steps, her own torch lighting the way. I followed, Swift right behind me.

'Don't forget this is a police investigation,' he called out, I've no idea why.

The steps went down around fifteen feet. At the bottom, the solid rock gave way to roughly built stone walls. It seems they'd cut through the layer of rock then tunnelled below ground. I wondered how close to the lake we were and was surprised it hadn't poured in.

'The floor is slippery, take care,' Persi called back to us.

She was right. My boot slid as I trod from the bottom step onto the flat surface. We caught up with her as she paused in what looked like a small chamber with a cave-like ceiling. My hair brushed the wet stones, moisture dripped onto my head and sent trickles of icy water down the back of my neck.

'Which way?' She shone her torch down one passageway and then another.

'The one on the left must go under the great hall,' I said, judging by the direction.

'We'll take that one,' Swift decided and led the way.

It didn't go very far, more or less to the far side of the building.

Persi shone her torch upwards into a vertical shaft, almost twenty feet in height. It was made of dressed stone, round, like a well. 'It's under the fireplace.'

'An emergency escape route.' I recalled the sticks and debris in the hearth. 'Would it be visible?'

'It's unlikely, these things were disguised.' She ran a hand over the mould-blackened wall. 'I think there may have been a wooden ladder attached to the stones.'

'Wouldn't there be a route out, under the walls?' I asked.

'The castle was surrounded by a moat, Lennox,' she replied dryly.

'Ah…yes.' My mind had been on Lady Rosamond and her flight from the murderous King John. 'If Lady Rosamond did hide down here, she would have been trapped when the castle was burned.'

'Yes,' Persi agreed. 'The roof would have collapsed; the fallen joists and slates would have made it impossible to open either of the trapdoors.'

'And everyone was killed, so no-one came to lift the debris away.' Swift was sombre.

'She's still here somewhere, isn't she.' I turned and headed back to the junction.

We took the unexplored tunnel out of the chamber. It dropped down a step and the ceiling lowered with it.

'Damn,' I cursed as I banged my head on a jutting stone.

'Lennox, time is passing.' Swift lacked sympathy.

'Yes, Swift, I know,' I retorted and carried on. The tunnel went steadily down, and I'd expected to find catacombs or caves or some such when we rounded a bend.

'These are going up.' I hesitated. We'd arrived at another set of stone steps. 'Have we missed something?'

'There weren't any other openings,' Persi said from behind me.

I started the ascent. The steps were made from smoothed stones, confined within a narrow passageway and the walls curved in a wide spiral as we went up. I stopped all of a sudden as realisation hit.

'We're within the walls of the tower.'

'What?' Swift shouted.

'This is the Lady Chapel, I'm sure of it. Think about the direction.'

'You're right.' Persi sounded delighted.

'And no-one knew about it?' Swift was astonished.

'No, of course not,' Persi replied bluntly. 'The tower wall is at least eight feet thick and the stairs were built inside. It's the perfect hiding place. No-one could have imagined it was here.'

I'd carried on, taking the steps two at a time. I reached the top and stopped.

'What is it?' Swift came in behind Persi.

We'd arrived in a circular chamber. I ran my torch about, the ceiling was barely high enough for me to stand upright. The floor was laid with simple terracotta tiles in a concentric pattern and the encircling wall held four niches. Each niche was rectangular with an arched top, framed with red sandstone, as a window would be. A stylised dragon was carved into each keystone, and more decorations were visible in the framework. The openings were obscured with rotted tapestries, dank and dark, reduced to grey shadows of whatever glory they once possessed.

'It's a hidden chamber,' Persi said. 'It's ingenious, nobody ever guessed it was here.'

'The guard room is above,' I replied.

'And the Lady Chapel below,' Swift added.

'The entrances are at different levels,' Persi continued. 'The door to the Lady Chapel is on the ground floor, but the guard room can only be accessed from the battlements.' She laughed. 'It's so simple...'

'The trompe l'oeil on the ceiling of the Lady Chapel must have helped in the deception,' I mused.

'Yes, and it's up so high, it's impossible to even tell it's flat without a ladder and a modern light.' Persi was enthralled.

Swift was more interested in the niches. He used his torch to lift the tapestry away from the nearest one to him. It shed mildewed threads as he pushed it carefully aside, but remained relatively intact. It revealed a recess, the length of a bed and about a yard and a half high. It had been carefully constructed of red stone, vacant except for blackened debris on the flat base.

'Straw,' Persi observed. 'Rotted away.'

'How far does the alcove extend?' I asked, leaning close to her for a better look.

'About four feet.' She aimed her torch at the interior. 'Half the depth of the wall.'

'And the steps stopped at this level,' I mused, realising the whole tower had been designed around this chamber and its four stone alcoves.

Swift had moved to the next opening. 'Look,' he said quietly.

We crossed the floor to join him.

'Is it her?' I asked in a whisper.

The form was covered with a sheet so fine it was almost transparent. The unmistakable shape of a skeletal body could be made out below the fabric.

Persi leaned over and carefully raised the shroud back from the head. Blonde hair, thickly plaited, was stuck to the skull, which I hadn't expected. I reached a hand to stroke the lightest caress across a plait but it disintegrated into a thousand motes of dust under my touch. My heart suddenly lurched and I felt horror creep under my skin.

'Don't touch,' Persi told me. She continued to lift the sheet.

Lady Rosamond was reduced to bone, her jaw fallen open, small pretty teeth smiling as only the dead can. The neck had mostly crumbled, the shoulders collapsed like piles of thin sticks.

'An injury.' Persi aimed her beam on the top section of rib cage. 'She was stabbed. It would have caused internal bleeding, probably into her lungs.'

'Lady Penelope said she fought with the King,' I murmured, oddly distressed by the thought.

Swift aimed his magnifying glass and muttered something under his breath. Despite the toughened exterior, I knew he was a Galahad at heart, always trying to come to the rescue of the weak and defenceless.

'Has the sheet been lifted since she died?' I asked.

'I think so.' Persi replied. 'It's coming away easily, and there are shreds of skin and old cloth stuck to the fabric. I'd say someone found her before us. Should I stop?'

'No, carry on,' Swift told her.

We waited with bated breath as she slowly peeled back the sheet. She suddenly stopped when she reached the chest and we all let out a gasp. The fine bones of the fingers were pushed aside. An indent had formed on her breastbone, the clearly defined shape of a heavy cross lying in faded fabric on her chest.

'They took it from her grasp,' Persi uttered.

'The gold cross,' I stated.

'Thieves,' Swift growled.

'Her hands must have rested across it.' Persi spoke softly. 'The weight of the cross preserved the fabric of her dress.'

Swift was angry. He paced over to the other alcove and moved the ragged tapestry aside. 'There's another body.'

'What?'

We joined him in two quick strides.

'It's a woman, probably her maid.' Persi observed the skeleton. 'She must have outlived her mistress, poor soul.'

The remains were curled up, one fleshless hand out-stretched, the other tucked under the skull. Her frail form was without a protective cover and her hair and fabric had decayed to nothing. The bones had collapsed onto the bare stone. She looked somehow tragic and very small.

'She must have laid her mistress out.' Swift was subdued.

'And died here, alone in the dark,' Persi said.

'God bless,' I murmured and sent a silent prayer to the man upstairs, because she must have died a slow death from starvation and despair.

Swift went to the remaining niche and lifted the curtain, then pulled it down with a sharp tug. 'Here,' he called, his voice too loud.

I strode over.

'Is it him?' Persi came to stand at my side and I put my arm around her shoulder.

Swift shone his torch on the decayed corpse lying in the alcove. 'I'd say so.'

It seemed we'd found the earthly remains of Randolph St George.

Swift took over, professional, calm and thorough. He observed the body, the skin shrivelled from the face, exposed teeth gleaming white, hair falling away. Persi held the torch while he made the examination.

The clothes were old fashioned by today's standards. A thick woollen jacket in Victorian style, moleskin trousers, a flannel shirt, tweed tie, knitted cream socks, hobnail boots. Practical, unadorned gear worn for travelling.

'Was he shot?' I asked.

'No.' Swift sounded distracted. 'Did you expect him to be?'

'Yes… no.' I had actually. I went to perch on the edge of the only vacant alcove, depressed by the find, although I knew I was being ridiculous.

'There's a crack just below the eye socket,' Persi stated.

'And the back of his skull is smashed. Perhaps Sinclair knocked him down then hit him with something heavy.'

'The cross?' Persi suggested. She was watching Swift closely as he carefully turned the cadaver over.

'It's possible, the wound indicates a sharp object,' Swift replied, his voice muffled as he leaned forward. He straightened up, his face grim. 'He stole it.'

'Penelope said his hair colour was the same as mine,' I told them.

'It's similar,' Persi replied.

'We need more than that for an identification.' Swift was still in professional mode. He began searching the clothes.

'There's a watch, it's engraved.' Swift peered at the back of a gold fob watch. 'Randolph St George, M & P.'

'Mama and Papa,' Persi suggested.

'Um.' Swift handed it to her. 'It suggests we're dealing with the right man.'

Persi came across to me.

'Would you keep this?' She offered the watch.

'Of course.'

'At least we've found him, Heathcliff.' She looked up, sympathy in her grey-blue eyes. 'It will bring the family some peace.'

'Yes…erm, not Heathcliff, old stick.'

'Lennox.' She slipped her arms around my neck and gave me a hug, then returned to help Swift.

'A few coins, a key, possibly from his travelling trunk.' Swift paused. 'I can't find a wallet.'

'It may have been in his case,' Persi suggested.

Swift muttered something in return and continued his search. 'Wait.' He carefully drew an envelope from inside Randolph's waistcoat pocket. He turned away from the shrunken corpse to focus the torch light on the letter.

'What is it?' I moved to join them.

He turned it over in his hands. 'It's addressed to Mrs P. St George.'

'Penelope wouldn't have had the title when she was married to Randolph,' Persi said.

Swift hesitated. 'Should we give it to her first?' He could be surprisingly sensitive.

'She's a suspect,' I reminded him.

'Yes, but...'

'Open it, Swift.' It was my turn to be practical.

'I think you should,' Persi agreed.

'Very well.' He slipped a finger under the sealed fold and pulled away the flap. The letter had been written on cheap paper, fragile and thin, it was foxed with red mould, the ink faded to a dull sepia.

'*Dearest Penny, how much I miss you and I haven't even left Lanscombe yet. We worked on the induction balance for three solid days, making sure everything was tip top, no loose wires or broken solders to hamper our efforts. We are ready to prove its worth in the goldfields, and have high hopes of selling the patent to American investors in new technologies.*

But I have even more exciting news to impart, we have found the tomb. Is it not extraordinary news! After all these centuries, we have discovered Lady Rosamond with my induction balance, the most modern invention to reveal the most ancient mystery. We were testing the I.B...' Swift broke off. 'That must mean Induction Balance.'

'Yes, of course it must.' It was my turn to be tetchy. 'Carry on.'

He turned the page over. '*We found a signal at the castle, it was made by a ring of iron under the earth. After much digging and removal of debris, we uncovered a trap door. It was utterly remarkable. Naturally we explored, our scientific testing forgotten in our haste. The tunnel led down, then up,* and took us to steps within the very walls of the tower. There we discovered a secret chamber above the Lady Chapel. It is as below, circular, but with beds of stone set in cosy alcoves. In one such, we discovered the Lady, lying as if she were merely asleep – although much decayed. In her hands she held the Cross of St George, made entirely of gold. It is much smaller than we'd believed, but very fine. I was almost overcome, tears stole into my eyes at the sight of her, our own lost Chatelaine. Sinclair was cock-a-hoop, he wanted to take the cross to America, saying it would fetch a fine price among the merchants and collectors of antiquities.

I forbade it entirely. The cross belongs to Lanscombe and should remain in the hands of Lady Rosamond until the family have chance to discuss the matter. He was piqued, but after some sharp words he understood my sentiment and offered an apology. And so, when you have regained your health, my darling, I gift you this fine task – go and find the Chatelaine on her bed of stone and retrieve the cross. Then you and dear old Ma and Pa can decide how best to proceed.

I will write much and often, with gladness in my heart, content that we shall both have adventures and mend our fortunes. I am confident I will return with pockets full of sovereigns and a name as a man of invention – or, more modestly, as a man of practical ability and good intent. God bless you, my beloved wife. I think of you each and every day. I dearly miss you and our two babes.

This year of absence will set us up for life, and is but a small sacrifice for our future. We will live out our days at Lanscombe, happy as larks with our children about us.

Your ever-loving husband, Randolph.'

The words fell heavy, the silence that followed even heavier. I'd have killed Sinclair myself after reading that letter. Swift folded it and carefully placed it in his inside pocket.

'They must have returned for some reason and Sinclair attacked him,' Swift concluded.

'And killed him,' Persi said. 'Perhaps he lured him here, intending to do so.'

'Probably,' Swift replied solemnly. 'It would be almost impossible to drag a body down those steps.'

'Yes, and this is a perfect place to leave him hidden,' I said.

'It was evil, wasn't it?' Persi began.

I reached for her hand and squeezed it.

'We should go,' Swift said. 'It will be growing dark outside.'

'Yes,' I agreed. 'And we need to bring this to an end.'

CHAPTER 23

Dusk was gathering, the mist creeping back across the lake. Fogg was sitting by the trap door and he rushed to me as we emerged, tail wagging frantically. I picked him up to give him a cuddle.

'We should close it,' Swift said.

He was right. It didn't take long to lower the stone lid and shovel the earth back into the hole. I stamped the turf down, it wasn't perfectly concealed but it was unlikely anyone would find it in the dying light.

Swift made a fuss about returning the metal detector and closing the workshop. We waited while he did, then we returned to the house with our minds reeling.

'Ah, sir.' Greggs was in the St Georges' kitchen, apron to the fore. 'Are you partaking of dinner?'

I don't know where he learns these words. 'Yes, Greggs, of course we're partaking.'

'I thought you may be dining in the neighbouring quarters, sir.'

'Well, we're not,' I told him.

We'd already decided against dinner with Lady Penelope and the family. The knowledge of Randolph's murder was too disturbing to hide under a cloak of politeness. And, in theory, they should be in mourning for Sinclair.

'Will there be enough for us all?' Persi asked.

'We have baked a chicken pie, ma'am,' he replied. 'There is more than sufficient.'

'Chicken?' Swift raised his brows. 'Not one of the chickens in the orchard?'

Greggs looked down at Fogg. 'I'm afraid there was an unfortunate incident earlier, sir.'

'Ah, it's been a day for bodies,' I remarked. 'We'll see you later, old chap.'

I made for the stairs, Swift and Persi followed and we all took chairs around the fireside in my bedroom. Swift produced the flask of Braeburn malt and passed it round. I thought he must have a secret supply because we'd almost emptied it earlier.

'I can't face them,' Persi stared into the blazing hearth.

'We can't tell anyone yet, it must wait until we know who the murderer is.' Swift was adamant.

I glanced at him. I knew who it was, or I was pretty sure anyway. Everything had pointed toward one suspect, but this had been cleverly devised and why would a clever killer make such a mistake?

'It's dreadful, I never thought it would be like this.' Persi was close to tears.

'Perhaps you'd like to go home…' Swift tried some sympathy.

'No.' She cut straight across him. 'We have to see it through.'

Swift took a sip of whisky, 'Lennox, what do you think?'

'I think we need dinner.'

The gong rang downstairs as I spoke and we all rose as one. A hearty chicken pie was just the thing for troubled minds.

Confronting the St Georges was another cause of perturbation, and we struggled to find light words while knowing their son's body lay in the tomb. We did our best but said our goodnights as soon as was polite.

'Persi,' I called softly as we left the kitchen.

'Yes?' She turned towards me.

I took her hand and led her through the dusty corridor between the old wing and new house. 'Lady Penelope must call the police. We need Scotland Yard here as early as possible in the morning.'

'I'll persuade her, don't worry.' She gazed up at me, her eyes dark under the shadows cast by the feeble lightbulb above us. 'Do you know who's done this?'

I nodded, not wanting to answer questions. 'It's going to be traumatic. I don't think you should be there when...'

She cut in. 'Lennox, I'll be there.'

I wasn't convinced, nor was I sure if our blossoming relationship would survive the storm of emotion. 'It's going to hurt your family, Persi.'

'Heathcliff,' she whispered and put her finger on my lips.

I sighed and took her in my arms.

'Lennox?' Swift came through the door, then broke into an apology. 'Oh, erm, sorry.'

Persi giggled. I let her go, although she remained close to me.

'What?' I demanded.

'I… erm, should I go…?" He dithered by the door.

'Don't worry,' Persi told him.

'Fine, yes, but the thing is, someone must call Scotland Yard. We can't…'

'Persi is going to arrange it, aren't you, old stick?' I smiled down at her.

'Yes. Really, I promise.'

'Right, all in hand then… erm, Goodnight.' Swift made a retreat.

'I need to talk to him,' I told Persi once we were alone again.

She smiled, wrapped her arms around my chest and hugged me tightly. I bent my head and gave her a lingering kiss, then let her go.

'And, Persi,' I called out as she went off towards the house.

'I know, not Heathcliff.' She laughed.

I watched her leave, then slipped into the old wing and made my way to Swift's room. He was just settling at his desk, notebook open, pen in hand.

'Swift, this isn't going to be easy,' I said as I sat down.

We argued until late about who did it, why, and how to nail the culprit, then finally turned in for the night. I slept fitfully until the light of dawn slipped between the curtains.

'Breakfast, sir.' Greggs appeared with a tray bearing a covered plate and an aroma of fried delights.

Tubbs and Foggy scrambled from among the bedcovers to sniff the air.

'Excellent, old chap,' I told him.

'I perceived an undercurrent of disquiet last evening and thought you may prefer to eat in your room.' He lifted the silver cover with a flourish. 'And there are dishes for Mr Tubbs and Mr Fogg.'

'Chicken, I assume?'

'Not for Mr Fogg, sir,' he replied solemnly and left.

I'd barely begun eating when Swift walked in.

'There are sirens, I heard them coming up the drive.' He was dressed in suit, hat and overcoat. 'I'm going out to meet them, you should come.'

'Why?' I said as I speared a sausage.

'Because we've carried out an investigation and...' He was itching to join the police who were probably on the doorstep. 'Well, we have to tell them what we've found.'

'Drawing room, in one hour,' I reminded him between mouthfuls. 'As agreed.'

'But I thought we should warn them, you know, prepare the ground.'

'No, let's stick to the plan, Swift.'

'Right, fine,' he said and reached for his belt to tighten it, realised he wasn't wearing his trench coat, sighed and went off.

I looked at my little pet duo and they gazed back; wide eyed, innocent – apart from the chicken killing, that is – and bereft of malice. I sometimes wish we humans lived lives as uncomplicated as a small fat cat and a happy little dog.

The next hour was spent in making lengthy notes and trying to put my thoughts in cogent order.

Greggs arrived. He was wielding a feather duster. 'Inspector Swift asked me to remind you of the time, sir.'

'Spot of housework, old chap?' I asked, as I pushed my chair back from the desk.

'Lady Millicent and I are dusting shelves, sir.'

'You haven't mentioned the get together in the drawing room, have you?' I asked as I pulled my jacket on.

'I have not, sir. Although her ladyship was rather bemused by the police activity in the grounds.'

'Right, well keep her and Sir Bertram occupied and out of the way.'

'I will, sir.'

'And I'll take Fogg with me.' I picked him up and put him under my arm.

'Very well.' He paused. 'And may I wish you good luck.'

'Thank you, Greggs,' I said and made for the door.

'Sir,' Greggs called.

'What?'

'The stick,' he reminded me and retrieved it from the corner.

'Right.' I took it from him, gave a cheery wave and cleared off.

It didn't take long to reach the dusty corridor and enter the palatial splendour that was Lanscombe Park. I strode through the state rooms, where maids and footmen had gathered in small knots at the windows to watch the police searching the grounds outside. I wondered if they'd recovered Sinclair's body yet.

Mullins was guarding the drawing room doors. He was dressed in butlering garb, so I assumed his new position had been sanctioned.

'Sir.' He bowed.

'Mullins.' I gave him the stick. 'Look after this, will you.'

'Certainly, sir.' He took it with white-gloved hands.

'And guard the entrance, no-one is to leave until I say so.'

'We are ready and prepared, sir.' He stood smartly to attention. There were a number of footmen in the corridor and one of them opened the door for me.

'Ah, Lennox, there you are.' Swift was already in the drawing room with a group of police officers. He indicated a tall, dour-looking chap in trench coat and trilby. 'This is Detective Chief Inspector Robert Billings.'

Billings came forward to shake my hand. I put Foggy down in the spirit of co-operation and he raced about barking.

'Scotland Yard,' Billings announced.

'Ashton Steeple,' I replied.

'Heathcliff.' Lady Penelope came to speak to me. She was very pale and looked as though she hadn't slept at all. 'I… I think we are ready. I've asked everyone to come.'

'Thank you. Could you sit down, please?'

She hesitated, raising troubled eyes to mine, but then turned away and went to settle in her usual spot by the hearth. The police stood in a group with Swift, watching every move.

Persi arrived first. She came straight to me and took my hand. 'She agreed to everything.' She nodded towards Lady Penelope.

'Persi, you mustn't become involved, old girl, however much it upsets you…'

'I understand.' She spoke quietly, her face pale in the sunlight streaming in. She squeezed my hand, then went to sit near the sofas grouped around the fire.

Max arrived next, glowered at me and went to join his mother. Lydia and Jerome came in together, but neither spoke as they went to sit on a sofa opposite the rest of the family.

Finn was the last to arrive, late as usual. He wore a casual outfit and offered a grin, his jauntiness back in place. He crossed the room to join the others.

A whistle blew beyond the door, a tramping of feet was heard and a dozen bobbies entered and positioned themselves against the walls. Mullins followed and carefully closed the door behind him.

Swift had been in close conversation with Billings. They waited as the troops assembled and found their places, then they came over to join me.

'Major Lennox,' Billings began. 'I've got my own way of doing things, I'm a man of method and procedure. Swift has convinced me you know what you're about.' He leaned forward until I could see the broken veins on his nose. 'Now, he'd better be right, and you'd better finger this perpetrator, or I'll have both of you up for wasting my time.'

I took a long breath and let it out. 'Well, I'll get on with it then.'

'Ladies and gentlemen.' Swift stepped in front of the fireplace. 'I must caution you all that this is a police enquiry, what you say and do can be used against you.' He turned to me. 'Lennox.'

It was beginning to feel like theatre. I went to stand in front of the fire as he moved aside. Fogg came to sit at my feet with his tongue hanging out, Persi rushed over to pick him up and took him back to sit on her lap.

'Sinclair is dead, murdered,' I began, then looked over at Billings. 'Has he been removed?'

'He has,' the chief inspector replied cautiously.

'Why was he murdered?' I asked.

No-one answered.

I took a few paces across the fireplace. 'His was the third murder within a week. The first was Monroe, his death was made to look like an accident.' I took a breath. 'Monroe was a professional driver, he was Lord Sinclair's chauffeur and bodyguard, he was trained to react to danger. And that's exactly what he did on the humpback bridge crossing the ravine.'

I nodded to Mullins who marched in smart style across the room. He handed me the stick, saluted and returned to his post.

The stick was grubby with homemade fingerprint powder and utterly unimpressive, but I held it up anyway.

'Monroe drove at speed into the Dell. It's a place full of shadows and last Sunday, it was wet from a downpour. Monroe would have had his car lamps switched on. As he crossed the bridge, his headlights suddenly fell onto a figure wearing a coat almost directly in front of him. This figure was so close it must have seemed impossible to avoid, but Monroe tried, he swerved to prevent an horrific collision.' Dubious silence met my explanation.

'Billings, could I borrow your coat?' I asked him.

'What?' the man grunted.

I held out my hand. He grumbled as he shrugged himself out of his pale-hued trench coat.

'Someone had placed a coat on the ends of this stick.' I fitted the 'y' branched end into the shoulders of Billings' coat and held it aloft. 'They stood behind the wall of the bridge and waved it just as Monroe cleared the brow. He had a split second to react and his instincts cost him his life.'

'Can you prove this?' Billings asked sharply.

'No.' I handed him his coat back, still on the stick. He wasn't impressed.

'The branch had come from the sweet chestnut trees near the old Church.' I mentioned. 'The murder took place at five thirty last Sunday evening. The police enquiry established that none of the servants were absent long enough to go to the Dell and back.' I paused to look at some of the bobbies, one of whom nodded to me. I realised he was the local sergeant.

'That's right,' he said. 'We interviewed them about it.'

'Not the family?'

The Sergeant's cheeks reddened. 'It was believed to be an accident, and it was made clear that His Lordship didn't want us bothering them.'

'One of the people seated around the fire here caused Monroe's death,' I said. 'And then killed twice more.'

A hiss of outrage followed that statement.

'Chief inspector.' Jerome stood up and addressed Billings. 'I must protest, Major Lennox is utterly unqualified to make these statements.'

'I'll be the judge of that,' Billings rapped his reply.

Jerome looked affronted and sat down again. He was dressed as usual in a tailored city suit. Lydia was sitting close to him, looking pretty in blue.

I carried on. 'Monroe was Sinclair's bodyguard, he kept him safe from harm. Once he was removed, the murderer could stalk the next target.'

'But the accident to Monroe might have merely injured him,' Max cut in. 'Your so-called murder was hardly precise.'

'An injury would have worked just as well,' Swift answered. 'He didn't have to die.'

'No, perhaps not.' I walked in front of the fire again. 'Trent had a soldier's mind. He served to protect, just as Monroe had done, and he probably saw the danger to his employer more clearly than Sinclair himself. He was killed for the same reason as Monroe, to clear the way to Sinclair.'

'What about the gun?' Lydia called out.

I wasn't inclined to be diverted, but they were all staring at me. 'You know it was taken from Randolph's room.'

'Yes, but who did it?' Lady Penelope asked.

'The person who murdered him,' I replied and went to the sideboard for a tumbler of water. Mullins poured it and I drained the glass.

'You all know how Trent died,' I carried on. 'Electrocuted in the fuse room. It was a cleverly devised death, a broken lamp to trip the fuse, a puddle of water on the floor and a single strip of copper jammed into the live cable. It was positioned to run alongside the handle of the power-switch. Trent died the instant he touched it.'

'Do you have the copper strip?' Billings cut in.

Swift extracted it from his inside pocket and handed it over.

There were a few gasps of surprise in the room.

'The killer had hoped to reach the fuse room ahead of Swift or me.' I recalled the jostling scramble downstairs and into the dark corridor where Trent lay dead. 'They failed. We found it and removed it. It's probable the killer returned to try to retrieve it in the night.'

'There were guards at the entrance to the passageway,' Jerome called out. 'They stayed up all night.'

'What about the cellars, were they guarded?' I questioned him.

I waited for an answer and Mullins provided it.

'No, sir. They were always kept locked, it wasn't considered necessary.'

'But Monroe had a key, didn't he?' I asked.

'He did, sir,' Mullins answered.

'The cellars connect this part of the house and the old wing where the St Georges live, don't they?'

'They do, sir.'

'The culprit took the key from Monroe when he was killed.' I concluded, although I couldn't actually prove it. 'And used it to sneak out of the back door into the old orchards. They also used it to access Randolph's rooms.'

'But Monroe wasn't killed until after the gun had been given to Sinclair.' Max had been listening closely and now called out the discrepancy.

'No, but the murderer knew where the gun was, you'd all gone up there with Lydia. It wouldn't have been difficult to slip through the house and enter in the afternoon when Sir Bertram and Lady Millicent were taking a nap.' I walked across the front of the fireplace, then stopped. 'The ability to leave the house without being seen was important to the final performance of this three-act play. The last act was to lure Sinclair out of the house and down to the lake. It was meticulously planned. One of Randolph's coats had been removed from his rooms, all that was needed was a misty morning. The murderer didn't have long to wait; mist is synonymous with autumn. Yesterday morning was perfect, the trap was set and Sinclair took the bait.'

'But why, what bait?' Lady Penelope called out, her face pulled with tension.

'The secret about Randolph,' I replied. 'Just as Lydia had always believed – it was all about Randolph.'

'What about him?' Max demanded.

'Sinclair murdered him,' I replied and stood back to watch the terrible realisation sink in.

CHAPTER 24

Lydia's hand shot straight to her lips, her eyes wide. A moment of triumph followed by a gasp of horror as she turned to look at her mother.

Max was faster, he reached for Penelope as she stared in bewilderment.

'Mama,' he uttered.

Colour drained from her face, her lips trembled as she tried to form words and then tears seeped from her eyes to trickle down her cheeks. 'No.' She let out a long moan.

Swift offered a handkerchief as though he'd been waiting for the moment. She took it to grip it in her hand.

'What the hell do you mean by that?' Max yelled.

'Exactly what I said,' I replied coldly.

'Sinclair murdered Randolph.' Jerome's diplomatic tact evaporated. 'You'd better have proof of that or I'll have you prosecuted for this travesty.'

'We have proof,' Swift told him quietly.

Their faces variously showed disbelief, grief and

anguish, except for Finn who was lounging in his seat with an arm resting along the back of the sofa.

I turned to him. 'You knew, didn't you?'

All eyes flew to the American.

'Yeah, I knew,' he admitted with a brief nod of the head.

The atmosphere was tense, the moment of silence stretched like a tightly wound spring.

'How?' Max broke in with a snarl.

'Because your mother still lived in Dawson,' I prompted Finn.

'She did,' he replied quietly, the comic's mask gone.

'When you came here to meet your father for the first time, you were curious.' I watched him as I spoke. 'Here was the family you never had, and there was much to see and learn. Riches beyond your experience, a life of opulence and ease, and you learned of the strange route Sinclair had taken to dominate Lanscombe Park after the death of Randolph St George.' I continued. 'Lydia told you all about Randolph, so when you returned to Dawson to see your mother again, you asked her about him, didn't you?'

He nodded.

'Did you tell anyone?' I asked.

'No,' he snapped back.

'Is that the truth?' Swift cut in. 'Because whatever you say here will be used in a court of law.'

That brought a dash of icy reality to the room. This didn't end here, it was a road to jail, justice, and the hangman's noose.

'It's the truth,' Finn shouted back.

'Are you saying Sinclair cut the fuse short on the dynamite in Alaska?' Jerome asked.

'No,' I replied. 'Randolph never went to Dawson, he never left Lanscombe Park.'

There was a louder gasp, and then they began shouting questions that I wasn't ready to answer. I returned to the sideboard and another drink while that bombshell hit home. I was tempted by the decanter of brandy, but noticed Billings watching me and decided to stick to water. Persi was sitting quietly some distance away, Foggy on her lap. I caught her eye and she gave a wan smile, although she looked as strained as everyone else.

'What the hell are you talking about?' Max demanded when I returned to stand before the fire.

I ignored him and turned to Finn. 'Tell them the story, Finn.'

He shifted in his seat, uncomfortable under every eye in the room. 'Kerri, my real mother, never left Dawson.'

'Kerri hoped Sinclair would look after her?' I prompted.

'Yeah, he took a shine to her, she showed me photographs, she'd been pretty. She had the Irish charm, funny and quick witted, she must have charmed him.'

'Until you came along,' I reminded him.

His face clouded. 'You've all heard that story.'

'What did Kerri tell you about Randolph?' I brought him to the point.

He looked beyond me, dropping his eyes. 'Nothing, she never heard of no Randolph.'

Lydia lifted her hand to cover her mouth.

'And after you asked her that, did you go and search the records in Dawson?' I demanded.

He nodded. 'I did and found out that Randolph had never arrived. I figured Sinclair must have killed him.'

'And you thought you'd use the information to black-mail Sinclair one day,' I stated the cold facts clearly.

'Where is Randolph?' Lady Penelope cried out, her voice broken with emotion.

'That's the question the killer wanted answered,' I replied. 'That's why Sinclair was murdered.'

I think they were beginning to hate me, spinning this tale of terrible truth, ripping away the lies behind the luxurious life Sinclair had built from murder and deceit.

'I... I don't understand,' Lydia stuttered, bewilderment in her voice.

'Sinclair murdered your father here, in Lanscombe,' I explained as calmly as I could, although I felt a tremor of remorse as I spoke. This wasn't the way to break such heartrending news to anyone and yet, if I wanted this murderer exposed, I didn't have a choice.

'But where is he?' Lady Penelope cried out again.

'There was only one person who could have answered that, and that was Sinclair,' I replied.

She looked close to collapse. Lydia started crying and Jerome drew her to him and comforted her as she sobbed.

I waited until the room quietened.

'Monroe was eliminated, Trent was killed, Sinclair was isolated. The killer wanted to know what Sinclair had done to Randolph and where he was buried,' I stated.

'Sinclair was lured from this house by a note, he found it in his office yesterday morning at six o'clock. That note pretended to be from Randolph.' I nodded at Swift, who took it from his wallet and handed it to the chief inspector.

'*Sinclair, I'm at the workshop. Randolph,*' Billings read slowly.

'Sinclair knew it wasn't from Randolph, but he realised someone had uncovered his secret,' I continued. 'He stalked out, heading for the workshop. There was a figure in the mist. He could barely make it out, but the clothes were Randolph's. It must have looked like a ghost had returned, but Sinclair wasn't a fearful man. He followed this apparition down to the boathouse where the killer was waiting to cosh him on the back of his head with a fishing priest.'

Swift had that too and proceeded to wave in the air. Everyone watched, mesmerised, as he handed it to Billings.

'Sinclair was knocked out and man-handled into a life jacket. The killer started the motor boat and threaded the stern line through the back of the jacket. Sinclair was dragged from the dock as the boat took off. His head hit the side as he fell.'

'How can you be sure of all this?' Max demanded.

'A trail of evidence,' Swift answered, 'and investigation.'

And a fair amount of guesswork, I thought but didn't say.

'We don't know exactly what happened next. Sinclair may have been dragged behind the boat, or he may have been set adrift. The killer wanted to know where Randolph was buried. What better way to force the truth than circling him in the boat, shouting out the question, demanding answers. 'Where is Randolph? What did you do to him?'

I paused to take a breath, then continued. 'Sinclair couldn't escape, he was trapped in the middle of the lake. The fog was thick, the water freezing, he must have been in total shock. He had a heart attack and died.'

'Did he tell where Papa was buried?' Lydia asked from within Jerome's cradling arms.

'We assume not, because later in the day some papers were left for us in Sinclair's office.'

Swift withdrew the passenger list from inside his jacket pocket. He handed it to Billings, who read it with a frown.

'It was proof that Randolph had never sailed on the ship crossing the Atlantic,' I explained. 'Sinclair's name was there, he had a double cabin to himself.'

'So it was all for nothing,' Lady Penelope murmured. 'All these terrible murders and we still don't know where he is...'

'No, it wasn't for nothing,' I told her. 'It was for a very good reason; a cold-blooded logic.'

'Do you know who did it?' Billings asked plainly.

'Yes, it was Max.' I replied, watching reactions very closely.

That caused an outcry of denial and anger; I waited for the shouting to die down.

'Max, you found out about the patent, that was the first clue, wasn't it?' I aimed the question at him.

Swift took the lawyer's letter out and waved it. His new coat must have deep pockets since he seemed to have stuffed everything into them.

'Sinclair took out a patent on your father's invention the moment he reached New York. That letter of renewal arrived two weeks before Sinclair's birthday and you found it, Max. You requested the passenger list, it confirmed your suspicions and you began your campaign to find your father.'

'No, I did not,' he yelled back.

'Perhaps you didn't,' I replied quietly, causing confusion. 'Lady Penelope, what would you have done?'

She was shaken to the core. She stared, barely comprehending the question, then she whispered. 'I'd have killed Sinclair.'

'Mama, don't say that,' Lydia pleaded.

'In the way I've described?' I continued.

'No, I couldn't have done that to Monroe, or Trent.'

'Would you have asked anyone to do it for you?' I glanced over at Mullins. His white brows drew together.

'No, of course not,' Lady Penelope answered.

'Lydia?' I asked.

'I would have told Max,' she replied shakily.

'Max?' He watched me warily. 'You knew didn't you? You tried to force us out of Lanscombe right from the beginning because you knew what Sinclair had done and that someone was seeking revenge.'

'Yes,' he admitted.

'Where did you find the papers?' I asked.

The room had fallen utterly silent.

His eyes dropped, then rose to gaze defiantly back at me. 'They were in my workshop. I don't always lock it. I came in one morning and they were lying on top of my drawings.' He shook his head, a grim twist to his lips. 'I barely glanced at them. I had an idea for a fuel pump, I'd been working on it and...'

'When did you realise what they were?' I continued.

'After Sinclair's party and that package with the gun. I was surprised, there was a lot of underlying tension and I thought about the papers left in my workshop. I went back and read them, I realised what it meant, and what had happened to my father.'

'What did you do?' I asked quietly.

'I considered going to the police, but I decided to confront Sinclair instead. Then Monroe was killed and you two arrived.' He paused to look at me. 'Lydia said you'd come to mend fences with Persi. I didn't believe that, but I suddenly feared she could have been behind the vendetta somehow. I couldn't see how you fitted in, but she's become so virulent about Sinclair recently...'

Lydia moved to argue with him but Lady Penelope spoke first. 'Max, why didn't you tell me?'

'It could have been you, for all I knew.' He raised his voice as the pressure weighed down. 'I thought someone was inciting me to murder Sinclair, and after I realised what he'd done, I felt like killing him myself...' He paused. 'I left the papers on Sinclair's desk for you to find yesterday.'

'You should have given them to us earlier,' Swift snapped.

Max looked away.

'Why didn't you?' I pressed him. 'Was it because you wanted Sinclair to die?'

'I didn't know he was going to die.'

'Yes, you did. It must have been obvious to you after Trent was killed,' I shouted.

'Very well, yes.' Max admitted. 'And he deserved it.'

Well, at least that was the truth.

'Why did you fix the boat the day before Sinclair was killed?' I asked the question which had been bothering me.

'Lydia said she and Jerome wanted to go out on a picnic to the island, they were going to take you and Persi as a surprise.' He shrugged. 'So, I checked the engine.'

'Lydia?' I looked at her.

She nodded mutely.

'Max,' I rejoined. 'Do you know who killed Sinclair?'

'No.'

Brows drew in puzzlement and all eyes flicked back to me.

I took another pace across the fireplace. 'Randolph has been at the centre of it all; the mystery of his murder, his missing body... But what if the search for his remains was nothing more than an act of theatre designed to disguise the real motive?' I turned and paced again. 'Everything points to you, Max. So what happens when you're hanged for this crime?'

I turned to look at Lady Penelope. 'Lady Penelope, you inherit Sinclair's business. Would you let Jerome continue running it for you?'

She looked confused. 'Yes… he has to, we don't know how to do it.'

'And Lydia would become the sole owner of Lanscombe Park, wouldn't she?' I stated

Lady Penelope nodded mutely. I carried on.

'Jerome will run the company and next year he will marry Lydia. He'll control the money and become master of Lanscombe Park. With Max out of the way, Jerome will have it all.'

I turned to look at Jerome at the exact same moment everyone else in the room did. He glared back, his dark eyes fixed on mine.

'Absolute drivel,' he shouted.

'Sinclair took you on because you were as ruthless and devious as he was. And you knew exactly how the company was run. You had access to Sinclair's papers, the blueprints, the accounts, everything. When you saw the letter about the patents taken out on Randolph's invention, you realised what Sinclair had done. And you were worried, weren't you, Jerome? Worried that Sinclair would hand the company to Finn, his own son, and a damn good businessman.' I paced again. 'So you began to plan. You sent for the passenger list in Sinclair's name. It would be brought to you first, because you always got Sinclair's post to sort through. Then you left all the papers in Max's workshop, thinking he would act. When he didn't, you acted on his behalf and you made sure to leave clues that would point to him. The copper strip, the boat, even the stick came from the trees near his workshop...'

'It was you,' Lydia suddenly shrieked in horror. She recoiled from Jerome and ran to sit with Lady Penelope. 'He lied the day Monroe was killed in the crash... I saw the clock in the hall when I came in, but he told me it was wrong...'

'Shut up,' Jerome shouted.

'You killed them, Jerome.' I spoke quietly. 'You wanted the money, you wanted Lanscombe, you wanted it all.'

'It's true.' Lydia was almost screaming. 'You wanted to marry me for money, you killed them for money. Mama, keep him away.' She turned to bury her head in her mother's arms.

'Jerome.' I swung on my heel to face him.

'You can't prove anything, I haven't... I didn't... you've driven her mad with your twisted story. Lydia, stop it.'

'Will you testify?' Billings stepped forward to ask Lydia.

'Yes, yes, I can tell you, he lied about the time and he was the one who talked about the boat and the picnic, it was him...'

'You framed Max, didn't you, Jerome.' I turned the knife. 'You tried to incite him to kill. When he didn't, you executed the plan on his behalf.'

'It was all a sick pretence,' Lydia cried out. 'Max would have hanged and he would have watched them do it...' Lydia burst into heaving sobs. Penelope wept with her.

Persi got up and moved towards them. 'Oh, you poor...'

Jerome suddenly leapt to his feet and grabbed her. He pulled a gun from his pocket and pointed it at her head. The police lurched forward.

'Get away. Go on, move back,' Jerome yelled, his mouth a vicious snarl. 'I'll kill her.'

He was a fool to have picked Persi. She kicked back with all her strength.

'Ahhh,' he cried out in pain as she caught him on the kneecap.

I pulled my own gun from my pocket and levelled it at his head. He jerked away, trying to catch hold of her again, but a shot rang out and his mouth opened in a silent howl. Blood seeped from his temple, then bubbled and flowed to drip down his face before he slumped to the floor.

I looked across the room. Mullins held a smoking gun, he had said he was a sharp shooter, and he'd just proved it.

CHAPTER 25

Mullins was placed in handcuffs. Personally, I thought he should have been commended.

Lydia sobbed more loudly and Persi helped her and Lady Penelope from the room. I wandered to the windows to leave the police to surge into action. Max was cautioned and made to stay where he was. Finn came to join me as attention moved to the still bleeding body of Jerome.

'Well, he sure had me fooled,' Finn said as we both stared into the expanse of the gardens.

'Did he?' I replied.

Finn glanced at me. 'Maybe not... I don't know,' he shrugged. 'I don't think like you do.'

I didn't reply to that.

'How d'you figure it out?' Finn continued.

'Logic, I suppose.' I was weary, and sick of the sight of death. 'You have to stand outside of the scene, look through other people's eyes...'

'Why is that logic?'

307

'It's their logic, not mine.' I don't think I was making much sense. 'You were going to blackmail Sinclair, weren't you?'

'Yeah,' he admitted. 'If I had to. I wanted the company, I didn't trust him to hand it to me.'

'A chip off the old block?' I remarked wryly.

'I draw the line at killing.'

'I'm pleased to hear it.'

'Would Jerome's plan have worked?' he carried on.

I watched a skein of geese fly across the blue sky. 'Possibly… Sinclair got away with murder all this time.'

'I reckon he was using the intercoms to listen in on folk.'

That was interesting, I hadn't considered that. 'I suppose he may have been.'

'You believe it's true that Jerome acted because he was scared I'd get the company?'

'Yes,' I said coldly. I doubt it was the answer he wanted to hear.

Swift came over. 'Finn, they want to question you.'

I turned to see the police had set up a group of chairs near the piano. They were already loading Jerome's body onto a stretcher. It was all very organised, you'd think they did this sort of thing all the time.

Finn went off and Swift handed me his silver flask. It was full again

'You did well, Lennox.'

'Did I miss anything?' I took a long slug from the flask and gave it back.

'Billings asked what happened to Randolph's coat.'

'Ha, he really does like it cut and dried,' I said and considered it. 'Tell him it's probably at the bottom of the lake weighed down with a stone.'

'Jerome should have done that with Sinclair, rather than make it so obviously a murder.' He took a swig from the flask himself.

'He'd never be able to pin it on Max if he had.'

'Yes, but he must have hated Sinclair to torture him like that.'

'I suspect he did,' I replied. 'Why don't you take Fogg for a walk,' he suggested.

I looked at him, then down at my little dog who had come to sit at my feet after Persi left. I knew he'd be upset by the presence of a body.

'Foggy,' I said and made for the stairs.

Persi was coming down from the upper floor. 'I've called the doctor.'

'Come with me.' I stopped and waited for her.

'I should stay…'

I took her hand, and then pulled her to me.

'We need some time together, and I want to talk to you.'

She nodded and we walked out into the sunshine. Our footsteps led us down to the folly. The police were still occupied indoors so we had the place to ourselves.

We sat together on a marble bench, Fogg ran to the lake to chase ducks and a pair of swans drifted by.

'Persi,' I began.

'Yes?'

'We shouldn't waste our lives.'

'No.'

'Love is… it's rare.'

'I know.'

'It's been difficult for me to leave the past behind.' I thought of all the meaning behind those words, then carried on. 'But I can do it. I've realised I want to live life with all it's complications and irritations. Even talking to people I don't want to…'

She smiled.

I dug the ring out of the pocket I'd tucked it into some time ago.

'Persi, if you don't promise to marry me, I'm going to throw this ring in the lake.'

That made her laugh. 'You're such a romantic.'

'No, I'm not,' I remarked. 'Do you promise?'

Her face lit up with a dazzling smile. 'Yes, I promise.'

I slipped the ring onto her finger, took her in my arms, and kissed her.

EPILOGUE

It was a chaotic couple of days; we had to steel ourselves to break the news to Sir Bertram and Lady Millicent, which went predictably badly. Greggs stepped in and provided stalwart support like the old soldier he was.

The police infested the place. Everywhere we turned there was a bobby or two taking fingerprints, spreading dust over polished surfaces, aiming torches into dark corners or rifling through drawers. I've no idea what they were looking for.

Swift was in his element and joined forces with Billings to direct the recovery of Randolph's body. Max was let off with an official warning, Mullins spent two nights in the cells and was delivered back to the fold with orders not to go anywhere.

Persi and I endured the first day; on the second we packed a picnic and took the boat to the island. We spent a heavenly afternoon under a glorious sun, basking in the warmth of the waning autumn weather.

On the third day the police upped sticks and decamped. Shortly afterwards, a trickle of relatives started to arrive. They were round-eyed with astonishment and came offering support, baskets of goodies and asking no end of curious questions. I met Persi's parents again. I was polite, then I escaped and ordered Greggs to pack. We were home in time for tea.

I had warned Persi this time, and she even came out to wave a farewell.

Her letter arrived a few days later.

'Dear Heathcliff, I know, it's Lennox, but I can't call you Lennox for ever. The family have gathered around and are behaving quite well in general. Aunt and Uncle St George are adjusting, although Aunt Millie wavers between fantasy and reality. Lady Rosamond is to be moved, she and her maid will be buried alongside Randolph. We're arranging a proper funeral for them, I think everyone will remain until then. It's quite jolly actually, in the strange way of family parties and funerals.

Lydia took to her bed and we're mollycoddling her until she feels more the thing. Penelope is sad and very quiet, but she has Mullins back now and he is an absolute brick; no-one has mentioned a word about him shooting Lydia's murderous fiancé.

Max is hiding out in his workshop, he doesn't like crowds either. Finn has been forgiven and is keeping the congregation amused. I swear he could talk himself out of the direst spot. He's managing Sinclair's company until it can be sold, nobody else here wants anything to do with it.

I miss you. I hope you feel you can come and visit. I will stay on at Lanscombe for a while, there's a great deal of tedious formalities to endure and no one seems inclined to do anything about it.

You're quite the hero amongst the family now. I've warned them all that you're likely to throw out accusations of murder if you're plagued, so they're suitably wary and have sworn not to bother you.

Give Fogg and little Tubbs a hug from me, your loving fiancée,

Persi xxx

I sighed and folded her letter carefully to place in my jacket pocket.

'Have you seen the missive from Inspector Swift?' Greggs enquired as he arrived with the tea tray.

My eyes moved to the mantlepiece. 'Yes, it's over there.'

He put the tray down with a sigh, poured tea and then fetched the envelope to present it in the proper manner.

'Thank you, old chap.' I gave him a grin.

He'd been in a finicky mood since we'd returned. I had the impression he'd wanted to stay at Lanscombe, particularly now it was free from the autocratic rule of Godolphin Sinclair.

Swift's letter began in his usual direct style.

'Lennox, arrived home in good order. I travelled to London with DCI Billings, before continuing to Braeburn. Billings was complimentary about the investigation, although felt we should have been more rigorous in method.

Florence sends her love, Angus is thriving, he has teeth coming and he's already trying to speak. He's incredibly advanced for his age, Florence is singing to him, she says it will help him along.

Apparently my contract with our whisky agent, Montague Morgan, is not negotiable. Florence thinks we should take a commercial approach to the situation as it stands, but we will be seeking properly legitimate outlets. It is outrageous that Morgan did not inform me that he was selling the Braeburn Malt into America.

We also discussed your idea to hold your wedding at Braeburn. Florence thinks you really should talk it through with Persi. A winter wedding in the Highlands will make it very difficult for any guests to attend. Why don't you hold it at Melrose, or Lanscombe? They're both much more accessible?

Wherever you decide, we will be there, and I'll be honoured to stand by your side as best man.

Yours etc,

Swift.'

I folded the letter and put that into my jacket pocket too. Cook had made Madeira cake and a couple of slices had been delivered with the tea. I took a bite from the largest.

Sir.' Tommy bounced in. 'Aunty says I have to wear velvet britches when I'm a page boy. Everyone's goin' to laugh, sir. I don't have to, do I? You wouldn't want to wear velvet britches...'

'Tommy, neither of us are going to wear velvet anything.' I interrupted the flow. 'Now sit down and have some cake.'

He grinned. 'Aye, sir. Auntie says, if you have the wedding here, all the village will want to come and we'll need a good clean up. And the garden needs cutting back and the gates ain't mended yet an...'

I ate my cake and gazed out of the window as he prat-tled on. Weddings, it seemed, were far more complicated than unravelling murder.

Author's Notes

Please don't read or listen to this until you've finished the book.

The technological era was burgeoning in the 1920s. Inventions and discoveries in the 1800s led to many devices we are familiar with today. The telegraph and telephone had transformed communication, the steam engine, motor car and aeroplane were spreading technology at an inexorable rate. The old world was melting away under the wheels of invention and industry.

The metal detector, or induction balance, had been devised as early as 1830 by mining engineer R W Fox. Innovations were added with the intention of improving accuracy; some to detect precious metals, others for medicinal purposes, such as locating bullets embedded in flesh. One famous example is Alexander Graham Bell's attempt to save the life of American President, James Garfield.

President Garfield suffered an assassination attempt in 1881. He was shot and injured, one bullet was removed, the other lodged among vital organs including the pancreas. Despite probing by doctors, the bullet could not be located and the President's life was in grave danger.

Simon Newcomb of Baltimore had been working on an improved form of metal detector and offered it to the President's doctors. But Newcomb's device had a deficiency, the hum emitted by the device when metal was located was too faint to be heard easily by the human ear. Alexander Graham Bell stepped in, he offered his expertise to amplify the sound of the signal by attaching it to the invention which had made him famous – the telephone.

Experiments followed, Newcomb's detector was proved to work when paired with Graham Bell's receiver. Full of high hopes they were shown into the President's sick room, but after numerous attempts, the experiment was declared a failure. Graham Bell's telephonic receiver gave off a constant hum whenever the detector was placed near the President.

The inventors were devastated, and a short while later, President Garfield died.

It was only some time afterwards that the explanation for the failure of Newcomb's and Graham Bell's combined device was discovered. The President had been presented with one of the very latest inventions in mattress technology. His new bed had been manufactured with coil springs made of metal and it was this that had set off the metal detector.

King John has been the only John in Britain's list of sovereigns. By all accounts he was as bad as he was painted, it doesn't take overmuch research to uncover records of his wanton acts of terror and cruelty. The Barons eventually revolted and Magna Carta was drawn up. It brought democracy of sorts to England, although its laws were intended to protect the rich and powerful rather than the commoners.

John signed Magna Carta in 1215 but refused to follow its precepts. The Barons invited the French prince, Louis, to take over the throne in John's stead and civil war broke out as a consequence. John's death in 1216, brought the war to an end and Louis' presence was no longer welcome. He returned to France. The account of Lady Rosamond's murder and the destruction of the castle are entirely fiction on my part.

Prohibition was enacted in America in 1920 and remained in place until 1933. Bootleggers, rum runners and gangsters made fortunes from illegal sales. But not all sales of alcohol were illegal, loopholes existed. Liquor could be legitimately supplied in two cases, for sacramental or for medicinal purposes.

To obtain alcohol for medicinal purposes, one needed a doctor's prescription. The patient was not actually required to be examined by a doctor, a telephone call was deemed sufficient. Whisky, brandy, gin et al, were considered appropriate remedies for flu, diabetes, insufficient lactation, anxiety and depression among others.

In 1932 Winston Churchill was involved in a minor car accident in New York City, as a consequence he was given a prescription by local doctor, Otto Pickhardt. It read *'This is to certify that the post accident convalescence of Winston Churchill necessitates the use of alcoholic spirits especially at meal times. The quantity is naturally indefinite but the minimum requirements would be 250 cubic centimeters.'* Which is 250 millilitres – a bottle of Scotch is 750 millilitres.

I haven't discovered which pharmacy fulfilled Churchill's prescription but he could have gone to one of Charles R. Walgreen's stores where whisky was kept under the counter for just such measures. Walgreen was already a successful businessman; when prohibition began he had 20 stores, by the end he had over 600.

Prohibition did not prevent Americans from drinking alcohol. As Oxford University Press notes, more hard liquor was consumed during Prohibition than before, with spirits accounting for 75 percent of all alcohol consumed.

Liquor, or more accurately, Braeburn Malt, will play a central role in book 7 of the Heathcliff Lennox series; The Mystery of Montague Morgan.

I do hope you enjoyed this book. Would you like to take a look at the Heathcliff Lennox website? As a member of the Readers Club, you'll receive the FREE short story, 'Heathcliff Lennox – France 1918' and access to the 'World of Lennox' page, where you can view portraits of Lennox, Swift, Greggs, Foggy, Tubbs, Persi and Tommy Jenkins.

There are also 'inspirations' for the books, plus occasional newsletters with updates and free giveaways.

You can find the Heathcliff Lennox Readers Club, and more, at karenmenuhin.com

* * *

Here's the full Heathcliff Lennox series list. You can find each book on Amazon.

Book 1: Murder at Melrose Court
Book 2: The Black Cat Murders
Book 3: The Curse of Braeburn Castle
Book 4: Death in Damascus
Book 5: The Monks Hood Murders
Book 6: The Tomb of the Chatelaine
Book 7: The Mystery of Montague Morgan
Book 8: The Birdcage Murders – ready to pre-order now, previewed for release in Summer 2022

All the series can be found on Amazon and all good book stores.

And there are Audible versions read by Sam Dewhurst-Phillips, who is amazing, it's just like listening to a radio play. All of these can be found on Amazon, Audible and Apple Books.

A little about Karen Baugh Menuhin

1920s, Cozy crime, Traditional Detectives, Downton Abbey – I love them! Along with my family, my dog and my cat.

At 60 I decided to write, I don't know why but suddenly the stories came pouring out, along with the characters. Eccentric Uncles, stalwart butlers, idiosyncratic servants, machinating Countesses, and the hapless Major Heathcliff Lennox. A whole world built itself upon the page and I just followed along...

An itinerate traveller all my life. I grew up in the military, often on RAF bases but preferring to be in the countryside when we could. I adore whodunnits.

I have two amazing sons – Jonathan and Sam Baugh, and his wife, Wendy, and five grandchildren, Charlie, Joshua, Isabella-Rose, Scarlett and Hugo.

I am married to Krov, my wonderful husband, who is a retired film maker and eldest son of the violinist, Yehudi Menuhin. We live in the Cotswolds.

For more information my address is:
karenmenuhinauthor@littledogpublishing.com

Karen Baugh Menuhin is a member of
The Crime Writers Association

Made in United States
Orlando, FL
16 May 2022

17912202R00180